I NEED YOU . . .

She pushed her face into his chest, but he took her head in his hands and tilted her face to the moonlight. He stared at her with eyes so deep and dark that she trembled with the intensity of her emotions. She felt tenderness pouring from him, drawing forth a torrent of love from her heart.

"My God," he whispered, and kissed her yearning lips. They locked together in an embrace of such intense passion that they were forced to draw apart in breathless surprise. They kissed again and again, covering each other's faces with a rain of murmured endearments, while a tide of desire swept through them stirring a need that could not be denied. . .

Other Avon Books in the
Finding Mr. Right Series

BALANCING ACT
by Pamela Redmond Satran
BEST LAID PLANS
by Elaine Raco Chase
DANCING SEASON
by Carla A. Neggers
LOVE FOR THE TAKING
by Beth Christopher
MIRRORS OF LOVE
by Jo Calloway
· PAPER TIGER
by Elizabeth Neff Walker
UNTIL LOVE IS ENOUGH
by Laura Parker

Coming Soon

BEST OF FRIENDS
by Betty Henrichs

*FINDING
MR.RIGHT*

OPPOSITES ATTRACT

ALICIA MEADOWS

AVON
PUBLISHERS OF BARD, CAMELOT, DISCUS AND FLARE BOOKS

OPPOSITES ATTRACT is an original publication of Avon
Books. This work has never before appeared in book form.

AVON BOOKS
A division of
The Hearst Corporation
1790 Broadway
New York, New York 10019

Copyright © 1983 by Mr. Right Enterprises
Published by arrangement with Mr. Right Enterprises
Library of Congress Catalog Card Number: 83-91039
ISBN: 0-380-84111-8

First Avon Printing, September, 1983

AVON TRADEMARK REG. U.S. PAT. OFF. AND IN
OTHER COUNTRIES, MARCA REGISTRADA, HECHO EN
U. S. A.

Printed in the U. S. A.

WFH 10 9 8 7 6 5 4 3 2 1

Chapter One

"YOU'VE ALLOWED YOURSELF to be brainwashed by a lot of liberation drivel, Susan," her husband jeered. "A search for fulfillment! You sound like a goddamn soap opera!" Jeffrey's corrosive scorn sent a quiver of dismay through Susan Blaine. "I can't believe it," he breathed angrily, his blue eyes alive with electric sparks that she had seldom seen before. "We have a good marriage and you're going to throw it away to chase some damn fool will-o'-the-wisp."

Susan's packed suitcase stood on the living room floor between them where she had dropped it when Jeff had caught her before she was able to escape. He held her farewell note clenched in his hand, waving it at her as if it were the enemy.

"I'm sorry, Jeff," Susan replied with calm dignity, her serious gray eyes filled with shadows of distress. "But you can't be surprised at this." Susan could hardly bear to say the actual words that would dissolve their marriage. She had tried to avoid this scene. But the marriage had been over long before this night. "The six-month moratorium hasn't worked. Be honest," she pleaded, willing Jeffrey to join her in her attempt at a quiet severance.

All her life Susan had opted for the quiet choice as if any other recourse were a capitulation to weakness. Emotional displays were a self-indulgence that only the immature allowed themselves. Her father had taught her that precept early in life, and she had never questioned her revered parent. It did not occur to her that her present predicament had been purchased by past worship at false shrines.

Still something nagged uneasily at the fringes of her

mind. "I tried it your way—I really did. I desperately wanted us to find a—" She hesitated, searching for kind words that would be brief as well as true—"deeper significance in our relationship, but we're right where we were last January."

"And what's so bad about that?" Jeffrey's belligerence continued to surprise Susan. In all their married life he had never raised his voice to her.

"There's nothing bad—but nothing . . . urgent either."

"Urgent! Significant!" Jeffrey sneered derisively. "You're only mouthing words, trying to mask your betrayal in lofty semantics—more of that pseudopsychology you've embraced. Why don't you speak plainly?"

"I'm trying to, but you won't listen," Susan shot back in a flash of anger. "And your scorn doesn't intimidate me, Jeff. My mind is made up."

They faced each other across five years of marital mediocrity that their academic world had lauded as an exemplary success. But the formula of compatibility had failed, at least as far as Susan was concerned. Somewhere in the formative years of her middle-class upbringing a rebel strain had developed unnoticed, and, starved on a diet of restraint and denial, it had burst forth this past year a burning desire demanding self-fulfillment. It could not be smothered by pleas made to duty or even tempered by promises of reform.

No. Freedom was its command, and Susan was prepared to obey.

"You aren't using your mind," Jeffrey attacked. "Certainly not the good sense you were born with."

It was painful to observe her husband's bewildered hurt, but Susan had a spine of steel that would not bend once she had reached a decision. And she knew Jeff would recover from the hurt more easily than he believed at the moment. Besides, he was the one who had precipitated the rupture by his recent philandering with Gina. The aborted affair had shocked Susan out of her dream of the perfect marriage. The discovery of his infidelity had forced her to stand back and evaluate what she and Jeffrey had built between them.

2

The results of that reflection were devastating. Susan discovered that Jeffrey's foray into adultery caused her so little grief as to be demoralizing. She tried to explain her altered perspective more than once without being cruel, but the message did not penetrate Jeffrey's bland assurance that it was merely a temporary aberration on her part. Like the sensible girl she had always been, Susan would revert to type and conform.

"We are two people who are comfortable and compatible, Jeff, but not . . . *necessary* to each other. In the deepest core of our beings neither of us really needs the other."

Jeffrey ran his hand through the thick waves of his dark hair and took an involuntary step toward his aloof wife. He wanted to prevent Susan from walking out the door, but nothing in his thirty years of well-mannered development had prepared him for handling an explosive emotional crisis. His whole training was predicated on achieving the finished product of the WASP male—not that it was a fraudulent product or an image assumed by an imposter— not at all. Jeffrey Blaine was indeed a white, Anglo-Saxon Protestant. His family traced its roots to the Pilgrim founders of early Massachusetts.

The Blaines had settled in the little community of Edinboro, Pennsylvania, shortly after their marriage when Jeffrey had been offered the chairmanship of the biology department at Edinboro College. Susan and Jeffrey had both been raised in Lynde, Massachusetts, where their forebears had settled in pre-Revolutionary days, sturdy members of a God-fearing, hard-working band of Puritans. The imprint of that admirable but frostbitten ethic still etched itself firmly in Jeffrey's psyche. Dr. Blaine was decent, sincere, and successful. He passed through the corridors of Edinboro College with the cool detachment of the well-bred scientist. If there were no emotional fireworks in his cultural apparatus, there were no neuroses either. Jeffrey was dependable, charming, and bland.

"Susan, you're making a mistake you'll regret for the rest of your life," he exclaimed, trying to sound reasonable, but actually resorting to a veiled threat. It was not in character and he did it badly. The ploy only hardened his wife's resolve.

"It is something I will have to learn from experience." Susan was growing tired of the argument and became blunt. "As I see it now, neither of us has too much at stake here. Our easy camaraderie has been a mask of superficiality covering a lack of deep commitment."

Dr. Blaine paused, studying his stubborn wife.

"This is a side of you I never dreamed existed," he accused. "Our marriage has been a sound relationship."

"Not really," Susan countered wearily. "What appeared to be sound was a glib façade, easy, friendly and about as deep as"—she shrugged her shoulders searching for an apt analogy—"about as deep as tissue paper."

It surprised them both when Jeffrey suddenly lunged at Susan, catching her against his chest and kissing her with aggressive determination. At first Susan offered no resistance, but his kisses grew cruel and she began to struggle against his assault. He had never resorted to physical violence before and her rejection only stirred his passion.

"Stop it, Jeff! Stop!" Susan demanded, but he held her in a grip of steel and pressed himself against her so ruthlessly that she lost her balance as she staggered backwards and they fell to the floor. The wind was knocked out of her and she gave up the fight, but the sudden descent into absurdity halted Jeffrey's transgression, and he immediately lost heart. The chastened caveman helped his wife to her feet, apologizing profusely.

"Did I hurt you, Sue? Here, sit on the couch and let me pour you a drink." His solicitude was genuine. Jeffrey was restored to his well-behaved self, his wrath evaporated.

"No, Jeff. I don't want a drink." She smiled into his concerned blue eyes and patted his hand. "I'm okay. Don't look so alarmed."

"Are you sure?" he questioned contritely. "I don't know what the devil got into me. I'm sorry as hell."

Susan, who had already initiated divorce proceedings against Jeff, left town and headed west in her Datsun the following morning, after spending the night with a friend. Sue had no clear-cut destination, just a vague notion of taking time to think and maybe finding a new life in a new location. Always prudent, Susan had not quit her job but had taken a leave of absence from Ballinger and Curtis where she had been practicing law for four of the five years she had lived in Edinboro, commuting almost daily to the courthouse in Erie, the county seat.

She covered almost three hundred miles the first day, taking time to enjoy the springtime awakening of the countryside in early May. The past winter had been harsh and oppressive and it was with a heady sense of freedom and promise that Susan left the quiet Pennsylvania community which was still recovering from the trauma of cruel bouts with ice, wind, and freezing temperatures. She spent the first night in a cheerful motel outside Charleston, West Virginia, still enjoying the sense of life holding great promise. Adventure and discovery loomed glamorously.

The next morning was fine with bright sunshine and after a leisurely breakfast in the coffee shop, she propped herself once more behind the wheel, turned on the radio to some classical music and joined the mechanized caravan on Interstate 77 and pointed herself in the direction of New Orleans. Susan was one of those rare women who were good alone. She seldom felt bored, the company of her own thoughts a comfortable comrade.

The fourth day on the road the weather blew up a sudden thunderstorm with threatening black clouds and strong winds that seemed to push her little car off the road. Heeding nature's rather sinister counsel, she left the highway near a little town in Louisiana called Slidell, and drove in search of the Holiday Inn listed in her *Mobil Guide*. The storm was pelting the countryside with fury when she rushed from her car to register, and once in her room the first move she made was to draw herself a hot bath and soak out the tension of driving the last twenty miles through hostile weather.

She dressed in a pair of gray slacks and a red sweater before attending to her hunger, and turning up her nose at the motel dining room, she decided to venture into town and find a local restaurant that would provide atmosphere and a chance to sample some southern cuisine. The rain had subsided to a damp drizzle and mist, shrouding trees and buildings in shadows that blurred their outlines. Harsh neon lights glowed with smudged softness through the hanging vapors, creating an aura of romance and mystery.

After passing several sleazy bars and unappetizing diners, she found herself apparently headed out of town without having discovered a suitable eatery. Deciding that the deepening fog was neither romantic nor comforting, Susan returned to one of the roadside cafés, which announced that it provided food with the big, red letters E A T. She pulled into the gravel parking area and entered by a side door that seemed to be the entrance to the dining section.

As soon as she pushed the door open, she wished she hadn't. Despite the darkened interior, she perceived an ominous scene, a sixth sense warning her that she had chosen poorly, but pride would not allow her to retreat. Enduring the discomfort of a stranger in the midst of a foreign land and the unabashed curiosity of assorted rednecks at the bar, Susan strode with as much nonchalance as she could muster to the few check-covered tables she discerned in the shadows towards the rear. She seated herself along the wall and was planning her retreat in the shortest time possible—one drink and go! The thought of eating here was dismissed as soon as her eyes noted the stains and debris of ashes and crumbs littering the table.

Someone put money in a jukebox and Mickey Gilley started wailing his "two-timing lover" while a young blonde in blue jeans that fit like tights and wearing a stretch-knit top with blue stripes took her order.

A martini was hardly appropriate and Susan hated beer so she settled for "Wine, a glass of white wine, please." She heard the girl call out "Sauterne" to the bartender and mentally shrugged her shoulders. She could hardly expect Pouilly Fumé in this neck of the woods.

"Evenin', little lady." A blue-jeaned rodeo hulk sat himself across from Susan, who could only stare in surprise. "You must be a stranger to these parts," he suggested as his opening gambit. Susan didn't know what to do. Telling him to get lost was her first impulse but she feared antagonizing him—he looked alarmingly huge and aggressive. His tight curly hair was red and bushy and the hand holding his can of beer was large with tufts of hair on the knuckles. His plaid shirt strained over the muscles of his shoulders, which he hunched over the table as he leaned towards Susan who was unable to decide on a proper attitude.

"Yes," she answered noncommitally. She had no intention of encouraging conversation with such an oaf.

"From the East?" he questioned. His eyes were studying her with obvious calculation and they weren't friendly, although his lips smiled. She supposed some women would find him attractive, but muscle-bound masculinity turned her off unequivocally. She couldn't stand the blatant macho man.

Susan nodded assent without speaking and glanced hastily around the room, assessing her chances of escape. Her unwelcomed guest would not be easy to discourage. As a matter of fact, she knew he had made her a target for the night. She considered getting up and walking out just as the waitress set down her wine.

"Here let me," her admirer offered, but Susan was smart enough to forbid it.

"No!" Her voice was sharp. "I'll pay for it." She threw a five-dollar bill on the table.

Her friend laughed loudly and leaned back in his chair. "Hell, Marge, take her money and git," he said, slapping the girl's behind. Susan had to get out of there fast. This guy was going to be real trouble.

"Look here . . ."

"Billy-Jo," he answered, still watching her with a same confident calculation that made her skin crawl.

"I've had a long day, and I'm tired. I wouldn't be much fun." She looked him in the eye, having decided that

7

outright rejection was her best course of action, after all.

"Oh, I don't know about that," he replied and reached under the table and grabbed her thigh.

Susan's reaction was swift and instinctive. She, too, reached under the table and dug her nails in the back of his hand and hissed, "Take your filthy hand off of me at once!"

"What if I don't?" he replied softly.

"Then I'm going to raise the biggest pile of hell you ever heard," she answered levelly. Her heart was slamming against her ribs and she could scarcely breathe, but she stared him down and finally he let go of her thigh. Susan jumped up immediately; knocking over the wine and grabbing her purse, she marched out of the bar, fearing at every step that he would grab her. She could almost feel his hand on her shoulder. Once outside, her legs started shaking so badly she could scarcely walk. But Billy-Jo might follow, and if he got her alone he would be vicious.

Her hands were trembling, nearly preventing her from inserting the key in the ignition of her car; at last her tires screeched and threw up gravel as she swung around and raced out of the lot and down the highway back to her room at the Holiday Inn.

She didn't get any supper and she slept on top of the bed in her clothes. Despite her fatigue it seemed hours before she fell asleep, and when she did, she had a terrible dream about Jeffrey. He was dead and she was too late for his funeral and went searching for his grave in a cemetery filled with dense fog. The names on the headstones gleamed with a ghastly light and she was paralyzed with fear.

Susan woke trying to call Jeffrey's name, but her voice wouldn't work. Her body was drenched with a cold sweat and she could barely move in the oppressive darkness, but the fear was too terrible to endure and she lunged for the bedside lamp and turned on the light. It was three o'clock in the morning and a yearning to hear Jeffrey's voice filled her with dread and remorse.

What had she done? What aberration had sent her hurtling across the country to wind up in this godforsaken no-man's-land? She must have been crazy to cut herself off from everything she had ever known! What in the hell was she looking for?

The experience in the bar had finally shaken her free from the false sense of adventure she had been wrapping around herself since she left Edinboro. Susan was a woman alone in the world, without a place, without a job, without a man. She was in terrible jeopardy. And she had very capriciously placed herself there.

By sunrise she had fallen into a fitful sleep filled with distorted images of crowds of people that turned into grinning dwarfs that marched through her room and over her bed. Around ten o'clock the sun's angle slanted through the unshuttered glass doors striking her face and waking her. She sat up feeling stiff and sore, then looked around the room and grinned at her foolish nighttime delusions. By light of day Billy-Jo and the sense of jeopardy faded into an amorphous cloud of female willies that a modern woman did not permit to appear on her agenda. However, a layer of caution had been laid into Susan's subconscious. The meaning of Billy-Jo and Slidell would rise to the surface when future events triggered its messages.

When Susan reached Houston, she was ready for a break in her travels. A week behind the wheel of her compact and she began to understand her dream about dwarfs. Five feet five was hardly statuesque, but lately she felt she had grown to amazon proportions and was sick to death of stooping and untangling her legs from the seat and wheel and floor pedals of the car. She needed breathing space and Texas seemed the place to find it. The Houston metropolis with its futuristic architecture communicated an immediate sense of cosmopolitan vitality and verve that Susan responded to. There was so much to see and do that her brain reeled: air-conditioned underground concourses with shops and restaurants; skyscrapers connected by aerial walkways; the Astrodome and NASA; universities, museums, and historical parks and sites. It was a cornucopia tumbling over with tempting attractions and glittering diversions. But it was May and it was blistering hot already.

Walking was an exhausting, muggy affair, yet Susan spent hours sightseeing in Sam Houston Historical Park and touring the university. She also attended a Beethoven Concert at the Civic Center and a production of *A Doll's House* at the Alley Theater.

But it was a solo performance and she was tiring of her own company. After a few nights of dinner alone, she called the Hadleys, friends that she and Jeff had known in Edinboro. They had moved to Houston two years ago when Roger Hadley had accepted a teaching post at the university. Susan didn't relish the prospect of explaining her sudden appearance in their city—they were really Jeff's friends—but the need for companionship and conversation forced her to overcome her reluctance.

Marion Hadley was full of enthusiasm as soon as she discovered her eastern friend's presence in Houston and arranged to take Susan to dinner at Courtlandts where they treated her to rack of lamb amid a discreet Georgian décor.

"I'd never go back to that gray world of snow and ice," Marion declared, her pixie face alight with fervor as she lauded Houston's sunny life-style.

"But the humidity," Susan responded. "I feel like a limp dishrag after five minutes out on the street."

"Your body adapts in time, Sue. Your blood thins and besides everything is air-conditioned down here," Roger defended his chosen land.

"Oh, I don't mean to criticize, Roger. I'm agog with admiration for Houston. There's so much to take in . . . and the atmosphere pulses with such vitality that I can feel the potential for growth and success here."

"You've hit the essential point about Houston and most of Texas, Sue. It's wide open territory for anyone seeking to build a new life. Houston has all the promise that characterized America about twenty years ago—without many of the urban problems. And it's still early enough in the game that the newcomer has maneuvering space. The city isn't so tightly structured and hog-tied in settled patterns yet—there's room for innovation."

"Would you say my husband is sold on Houston?"

Marion chided. "But I don't blame him for singing its praises. Do you like to shop, Sue?" She didn't wait for a reply. "I love it. I never tire of searching and finding new boutiques to explore."

"And spending my money," Roger chuckled. "But enough paeons to Texas and its spirit of enterprise. How about you, Sue? It's quite an enterprising female who travels across the country alone. Where exactly are you headed?"

"I'm not sure, Roger. Maybe Houston." She smiled uncertainly. "I'm just looking around and taking in the sights for now."

"There's always room for a good attorney in a boom town," Roger suggested.

"Hope you're right, Roger, but I need to look around some more. I have a notion I might like San Antonio."

"You have?" Marion cried. Susan nodded while her friend charged on.

"You'll adore San Antonio. It's big and cosmopolitan but so romantic and atmospheric. It's very Spanish and . . . the Riverwalk, my dear, the shops and galleries—you'll adore it. And, oh my gosh, Roger, the Forsythes. Sue's got to meet the Forsythes."

Susan looked inquiringly at the couple, who were smiling brightly with enthusiasm. "The Forsythes?"

"Yes, yes," Marion cried. "They are very good friends of ours and have one of the oldest and most prosperous law firms in San Antonio. We just had dinner with Owen Forsythe in this very dining room not over a month ago. Oh, my dear, how absolutely perfect for you."

"Whoa, girl." Roger patted his wife's hand. "Slow down and let Susan catch her breath." He turned to Susan. "Marion's right, Sue. It does sound like a piece of good luck. The Forsythes are fine people and I'm sure they would be happy to talk to you, even if they couldn't offer you a position. I know they would provide an entrée into the right circles. I'll write them if you like."

And so it was that Susan left for San Antonio a few days later and fell in love. The San Antonio ambience, a mixture of old Spain and new America, captivated her imagination at once. The city had it all—elegance and charm amidst tropical trees and a sleepy river meandering through its center; the Riverwalk and open-air galleries and restaurants, history in the Alamo and Capistrano missions and modern skyscrapers and the Forsythe law firm.

Chapter Two

SUSAN PULLED HER blue Datsun into the parking lot across the street from the offices of Forsythe, Cramer and Forsythe—her new employers—and gazed up at the towering metal and glass building that was located in the heart of the downtown business district of San Antonio. Grabbing her briefcase from the backseat and slamming the car door shut, she walked to the corner to wait with the other pedestrians for the light to change. The temperature sign on the bank building read eighty degrees, causing her to grimace. It was not quite nine A.M. and already she was feeling the heat of the day. She wondered whether she would ever adjust to it, or if it would eventually drive her away from this haven under the sun.

Everything had fallen so easily into place since she came here and met Owen Forsythe, the tall angular man with sandy-colored hair and deep gray eyes who had hired her. He impressed her initially with his competence and his no-nonsense, all-business demeanor. Yet he had a certain grace and easy manner that permitted Susan to feel comfortable in his presence, and she sensed that he accepted her in much the same way; therefore she was not surprised when Mr. Forsythe offered her the job she sought. Of course, it wasn't just his decision alone. There had also been a formal meeting with the senior members of the firm, which included Owen's father Edward Forsythe, and his partner, Harold Cramer. After a look at her credentials, they were very willing to endorse Owen's choice.

The light changed and she joined the crowd that scurried across the thoroughfare to their appointed destinations. Then, stepping smartly through the revolving doors of the sleek new building's lobby, Susan made her way to the elevator that carried her up to the second floor.

"Good morning, Carol." Susan smiled warmly at the secretary she shared with three other junior partners at F.,C.&F. "Any messages for me?"

"Mr. Forsythe, Jr. wants to see you in his office as soon as possible."

Surprised, Susan's eyebrows rose questioningly, but the secretary only gave her a nebulous shrug of the shoulders.

"And Ms. Vargas is waiting to see you, too." Carol pointed to the client's lounge on her left and Susan turned to acknowledge the short, dark woman who represented Susan Blaine's first important case.

"I'll be with you in a minute, Ms. Vargas." Susan went into her tiny office, dumped her briefcase on the desk, her purse in the bottom drawer, and removed her light brown suit jacket to hang it over the black leather chair. Briefly she paused to look out of the long narrow window towards the San Antonio River and wondered why her boss wanted to see her before she turned to the work of the morning. Then, opening her briefcase, she pulled out the Vargas file and invited her client to step in. After putting Maria Vargas at ease with a joking comment about her cramped quarters, Susan addressed herself to the issues at hand.

"I've been studying your case, Maria, and before I file your suit in superior court, I have a few more questions for you."

"Ask anything you want if you think it will help me nail that jerk for sex discrimination."

"That's one of the problems, Maria. It still hasn't been clearly decided whether Title Seven of federal law includes sexual harassment as bona fide sex discrimination."

"It's gotta be. I was demoted because I didn't give into him sexually!" The sloe-eyed woman's response was swift and challenging.

"That's what you claim. But we've got to prove it in a court of law. And even then the case could be lost."

"Are you telling me I can't win?" Her client's eyes flashed questioningly.

"No, I'm not saying that, but it will be a struggle and

you have to be prepared for it. Some unpleasant accusations and insinuations will be made against you—"

"I figured as much," Maria cut in.

"And there is always the possibility we could lose."

"I'll take my chances," Maria responded defiantly. "I'm not going to let that guy ruin my life and get away with it."

"Good. It's important that you believe strongly in your position. Now let's spend a few minutes on some important details." Susan began by reviewing her client's previous statement. In it Maria Vargas claimed that after working five years for the brokerage firm of Howard Haas as a secretary and then as an assistant account manager, her dealings with Robert Harmon, senior vice president in charge of accounting, had been infrequent. So she had tolerated, on those rare occasions when they did meet, a playful hug that ended in a caress of her buttocks or breast and his sexual innuendos.

"And you never encouraged him?"

"Never! I put up with it because I wanted to keep my job."

Susan nodded and jotted down a note on the side of the typed brief which contained Maria's account. Her client's fortunes seemed to change quite suddenly, however, when Mr. Juarez, Maria's immediate superior, was about to retire. She was in line for the promotion and approached Harmon about it. He indicated that the job had certain "strings attached to it," and that it might be available if she "came across." When she threatened to go to the president of the company Harmon laughed, claiming he would convince Haas to have her fired for being an office troublemaker, for not having an appropriate attitude. At first she thought it was just an idle threat and she tried to talk around it to get out of his office. But he was insistent and wouldn't let her alone until she agreed to have dinner with him at his apartment. It was the only way he would let her go. Once freed, Maria reneged on her promise and vowed never to be caught alone with him again. Not long after that incident, one of the young male clerks much less experienced than she was chosen over her to replace the retiring Juarez. Even then it did not end. Harmon began to find fault with her work. He claimed she was inefficient and noted errors she made that Maria was certain were the result of sabotage although she couldn't prove it. He started a file documenting her shortcomings and said that she repeatedly broke appointments with him which were set up to "discuss and improve her work performance."

"Did you break those appointments?"

"Well, yes . . . but I was only trying to avoid him."

Susan could sympathize with Maria's predicament, but she knew it would be used against her at the trial. "And that's when you were given clerical duties to do besides your regular work." Flipping to the next page of the log, Susan reread the final paragraph. When Maria couldn't handle the extra work load, she was demoted. That's when she had had enough and went looking for a good lawyer. "What we need now are some corroborating witnesses. Who can support your case against Harmon?"

"I—I don't know for certain."

"Perhaps there are other women in the company who have experienced similar kinds of harassment. Has anyone confided in you or sympathized with you about your unfair treatment?"

"Well, Mrs. Hayes, Harmon's personal secretary, said to me that he had a short attention span, and it wouldn't last long. But when I asked her to help me by going to Haas, she clammed up. Didn't want to get too involved."

Susan wrote down her name on a note pad. "That's one possibility. Now who else?"

"There's Margaret Peron, an account executive. She's a tough egg, Ms. Blaine. When the gossip got around she came to me and said that it happens to all of us at one time or another, but that I should roll with the punches. Then I could fight when I was in a better position to do so."

"Mmm, I think I'd like to meet her." Susan smiled as she wrote Margaret Peron's name on her pad.

"I've thought of one more possibility—Jane Connery. She was going places with the company, and then one day she just up and quit. Afterwards there was some talk about Harmon and her but nothing very substantial."

"Where's she now?" Susan asked, her curiosity heightened.

"I don't know. I never saw her again."

"Damn! I'll have to put a tracer on Ms. Connery and see if I can have her located. She might be a valuable witness. I'll arrange for the tracer this afternoon, and I'll make appointments to see the other two women sometime this week. In the meantime, Maria, try to think of anyone else who might testify in your behalf. A *male* witness would do wonders for our case. Do you think Mr. Juarez would be of any help?"

"I—I don't think so."

"Perhaps I'll contact him anyway." Susan closed the file. "I'll be in touch with you in a few days to let you know what progress I have made." She walked to the elevator with her client and saw her off. It was only then that she recalled that Owen Forsythe wanted to speak to her.

Slipping the tan linen jacket over her yellow and green striped silk blouse, Susan hurried along the red carpeted corridor in the direction of the executive suite where the senior partners were in consultation. Before she turned the brass knob of the rubbed walnut door, she stopped to pat her short wedge of blond hair into place, then entered the outer office to a barrage of male voices. Owen Forsythe, his father, and Harry Cramer were deeply involved in a discussion with a tall dark-haired man in military garb.

"Ah, Susan," Edward Forsythe, the white-haired president of the firm, beckoned to her. "Come and meet Major Obregon. Carlos, this is Susan Blaine, the latest addition to our staff."

Major Obregon turned to greet her and immediately Susan felt the impact of the man. Large jet black eyes fastened searingly onto her own sky blue ones and then swept over her appraisingly. Finally a low lazy smile lighted up his chiseled Spanish features.

"Carlos is one of our most respected clients, my dear." Edward Forsythe continued to speak as a silent communication went on between her and Obregon. "Be sure to treat him well."

"I'm sure she will," Carlos said in a deep, rich baritone voice as his hand gripped Susan's in a meaningful way. The man's mere presence seemed to exude a sense of power that caused her to draw back and look to Owen Forsythe for support. He was standing slightly behind her. A frown creased his brow and he held himself stiffly.

"I didn't mean to interrupt, Mr. Forsythe, I'll come back later when you're not so busy."

"I'm not busy, Ms. Blaine. Major Obregon is here to see my father on business. I can see you now."

"We'll meet again soon, I trust, Ms. Blaine." The major flashed her a winning smile as she followed Owen into his office.

Susan was confused by her reaction to Obregon and to Owen's frown. Was it meant for her or the major? She decided to let Forsythe open the conversation and she would take her lead from him. He seated her firmly in one of his plush office chairs and handed her a cup of coffee before speaking; his tone of voice held no emotion. "So you have met Major Obregon."

"Yes, a very impressive individual," she was now able to answer calmly. "Has he been a client for a long time?"

"The Obregons have been doing business with the Forsythes for three generations. They own cattle, wells, and a wide variety of other investments."

"And Major Obregon is the head of the family?" There was an affirmative nod from Owen which raised another question in her mind. "I find it strange that he is in the Air Force then. I wonder why?"

"I believe that it's just a hangover from his macho upbringing, something he inherited from his father who died about a year ago. From what my father tells me—he handles the Obregon account personally—Carlos has a passion for planes, among other things." Susan thought she detected a slight sneer in Owen's voice. "I understand, though," he went on, "that he plans to make this his final tour of duty. But as far as the family businesses are concerned, he has enough uncles to carry on if he decides to remain in the Air Force. Quite frankly, in my opinion, his

temperament seems more suited to daredevil exploits than
to business."

Owen rose from the chair beside her, a signal Susan in-
terpreted to mean that he had spent too much time on that
subject. Instinctively, Susan picked up his cue. "You did
want to see me on another matter, didn't you?"

"Yes." Redirecting his thoughts, Owen took the chair
behind his long, sleek cherry wood desk. "Last evening I
received a call from Robert Harmon of the Howard Haas
Company."

The mere mention of the name of the key figure in her
client's case caused her some instant uneasiness. She tried
to look unruffled while Owen went on.

"He informed me that our firm was about to take on a
case for a Maria Vargas alleging sexual harassment."

"That's right. Why did he call you?" The defiant tilt of
Susan's chin assured Owen that she meant business.

"Because we are acquainted with him and he wanted to
see if I would—or *could*—stop you from accepting the case."

"And do you intend to?" Susan's eyes deepened to a midnight blue as they always did whenever she was challenged. This was a tense moment for her, maybe the most
important one as far as her fate with this firm was concerned. Owen Forsythe was evaluating her right now, she
could sense that. He wanted to see what kind of mettle she
possessed, and her response would provide him with at
least an initial appraisal of the kinds of skills she would
use in her legal work. Susan braced herself for his reply to
her question.

Owen placed his arms squarely on his desk top and
brought his steepled fingers to rest against his mouth. A
confident, jurisprudential pose, Susan thought. "Do you
have any idea how difficult it is to prove sexual harassment?"

"Yes, I've done my homework. I know as many cases
have been lost as won. Several cases right now are on appeal and one may even reach the Supreme Court."

"You're convinced this Vargas woman is telling the
truth, and that her case is worth the time and effort involving a court trial?"

"Absolutely. I believe we're looking at a case that could pave the way for an entirely new direction in litigation. Would you like to see my brief?"

"No, that won't be necessary. I hired you because I trust your judgment, Susan." Owen left his side of the desk and walked towards her pointing his finger. "Harmon is an influential man who does not want to end up with egg on his face in public. He's going to fight any way he has to in order to try and win. That has to be weighed against the real possibilities of achieving success for your client."

"I understand that, Mr. Forsythe, that's why I haven't filed a complaint yet. I'm in the process of developing an extensive list of details that I'm going to check out very thoroughly first."

"I'm sure you will, but let me give you a word of advice. There's little doubt that a sexual harassment case will attract the press. Be careful that sensationalism is not substituted for competent legal work."

"Then you are not going to ask me to drop the case?" Susan breathed a sigh of relief.

"Certainly not. If Robert Harmon is guilty of sexual harassment, he should be tried."

"I'm glad you feel that way. I know many men wouldn't share your opinion."

"I'm not going to deny that you are right. The understanding that women are something more than sex objects is slow in coming."

"That's why the Vargas case is important."

"If I can be of assistance in any way, be sure to let me know."

"Thank you, I will."

Susan put her cup on the console and rose to go. But before she could leave, Owen asked with a definite twinkle in his eyes, "I hope you won't take this amiss and begin building a harassment case against me, Susan. but I'd very much like to take you to lunch."

"Why, I'd be delighted . . . Owen."

"In about half an hour then?"

On cloud nine, Susan started back to her office. Not only had Owen given her his support to pursue the Vargas affair, but he had also invited her out socially for the first time, and she realized that he appealed to her more than just as an employer. His sharp wit, clear vision, and fair-minded attitude, not to mention his handsome appearance (in an intellectual way) had attracted her early in their relationship, and she had finally admitted to herself that she was hoping he would show something other than a mere professional interest in her.

When she entered the reception room, Carol signaled her frantically.

"What is the matter?"

"It's Major Obregon," she whispered excitedly. "He's waiting to see you. He's in your office."

"My office?" Susan was surprised. Why was Major Obregon waiting to see her?

"Yes. Oh God, I thought I'd die when that beautiful hunk of man came in here and asked for you."

"But why didn't you have him wait in the visitor's lounge like everyone else?"

"Are you kidding? I should treat Carlos Obregon like 'everyone else'?"

Susan grimaced, realizing the futility of wasting her breath trying to convince her moonstruck secretary that Major Obregon was just that—a mere fallible mortal. Instead she went to her office to find her visitor seated behind her desk with his legs propped up on it, reading one of her law books.

He smiled, showing a row of perfect white teeth. "That's rather boring material," he commented, then tossed the book aside and rose, filling the tiny office space with his manly presence.

He was tall for a Latin, perhaps six feet, Susan judged. She had to agree with Carol that he was quite a specimen of maleness. But too handsome for his own good, she was certain. Obviously every female he met fell all over herself hoping to be noticed by him. Carol was a case in point. Well, Susan decided, here was one woman who had no intention of melting because he had the features of a movie star.

Choosing to ignore his remark about her law text, she

Alicia Meadows

went on the defensive. "Major Obregon, I understood that Mr. Edward Forsythe handled *all* your business with the firm; however if there is some way I may be of professional assistance . . ." She left the rest of the statement hanging and, maneuvering lightly past him, picked the text up from the desk and replaced it on the shelf. If she had hoped to disconcert him in any way she was mistaken. The major proceeded to seat himself on the edge of the desk, blocking her exit and forcing her to sit down.

"Mr. Forsythe, Senior *does* handle all my business affairs. That's not why I'm here, *Miss*—or is it *Mrs.* Blaine?"

"Technically, it's Mrs.; however I prefer Ms. I'm divorced."

"So much the better." He smiled, surveying her crossed legs in an obvious way that made Susan feel suddenly very uncomfortable. "I'm glad the possessor of such classic Nordic beauty hasn't wasted all her energy on a career."

"Really, Major," Susan interjected indignantly, "I don't know what you've come here for, but certainly it was not to discuss my personal attributes."

"Oh, not entirely," he continued in that same self-satisfied manner, and Susan didn't know whether to be angry or amused. As was her habit when contemplating her options, she reached for a Marlboro, but before she could light it Carlos had slipped it from between her lips and crushed it between his fingers. Speechless, Susan glared at him. Who did this arrogant military playboy think he was anyway? In response to the anger he saw glinting in her eyes he responded, "I think you should be more careful in the way you take care of your beautiful body. You haven't been paying close enough attention to those reports about the evils of tobacco."

"I think I'm quite capable of determining what is right or wrong for me, Major Obregon!" she said adamantly as she reached for the cigarettes. But Carlos held on to the pack, wagging an admonishing finger at her.

"That's the trouble with women today. They no longer are willing to listen to the good advice of men." He tossed the packet to her. "But," he warned, "when you go out with me I must insist you refrain from smoking." Al-

22

though Susan's eyes continued to flash anger, resentment, confusion, and refusal Carlos went on. "That was my main reason for coming here: You must accompany me to lunch."

"That's absolutely out of the question!" she snapped back.

"Why? Because I clipped your cigarettes?"

"No!" she thought fast and remembered with relief, "I already have a luncheon date."

"Break it."

"I don't think Owen Forsythe would care for that," she replied smugly.

"To be sure." He grinned. "Well, then, we shall have dinner together."

"I think not, Major. I make it a policy never to date a client."

"I'm not your client, Ms. Blaine."

"Indirectly you are."

"Then I guess I'll have to cancel all my business with the firm so that even indirectly there's no business connection."

Susan didn't take his threat seriously for one second and called his bluff. "I suppose that is your privilege."

Obregon threw back his head and let out a lusty laugh. "Clever woman! Very well, Ms. Blaine, I shan't cancel my business with F.,C.&F., but I insist on taking you out to dinner."

"I'm sorry, Major, I've already stated my position regarding clients. Now you'll have to excuse me. I have work to do." Susan reached for some papers and he deliberately got in her way and refused to budge.

"Naughty, naughty." Again he wagged his finger, forcing Susan to blush. "I'm not going to leave until you've agreed to have dinner with me." Suddenly Susan's dilemma reminded her of Maria Vargas's plight and she instantly grew furious. No longer caring that Obregon was one of the firm's most influential customers, she cried, "This really is quite childish behavior, Major Obregon."

Carlos simply ignored her outburst. "The Green Grotto

is about twenty miles outside the city limits. It's a pleasant drive. I guarantee you'll enjoy it."

"Do you wish me to call the security guard and have you evicted?"

"I don't think Edward Forsythe would approve of such discourtesy. Now about the Green Grotto—"

"You really are very persistent, aren't you?" Susan's sigh of exasperation indicated to Carlos that his opponent was weakening.

"Ah, I knew you'd see it my way. . . ."

"I didn't say that. I've just decided to work around you." She failed to suppress a laugh in spite of her frustration and started to squeeze by him, but he rose from the edge of the desk and pinned her skillfully between the furniture and the window.

"These quarters are rather tight, Ms. Blaine," he warned, stepping close enough so that there was the slightest body contact between them, causing Susan's heart to skip a beat as she looked up into his compelling black eyes.

"Don't you think this is going quite beyond the bounds of a professional relationship?" She was unable to hide the panic welling up inside her.

A timely knock at the door brought Owen Forsythe into the room and Susan was relieved. All three of them froze for a moment and she wondered if Owen was assessing the situation accurately.

Carlos was the first to speak and, using his infinite charm, made light of the situation. "Owen, my good man, you must train your staff better. This young lady has refused my dinner invitation stating some flimsy professional reasons. Will you inform her that dinner is one of the better ways to promote good client relationships for the firm?"

"I find it hard to believe you need a spokesman, Carlos," Owen said without humor. "Nevertheless, Susan is free to accept or reject any invitation she wishes. It's a woman's prerogative these days, you know."

"That's what I like about you, Owen, your open-mindedness." There was a slight edge to his voice as he turned from Forsythe to Susan. "You see, dear lady, Forsythe is so typical of the modern American male that he cannot make a decision by himself. He must be 'democratic'—oh, how I loathe that word—and allow you to make your own choice. Tsk, tsk. It seems to me that no one has any appreciation at all today of male chivalry. What do you say, Ms. Blaine?"

"Well, I admire your attempt to resurrect chivalry as an institution." Susan was amazed at her own archaic admission, but recovering quickly she proceeded to explain, "I think our particular situation, however, calls for an uncomplicated professional association. I hope you will be chivalrous enough to accept my view on this, Major Obregon."

"You've had your answer, Carlos," Owen said, jerking open the door. "And now if you'll excuse us."

"For the time being." Carlos laughed as he retrieved his cap from the cabinet, gave a smart salute, and sauntered from the office.

"Damn," Owen swore under his breath and shook his head before turning to Susan with a disgusted look on his face. "There are no limits to the man's aggressiveness with women. He loves to intimidate them. Part of his background, I guess. But I must say you handled him rather well. And for that you really deserve a special lunch. Let's go right now and forget the whole incident."

Susan was as anxious as Owen to put Carlos out of her mind and enjoy the luncheon with her employer. They drove to the Buena Vista Country Club on the outskirts of the city where they dined in the Spanish *Sala*, a room designed in the Spanish Gothic style with a huge stone fireplace, large tapestry wall hangings of mounted Spanish knights, and a rich plush carpet of intricate and complex patterns. They were seated in red cordovan wing chairs by a discreet waiter who spoke with an appropriate accent. Their table near the sheer-curtained window gave them a panoramic view of the golf course.

Luncheon consisted of mushroom and avocado vinaigrette, onion soup, and chicken marengo. Over a dessert of cherries flambé, the focus of conversation centered on the country club itself, its clientele, and its lush green golf course.

"Confidentially, that's why our dues are so high," Owen quipped. "Do you play?"

"If you mean have I ever held a club in my hand, the answer is yes, but if you mean am I a golfer, the answer is no."

"It's one of my favorite pastimes."

Susan could have bitten her tongue for being so definite in her reply, but it wasn't necessary for in the next minute Owen was offering his expertise for helping her improve her game.

"I'd like that." She smiled beguilingly.

"So would I," he agreed, briefly touching her hand, which rested on a long-stemmed wineglass. "Let's begin this afternoon."

"Today? But I'm totally unprepared."

"I'm sure the pro shop can outfit you."

"But what about the office?"

"Do you have anything urgent, something that can't wait until morning?"

"No, I guess not."

"Well, then, I think that covers all the bases. Surely you're not worried that your employer would fire you?" he asked with a playful smile.

"He's a tyrant, but I have a sneaking suspicion he won't mind," Susan answered impudently before heading for the pro shop.

Within half an hour Susan found herself outfitted with a new pair of golf shoes, gloves, and rented clubs. Following Owen on to the driving range, she got in some practice shots. At first she was extremely nervous, slicing at the ball, but with encouragement and helpful hints from Owen, she began to relax and her strokes improved. Eventually they moved on to the greens where she continued to gain confidence under Owen's tutelage. Even so, her putting was poor. No matter how carefully she gauged her angle and the distance from the cup, her shot went wide.

"That's the most difficult part of the game," he reassured her as he studied his own putt. "It takes a great deal of time and practice, so don't get discouraged. You've done amazingly well." Owen adjusted his hands on the clubs, planted his feet firmly on the ground, and tapped the ball gently into the cup.

"I wish I could do that and make it look so effortless."

"You will, my dear, in time." Owen led her back to the golf cart. "Nine holes enough for one day?"

"You mean we don't have to finish all eighteen?"

"There's no law that says we must. Golf is a game of skill and it requires practice, but you shouldn't engage in overkill the first time out," Owen explained as he turned the cart towards the club house.

How considerate he was, Susan thought, remembering the few times she had played the game with Jeffrey. He had always insisted on finishing all eighteen holes, regardless of her feelings, just as long as his enjoyment wasn't jeopardized. She liked this man's style and his empathy.

They were seated in the club lounge sipping cool mint juleps when an elegant woman in a blue silk dress strolled into the room and headed straight for their table.

"I've been looking for you, my pet."

"Gloria." Owen rose unhurriedly. "This is Susan Blaine who recently joined F.,C.&F."

"Ms. Blaine." The woman extended a languid, jewel-encrusted hand. "I'm Owen's ex."

Susan was spared the embarrassment of having to reply as Owen asked, "When is the wedding, Gloria? I understood it was to be soon."

"It is! Quite soon. That's why I'm so anxious to settle the business over the company with you."

"Well, I have no intention of discussing it here and now, Gloria. You'll have to come to the office for that."

"Indeed?" Gloria eyed Susan and then Owen before concluding with obvious sarcasm, "Yes, you never were one for mixing business and pleasure."

Owen brushed her barbed comment aside. "I'm free after one tomorrow. Why don't you drop by the office then?"

27

"As you wish." She tossed her long blond hair and then drifted away.

"I'm sorry about that, Susan."

"Oh, please don't apologize to me—I have an ex myself."

Their eyes converged on each other's in a silent moment of mutual understanding and their fingers met fleetingly across the small table.

Long after Susan had returned to her apartment on Hacienda Drive, her thoughts remained on the afternoon spent in Forsythe's company. Although she enjoyed him and wanted to spend more time with him, Susan had no intention of becoming deeply involved with any man for the present. And if she read Owen accurately, his sentiments corresponded quite nicely with her own. This relationship would suit her needs perfectly for now. She could concentrate on her career and still have the male companionship she sought without letting it dominate her life.

On that practical note, Susan put the matter out of her head and opened a brochure from the San Antonio Women's Center to learn more about the women's movement in this section of the country.

Chapter Three

SUSAN MET Vera Banks at the San Antonio Women's Center during its annual Women's Day Conference. The attraction between the two was instantaneous, although they were very dissimilar in character and type. Vera was a dynamic redhead with an air of authority that complimented her statuesque proportions. It was she who organized the conference and hammered it into shape. But Vera was very feminine too, in the traditional style of the southern woman. She dressed in neat suits with soft bows at the neck and she wore her hair in feathery short waves that framed her lively face. Although she actively espoused women's causes, she liked men too. As a matter of fact, Vera was seldom seen without a man in tow. She had an infectious laugh that drew others to her and she won her battles as much by charm as by bravado.

"Although I advocate change, I never lose sight of the old truth about catching more flies with honey than vinegar, sugar," she informed Susan over their luncheon fare of chicken salad and ice cream during the noon break at the conference. "If there's one thing a southern lady learns at her mother's knee, it's how to wear the velvet glove."

"Then what I've always heard about southern women is true?" Susan questioned, enjoying her new friend's easy conversation and relaxed style.

"Yes, indeed! The South is a matriarchy and don't kid yourself into thinking all that lace and sweet cologne are symbols of subjection. Women hold the reins in magnolia land."

"Then why all this?" Susan gestured around the dining

room filled with several hundred babbling women all belaboring their personal push for women's rights.

"Because the old way is too covert, honey," Vera exclaimed. "Hell, Texas isn't just the South—it's the West, and honesty is our main act out here. I don't want women to get their way just because they're good in the bedroom—but the boardroom too!" she laughed. "Not that I have anything against the bedroom, mind you. That's what it's really all about."

"Is it?" Susan queried thoughtfully; a momentary image of Jeffrey flickered through her mind. "That seems a contradiction to this kind of action."

"I don't see why," Vera answered quickly and Susan sensed a sudden defensiveness from Vera that she didn't wish to tread upon. But the issue tempted her to pursue it. "Don't you think that political and social activism can drive men and women into adversarial positions?"

"Sure it can—and it does—but that's a necessary stage of passage towards the new synthesis of men and women unified and together instead of secretly antagonistic and hostile."

"That's a nice picture. It sounds so dignified and decent." Susan's natural instinct for reason and her training in self-discipline responded hopefully to Vera's attractive utopia of the sexes joined in mutual support. Susan was a woman committed to good sense and pragmatism—or so she believed. It didn't occur to her that leaving Jeffrey had been anything but sensible.

Later that afternoon Susan attended a workshop on women in nontraditional employment, which started off with a film showing women truckers, dockworkers, and telephone repairmen climbing poles and lugging heavy equipment. The film was slick and professional but superficial to Susan's critical eye. It hardly seemed liberating to encourage women to seek back-breaking labor and physical drudgery.

During the second workshop—on education and programs designed to help women define their goals and take control of their lives—Susan found herself in a more congenial atmosphere. She was agreeably surprised by the intelligence and openness of many of the participants.

There was one exquisitely beautiful woman seated towards the front of the room who reminded Susan of a young Liz Taylor. Her nose and chin were finely carved and her ivory complexion had the petal softness of a fresh gardenia. But when she spoke, she was much more than a pretty face.

"I have been listening all day to talk about women taking control of their lives and competing with men for equality. The whole program has been for Anglo women in an Anglo society. What about the Latinas and those of us in Texas who have not only society but our own cultural traditions to fight if we are to achieve personal freedom?" The girl spoke passionately and her words were supported by murmurs of approval from those in the audience who clearly bore the stamp of Latin heritage on their features.

"Your observation is a fair one, Elena, but it must be said that the Center tried to organize a faction from the Mexican-American community to address themselves to this very issue, but we couldn't find a spokesperson for your group. Why don't we take up some of those problems here and now?" the moderator suggested. "What are the cultural traditions that *you* refer to that hold back the Latin woman today?"

"Machismo!" The dark-haired girl answered quickly and the word echoed around the room in concert. "Women cannot escape the position of command held by the male in the Latin family."

This statement released a sudden torrent of commentary. Spanish was as thick as English. One expressive woman made a disturbing impression on Susan.

"I am an American," she said, "but I might as well be a citizen of Mexico. I think like an Anglo and I live like an Anglo, but I can never look like one. Just seeing me no one can tell if I'm an American or a Mexican from across the border. It's hell to look like a foreigner in your own country." The chorus of approval showed the speaker was not alone in her feelings.

Another young woman stood up and cried, "I wish I could squeeze every drop of Mexican blood from my veins."

The anguish and hostility were both pitiful and frightening. Here was an issue that went deeper than jobs and political action. Their very souls seemed caught in a wrenching ambivalence between family loyalty and a desire for independence. It was an insight Susan found upsetting. What must it be like to feel so outside of the mainstream of the dominant culture?

When the conference was breaking up, Susan spied the young beauty who had spearheaded the Spanish women's demand for equality talking to none other than Carlos Obregon in the foyer of the Center. The late afternoon sun flooded through the glass doors surrounding the couple in warm light where they stood speaking together in quiet agitation. The girl turned abruptly to walk away, but Carlos grabbed her elbow and swung her around to face him while he apparently delivered an ultimatum.

Was she his wife? Susan wondered. She wanted to avoid contact with the couple, but to turn around and walk in another direction would be too obvious. There was nothing left but to proceed through the entrance and out of the glass doors. Courtesy demanded a nod of recognition.

". . . *estudiar!*" Carlos was speaking to the girl in Spanish.

"*Bastante!*" the girl replied heatedly and pulled free of his grasp.

By one of those unpredictable movements in time both Susan and Carlos reached for the door at the same instant and ran into one another.

"Pardon me."

"Excuse me."

Carlos stood back and held the door, his gesture of courtesy costing him the chase of his companion who fled down the steps and into a waiting Camaro with a handsome young man at the wheel. They sped off before Carlos could reach them and he stood on the sidewalk watching their escape with obvious frustration.

Susan observed the little drama from the top of the stairs, trying to find an excuse to stall while Carlos decided his course of action. She opened her purse as if rummaging for car keys, but Major Obregon did not leave. Instead he shrugged his elegant shoulders fatalistically and turned to the embarrassed woman at the top of the stairs.

"Can I offer you a lift, Mrs. Blaine?"

"Uh, no, thank you," Susan answered, not understanding her overwhelming alarm at his offer.

"You are expecting a ride?" he questioned stubbornly.

Why doesn't he leave? Susan wondered while striving to find an excuse to send him away. She shook her head no, and he walked back to the stairs and looked up at her with dark, mischievous eyes.

"You are not afraid of riding with me?"

"Of course not." *Damn,* she thought. *I would leave my car at the office.*

"It is too hot to stand in the Texas sun so long. You are not used to it yet." It was as if he were compelling her acceptance. "Come." The major held out his hand and Susan felt too foolish to resist any further. She descended the stairs slowly and he smiled so charmingly that she had no choice but to allow him to lead her to the black Jaguar parked down the street.

"Now where shall I take you?" he queried once she was comfortably settled in the dark plush seat and the air conditioner was running.

"My car is at the office."

"Oh, but that is so short a distance. I was hoping to enjoy your company for longer than that."

"Sorry." Susan smiled, feeling triumphant. "Anyway, I thought I'd try to catch up on some paperwork."

"On this lovely Saturday? Why don't I take you for a cool drink at the Casa Rio instead?"

"No, thank you, Major Obregon," she returned firmly.

"But you will enjoy it. Casa Rio is on the Riverwalk."

"I've already been to the Riverwalk," Susan replied dampingly.

"Good. Then you know how enjoyable it is. Paseo del Rio is very charming. We'll sit outdoors under the trees." And without further discussion, the Major parked the car and led Susan to a riverside café where they sat under arching elms and drooping willows and drank coladas beside the jade green San Antonio River and listened to a string ensemble serenade them into twilight.

"This is very nice," Susan admitted and felt her reluctance to share the major's company dissolve under the soothing influence of pleasant surroundings and soft music. It was like stepping into a picture postcard and finding that the reality was every bit as charming as the glossy fantasy. And there was no denying that her companion was a strikingly handsome man.

Susan's ease was soon disturbed, however, when Major Obregon questioned her about her recent arrival in San Antonio. She had no wish to explain her reasons for coming to San Antonio to the major.

"I have always felt drawn to the Southwest," she parried evasively. Her partner made no comment, waiting for her to explain herself further. The lengthening silence became threatening and Susan was forced to speak despite her inner resolve not to. "In my imagination I conjured a life-style more open and free out here," she added while inwardly seeking a change of topic.

"And is it as you imagined?" the major persisted, unaware of his companion's discomfort. It seemed a valid topic between strangers getting to know one another.

Actually, Susan didn't mind discussing the Southwest, it was a natural subject, but she feared any discussion that might lead back to her marriage and Jeffrey. "Yes, there is much out West that is just as I imagined it to be. Certainly the sunshine and wide open spaces . . . but I hadn't expected the Spanish influence to be so dominant," Susan admitted and could have bitten her tongue. That last remark could be taken as a slur. "Not that I don't appreciate the Spanish culture," she claimed hastily. "As a matter of fact, it is the Spanish ambience that made San Antonio so attractive to me."

Major Obregon smiled knowingly, his dark eyes regarding Susan warmly as he said softly, *"Muy simpática, niña."*

Susan's heart lurched uncomfortably at the note of tenderness in his voice. This man was raising havoc with her composure. There was something so magnetically masculine about him that his very presence seemed to radiate electricity. She had to get away from him soon, or she might find herself drawn into his orbit. And for all she knew, he might be a married man.

"You're presently stationed at Randolph Air Base, Major Obregon?" Susan commented in an effort to divert the topic from herself.

"Yes, I have been stationed there for the last six months."

"That must be very convenient for you, with your home and business interests so close at hand."

"I was sent here as a flight instructor for the T-38." He paused. "The Talon is a supersonic jet."

"Flight instructor!" Susan was surprised. "That must be very dangerous work."

"Not really. The T-38 is a superb aircraft. Light, maneuverable and fast. It can climb at ten thousand feet per minute—very useful in combat."

"Have you flown in combat?" Susan was even more surprised.

"But of course. Vietnam was not so long ago. I have been a pilot for twelve years."

Susan could barely conceal her admiration for the man seated across from her. She had never known a man so blatantly virile and dynamic. He was too attractive for her to handle and a warning signal flashed red in the back of her brain. The more distance between her and Major Obregon the better off she would be.

Susan was scheduled to spend Sunday with Vera Banks. They were going to tour the San Antonio missions which were established by the Franciscan friars early in the eighteenth century.

Susan was surprised to discover that Vera did not come alone to her apartment at the Oaks. She arrived in the company of the Latin beauty who had spoken up at the Center yesterday and was later seen with Carlos Obregon. Susan's curiosity was intensified when she was introduced to Elena Obregon and discovered on closer inspection that the girl was quite young. She couldn't be more than twenty at most.

"I brought along a native of San Antonio so that you can have the benefit of a first-class guide, Susan. Elena's ancestors go back to the very origins of this territory. Obregons have been a part of the local history from the time that the Spanish first settled here when they received a land grant from the Spanish crown in the seventeenth century."

"That must make you very proud," Susan said warmly to Elena.

"Oh, indeed it does"—Elena smiled beautifully—"but sometimes I get weary of worshipping the past. My family can think of nothing else, it seems to me."

"Elena is a student at Saint Mary's University majoring in law," Vera offered. "I'm sure you two will find a lot in common."

"Law!" Susan exclaimed. "How wonderful! I know you'll make a splendid attorney. I heard you speak at the conference yesterday."

"I know," Elena smiled ruefully. "I'm also certain you couldn't help hearing me arguing with my brother either."

"Oh, is Major Obregon your brother?" Susan questioned, suppressing an unaccountable surge of happiness at the discovery.

"Yes, the mighty major is my brother, my mentor, and sometimes my jailer. He makes me so angry, that one!" Elena claimed heatedly.

Later that afternoon Susan found the Mission San José her favorite with its famous sculptured sacristy window known as Rosa's Window. Walking through the cloister arcades and sitting on a stone bench beside ruins of a wall which once surrounded the compound created such a vivid impression of the past that Susan could almost see the brown-clad friars marching solemnly to vespers while the chiming bell in the tower called the mendicants to evening prayer. San Antonio's past wove its elusive spell for Susan, echoing a bygone era when life was simpler and more accessible to the heart.

Chapter Four

IT WASN'T LONG before Carlos Obregon made another appearance in Susan's world. She returned to her office one morning after a particularly frustrating wild goose chase trying to track down Jane Connery for the Vargas case and discovered his invasion of her sanctum. Susan was fighting a nagging fear that the Vargas case was more than she could handle, and was in no mood to play cat and mouse with the likes of Obregon. The sight of him seated behind her desk once more started a slow burn in the back of her mind and with uncharacteristic fire she lashed out at him.

"I don't recall giving you the freedom of my office anytime you need a place to hang your hat, Major Obregon. What kind of training does the Air Force conduct these days? If this is military courtesy, it's a poor show."

"*¡Dios mio!*" the major exclaimed, jumping to his feet. "Forgive me if I intrude at a bad time."

His apology defused Susan's wrath immediately and she even had to smile at the major's display of alarm, however fake it might actually be. He was watching her with a dark uncertainty that stirred her ready sense of humor and she began to laugh.

Carlos's face brightened and he beamed a brilliant smile towards her. "I didn't know the Nordic types were capable of such fire. You're quite a woman, Susan Blaine."

The approval in his eyes was flattering and it was tempting to bask in the warmth of his admiration, but the man was too volatile a commodity for her to relax her guard openly.

"You're very kind, Major, but you must excuse me. If I

don't get my notes written up soon, I'll forget the results of my investigation." A business attitude was the best demeanor.

"But I too have very important matters that require attention."

"I'm sure the senior Mr. Forsythe is always ready to accommodate . . ."

"But, sweetheart, this is not that kind of business," he murmured suggestively.

"Major, I beg of you. I *must* get to my notes."

"Such dull, dreary business for such a lovely lady."

"Ladies have bills to pay too, my friend."

"Not if they have a man to look after them as they should."

"Oh, indeed!" Susan rose to the bait. "Am I to understand from that remark that ladies do not belong in the work world, or merely that it is only ignorant ladies who find themselves there?" Susan glared with her hands on her hips.

"I meant only that a woman as lovely as you should have better things to do with her time." Carlos reached out a hand and touched her hair.

"And better things, I suppose, are sex and seduction." Susan shook her hair free of his touch.

"I was thinking more in terms of love and romance."

"Those are merely euphemisms employed by predatory chauvinists to disguise their primitive instincts!"

Carlos raised his hands helplessly. "Peace, Madame Counselor, peace. I concede your forensic superiority."

Susan felt foolish and gauche. She had jumped on the soapbox and spouted nonsense because she was frustrated over the Vargas case. "Forgive me, Major Obregon. I spoke too hastily. I've had a very trying morning."

"De nada, niña. I like a woman with spirit." As Susan's eyes rekindled, he spoke hastily to derail her resurging ire. "My sister Elena tells me you are very impressed by our local history."

"The San Antonio missions were enchanting and your sister is a charming guide."

"Her brother is even more charming when given half a chance."

Susan studied the handsome face waiting for her response and weakened. What woman could resist such a desirable man and the flattery of his persistent attention? "And if I gave you half a chance . . . ?"

"I would reveal such marvels as only a privileged few are allowed to discover."

"My, my," Susan chided. "You sound like an advertisement for the Taj Mahal."

"Your mockery would change to wonder if you were to accept my invitation."

"You issued an invitation?"

"I want you to spend the afternoon with me at Hacienda Felicidad."

"Hacienda Felicidad. I haven't heard of it. Is it a museum?"

"It is my family estate."

"Oh." Susan was surprised. "I didn't mean anything . . . it's the name that threw me."

"It means house of happiness."

Susan heard the note of pride in Carlos's voice. "And is it a house of happiness?"

"Come see for yourself."

"The name sounds very appealing." Susan felt herself drawn to his offer, impelled by an inner vision of bright flowers and shadowy colonnades. "Is it far from here?"

"About twenty miles northwest of the city." The major waited patiently, allowing Susan's curiosity to work for him and prod her to accept his offer.

Susan was about to reach for a cigarette before answering, but the memory of his past censure held her back. "Very well, Major Obregon. Let's spend the afternoon at Hacienda Felicidad. I could use a change of pace right now." Carlos smiled with satisfaction. "Just let me speak to my secretary about these notes before we leave. I hope she can decipher my chicken scratching."

She ran into Owen in the hall and had to suppress a pang of guilt as she explained her plans for the afternoon. His disapproval was apparent, but he chose not to play the heavy by forbidding her departure even though he was her boss.

"I've had such a frustrating morning trying to scout witnesses for the Vargas case," Susan explained lamely.

Owen's face softened visibly. "There's no need to explain your actions to me, Susan. You're an adult and completely free to schedule your time as you see fit."

"I certainly don't want you to think that I am neglecting my responsibilities."

Owen smiled broadly, genuinely amused. "I know you wouldn't. I've seen how hard you work." He regarded her warmly. "You need a break. Go and relax and enjoy yourself . . . but not too much."

Susan smiled back happily. "Thanks, Owen. I appreciate your understanding."

Owen took her elbow as she turned to leave. "But a word of caution, Susan. Watch out for Obregon. He's a stalking panther. And you, I think, are an innocent lamb." He released her elbow and walked away while Susan thoughtfully studied his retreating back. She really liked that man. He seemed one of nature's noble creatures, and what a rarity that was.

The drive along Bandera Highway with Carlos at the wheel of his Jaguar was exhilarating. He drove at a high speed, but with such ease that Susan relaxed completely. His control was absolute.

Susan Blaine was unprepared for the grandeur of the Obregon estate. They sped down a tunnel of trees to an arched gateway of towering wrought iron, then continued farther along a curved drive that led to a low, sprawling villa surrounded on all sides by heavy white pillars that supported a red-tiled roof. It was a picture of old Spain; of shaded cloisters sheltering darkened interiors from the glare of the sun; of lush tropical flowers and cool verdure spilling abundantly from the grounds and trees.

"Oh, Carlos, how beautiful." Susan was captivated as the centuries seemed to dissolve and the Spanish aura penetrated her consciousness. "Your home is very appropriately named. This seems an oasis of peace and beauty."

"Thank you, *querida.* I knew you would be one to appreciate what is here." She sensed there was no artifice in his compliment, and he was offering her high praise. For Carlos there was nothing nobler or finer than his family home and all it represented. "This house has stood here many generations and endured many fortunes—some good and some bad—but it has stood strong and proud."

"I know. I can feel the long history as if the past were still present—invisible but here." Susan's face was filled with rapt admiration, as if deep streams of consciousness had been stirred and a subliminal recognition had occurred.

"You are very . . . *simpática.* Very sweet . . ." Carlos grasped her hand and placed a lingering kiss on her fingers.

Silence hung heavily in the warm summer air wrapping the couple in a magnetic spell of heightened awareness. Their eyes met and held and for a brief moment their spirits touched. The intensity was almost too strong to bear.

"What is that tree with the red flowers?" Susan questioned, seeking a neutral topic that would gently carry them out of the spell of hushed intimacy. "I've never seen one like it before."

"It is a frangipani. Not too many grow in the United States. It's a tropical variety."

"The perfume is very . . . distinct."

"Come, there's something I want to show you." Carlos took her hand and led Susan through tall french doors into a room lined with books and heavy dark furniture. Beside the red damask draperies there were two framed documents, yellow with age, hanging on the wall. "This is the original title to these lands. It is a grant for thirty thousand acres given to my ancestors by King Philip of Spain. If you look closely you can see the name Contreras Helotes Maldonado Valdez y Obregon. Come look." Carlos drew Susan beside him.

"Oh, yes. I can just make out Obregon. How marvelous. To think that a Spanish king so long ago gave this land to your family. You must be very proud."

He nodded his assent. "The other is a map of the territory as it was then."

"Everything belonged to Spain, it seems."

"It did."

"I wonder . . ." Susan let her thoughts drift.

"You wonder?" Carlos urged lightly.

Susan stopped herself before saying something impolite. She had no wish to engage in controversy with Carlos. "Oh, nothing. It's not important."

Carlos too had no wish to embark on a topic that might lead to dispute, and let the subject die. Instead he turned Susan to face himself and whispered, "Did I not promise marvels to discover?" He folded her in his arms, and she did not resist when he lifted her chin with his finger and kissed her tenderly on the mouth. It was a very sweet kiss of mutual discovery and exploration. They drew apart without further dalliance, but a promise had been made.

Lunch was served to them by an old manservant who spoke only Spanish. The patio where they dined was at the center of the house onto which the bedrooms and parlors opened. An attitude of repose and dignity emanated from the villa enfolding Carlos and Susan in a quiet intimacy, slowing their tempo imperceptibly until there seemed no need for talk. Occasional drifts of wind carried a faint bouquet of flowers that hovered and dissolved in the air, and the contemporary world seemed far away.

Susan wondered where Carlos's family was at the very moment he began to speak of them.

"My mother spends the month of August with my Uncle Tomás visiting members of the family in Madrid."

"Madrid? You have family in Spain?"

"Yes. There are more Obregons there than in the United States."

"I was wondering who lived here with you," admitted Susan.

"There is Elena, of course." Carlos looked troubled. "The girl is seldom home. She is studying law at St. Mary's."

"Yes, she told me. I think she'll make a fine attorney."

"She will never practice law." Carlos was very definite.

"She won't? Then why is she studying?" Susan was amazed.

"Because she created such a fracas, and it keeps her occupied for the present."

"Occupied! You mean pacified . . . like a child with candy!"

Carlos shrugged his shoulders indifferently, but a tight look had crept into his face.

"Why won't she ever practice law?" Susan prodded.

"She will get married."

"Can't she have both marriage and a career?" Susan challenged.

"Marriage is career enough for a decent woman." Carlos realized his error at once and looked sheepish. He glanced quickly at Susan to gauge her reaction and read her scorn accurately.

"Well, that certainly tells me what segment of society I inhabit in your little world!"

"Susan, I didn't mean to include you in my comment about Elena."

"And why not? I'm a woman and I practice law. Very indecent indeed!"

"But—"

"And furthermore, I walked out on a marriage—*repudiated* a marriage—very, very indecent indeed."

"You're magnificent. Such fire! You must be spectacular at the bar." His eyes glowed with admiration. "I pity your opponents. They don't stand a chance."

"Don't try to flatter your way out of your blunder, Major Obregon."

"I wouldn't dare. I plead guilty and throw myself on your mercy."

"I have none."

"No?" Carlos murmured seductively. "I don't believe it. There is mercy in the deep blue of your eyes and the sweet curve of your mouth." Carlos rose and stood behind Susan's chair. He placed a hand on her shoulder and she turned to look up at him. His eyes were warm with desire

43

and she obeyed instinctively when he raised her to her feet and drew her to him in a kiss of deep passion. She returned his kiss, allowing the heady wine of desire to melt her defenses and to compel her surrender to his passion. He kissed her long and lingeringly.

Later Carlos took Susan to the corral and showed her his collection of prize horses. The stables were clean and the stalls occupied by a line of animals matchless in aristocratic bearing and beauty. Susan fell in love with a sleek black stallion called Diego.

"Do you ride?" Carlos asked her.

She shook her head. "I've always wanted to learn, but I never had the opportunity."

"Then I'll teach you. We have a riding ring beside the paddock and a bridle path through the woods. Would you like a lesson?"

"Now?"

"Why not?"

"But I'm wearing a dress and heels—"

"And very lovely you are in the green linen, but I'm sure Elena has breeches that you can borrow."

"No, Carlos, I'd rather wait until another day."

"Don't be afraid, Susan. I won't let anything happen to you."

"I'm not afraid. What a silly thing to say." Susan was annoyed.

"Then why not start today? You will make a fine horsewoman, and someday I will let you ride Diego."

"You tempt me."

"Do I?" Carlos quirked a rakish eyebrow and circled her waist with his hands, drawing Susan against his hard body. "Mmm, maybe we won't go riding after all."

"I think I'll take my chances with the horses." Susan laughed, pushing Carlos away. "Let's find me the proper duds, as they say in these parts."

Susan's bravado wilted when she confronted Dulcinea a half hour later and tried to mount the animal under Carlos's watchful eye. She felt a damn fool when her foot slipped from the stirrup and she landed on her backside as she tried to hoist herself up.

44

"You have to brace your left foot in the stirrup and swing your other leg around," Carlos reiterated as he helped Susan to her feet.

She mounted on the second try but felt no triumph as she stared over the horse at the ground so far below. "Oh, God," she whispered as Carlos led her around the ring telling her to sit up straight with her shoulders back and feet flat in the stirrups, while she gripped the reins for dear life.

"No, no, *amiga,*" Carlos warned. "Firm, but not strangulation. You must be master, but at ease. Do you understand?" Carlos was exhibiting a style of command that Susan found extremely irritating in her heightened state of anxiety. But she had let herself in for the ordeal and was determined not to beg off before she had made an adequate show of spunk. Carlos sent her around the ring a couple of more times before he left her alone shortly and came back mounted on Diego.

"What are you doing? Where are you going?" Susan could not keep the alarm from her voice.

"Come on, I want to show you some of the land around the hacienda."

"You mean you want me to ride outside of the ring?"

"Of course. You are doing very well, *querida.* The ring was just for you to get the feeling of the horse."

"I really think I've had enough for one day, Carlos. Let's save the sightseeing for another time."

"It would be a shame to miss such a fine opportunity. Nothing will happen. You are perfectly safe with me." And he turned and led the horses out of the paddock towards the woods.

"Major Obregon," Susan called angrily, barely keeping an undignified screech out of her voice, "I prefer to close this session now!"

He looked over his shoulder and smiled condescendingly. "Remember to grasp the horse with your knees and keep the reins firm but relaxed." He nudged his horse into a canter and Dulcinea willingly followed behind.

Susan was stunned. Never before had any man so blithely ignored her wishes and cavalierly pursued his own way. His undisguised arrogance, his assumption of masculine dominion almost unseated her. He was simply ignoring her desires.

Susan bounced in the saddle until her teeth rattled and she finally grasped the fact that she had no control over the situation. She didn't even have time to work up a high-level grievance while she fought to stay in the saddle and evade the slapping leaves and poking branches that assaulted her through the woods. *Damn his Spanish hide,* she cursed inwardly and leaned low over the horse, clinging to its neck. *To hell with good form,* she thought viciously as she struggled to keep from falling.

Eventually they came out of the woods into a clearing that overlooked a vast expanse of rolling hills, green with waving grass which stretched for miles to a horizon glowing orange and red in the late afternoon sun. There were cattle grazing far below that looked like dark clouds moving across the distant ground.

Carlos dismounted and came to help Susan get down. She wanted to push him away, but she needed the support of his hands. Her legs felt wobbly and the ground too solid for her unsteady feet.

The awesome vista dissipated Susan's wrath. It no longer seemed of consequence in the midst of such natural splendor. What did it matter that Carlos had forced the ride on her if it resulted in this magnificent view?

"Tell me what you are thinking," Carlos asked of her after some moments of quiet.

"I find it hard to express. This is a grandeur that escapes language. Is all of it yours?"

"Yes. It has been in the Obregon family for many generations."

"And you expect it to remain so for generations to come."

"Of course."

"It's a great honor—something that I can barely understand—to be overseer of so much of the earth's goods."

"An honor and a burden," Carlos admitted frankly.

"A burden?"

"Such an inheritance imposes responsibilities and obli-

46

gations. Sometimes choices are not freely made." It was the first time Carlos had ever hinted that his life was not the carefree adventure that his flamboyant style suggested.

"You wouldn't ever give this up, would you?"

"No, never." Carlos was definite in his response. "But I sometimes wish that I was not the only son. If I had a brother, I might have entertained other notions."

"Really? Are you thinking of the Air Force? Would you make that your life?"

"Perhaps." Carlos was thoughtful for a long moment. "I know I could never give up flying. As much as I love this land, there is a feeling up there"—he looked to the burning blue above—"that is like . . . touching God."

Susan made no comment. She felt she had been given a private insight that Carlos seldom permitted outsiders. There was much more to Major Obregon than a handsome exterior and devilish charm. She felt a deep response within herself, as if hidden meanings were being revealed. This man was far more dangerous for having exposed a glimpse of his soul.

Carlos did not force Susan to ride back to the hacienda, but took her up onto the saddle in front of him and held her firmly clasped to his chest as he slowly rode Diego back with Dulcinea on a lead trailing behind. It was his first tacit admission that Susan's earlier distress was not lost on him, and she was amazed to find herself so gratified by his concern. There was something definitely treacherous to her newly liberated self in her ready capitulation to his masculine supremacy. They came up to the villa, which was now lighted by lanterns glowing softly beneath the colonnaded verandas. The house looked like a glowing jewel of gold and pink set in a soft velvet of muted blue and purple. The vision took her breath away and stole a corner of her heart. Carlos Obregon, his home, and his world, had taken on the dimensions of a dream. She felt her defenses tremble as a thrill of romance shivered delightfully along her nerves and touched her heart.

The day had been unexpectedly and deeply emotional for Susan. She felt compelled to see more of this exciting

47

man with whom she felt, so often, at great risk. On the drive back to San Antonio she eagerly accepted Carlos's invitation to a formal event that weekend, the precise nature of which Carlos typically left intriguingly mysterious.

Chapter Five

ALTHOUGH CARLOS'S PLANS for the coming evening were shrouded in mystery, Susan dressed carefully for the occasion because he had led her to believe it was to be a special event.

She was more liberal than usual with the amount of Norell she applied so deftly behind her small ears, over the full curve of her breast and along her slim arms before donning a sheath gown of blue silk with a low-cut bodice and a plunging back. After a final touch of "Royal Rose" to her lips, she viewed herself in the mirror. She was well pleased with her appearance and even more so when she saw the gleam of admiration in Carlos's eyes.

"You look absolutely magnificent this evening," he said in a low, husky voice that clearly intended to communicate much more by its tone.

"Why, thank you, kind sir." Susan was conscious of the desire that was kindling in his eyes, and in an effort to avert his hypnotic gaze, she rummaged aimlessly through her overnight bag.

"I'll take that." Carlos lifted it from her fingers, sending a delightful tingle along her arm as he held hers in a light grasp.

"I still can't imagine what kind of an affair this is where formal attire and a swimsuit are required," Susan commented as he helped her into his sleek black Jaguar. When there was no response from him she probed further. "Just where are we going, anyway?"

Sliding behind the wheel, he grinned and pinched her chin. "Curious as a cat, aren't you? But I told you, you must wait to find out."

"Carlos," Susan cried pleadingly.

"No, I wish you to be surprised," he said with finality and Susan sighed in acquiescence.

He started the engine and swung the car easily and quickly into the traffic. Soon they were traveling out of town along highway 35 passing New Braunfels. As the miles continued to click off on the speedometer, Susan grew uneasy. He was an able driver and handled his classic car effortlessly, but he was driving fast and seemed to be fascinated with the purring of its powerful engine. Susan tried to hide her edginess, but when they finally sped past the San Marcos exit, she demanded to know where they were going.

"Niña, you don't trust me?" In the warmth of his smile, Susan's distrust vanished and Carlos turned the conversation away from their destination to her job. Susan began explaining about her harassment case and the difficulties she was having in finding witnesses who were willing to testify on behalf of her client.

"It is only natural that no decent woman would wish to become involved in such a case," he stated baldly.

Susan tried to maintain a cool, logical exterior. "Correct me if I'm wrong, but are you saying that only *indecent* women would be involved in a case of sexual harassment?"

"Perhaps *indecent* is too strong a word. Let's say I do not think most women want it known that they have had an association with another woman who has allowed herself to be put in such a position."

"Has allowed herself?" Susan exploded. "She is the *victim!"* Now her composure was shattered. She hated whenever this happened to her, but she just wasn't going to sit back and accept this line of reasoning.

"This kind of thing should be settled out of court. There is no need to hang dirty linen in public."

"Dirty linen? This isn't some petty, private quarrel we're talking about. It's a serious problem, and as long as the public is unaware or unwilling to deal with the issue openly and honestly, it will continue to exist."

"Ah, but is there really an issue here, or are some women merely trying to make one?"

"Believe me, Carlos, I can show you statistics on just how widespread the problem is."

"Mmm?" he mused doubtfully. "Do you not think that these women are doing this to create trouble?"

"Oh, I am sure there are any number of those cases," Susan said, trying to be fair. "But in my client's case, absolutely not."

"If this is true, why didn't she just turn the job down?"

"Why should she? She was qualified."

"Have you considered the possibility that she tried to use her sexual wiles to get the job in the first place, and when it backfired she decided to get even."

"That's unfair! Do men use sex to get their jobs?"

"Of course not."

"No, of course not, because they dominate the work place, and they extort sex from women as the price they must pay to get ahead."

"Oh, come off it, Susan. Most men don't have to blackmail women into having sex . . . especially today. A woman like your client probably asked for it and she got what she deserved."

"My God, Carlos, where have you been the last twelve years? How can you be so unaware of the women's movement and the plight of some women?"

"Susan, to my way of thinking, there are two kinds of women: the wife and mother of a man's children who is protected by her role in society, and the sex goddess who knows how to take care of herself."

"Your classification of women is typical of the egocentric male chauvinist. You put a woman either in the kitchen or in the bed, but refuse to view her as an equal—especially in the work world. I hate that kind of condescension!"

Carlos was furious with himself. He realized too late where this debate was leading them and that now he had an angry, unhappy woman to contend with. The weekend would be ruined by his careless remarks. Suddenly he swung the car off the road and came to a stop, startling Susan.

"Niña." His voice caressed her, but she did not respond.

His hand rested lightly on her shoulder. She flinched away and Carlos sighed. "Susan, if I sounded condescending I apologize. You see," he explained, "I have been raised a chauvinist, and that is not easy to change. But perhaps between you and my sister Elena I can be re-educated." Carlos flashed his winning smile again, this time with visible traces of repentance that mollified Susan's wrath. "I promise it won't be easy. Do you think you're equal to the task?"

Susan discerned seduction through the thin veneer of his apology. She was convinced he could charm an eel out of a tree. "Oh, I'll gladly accept that challenge, Major Obregon. It will be a pleasure re-educating you."

He threw back his head and laughed loudly with Susan joining in. Then he swept her into his arms. "One kiss, my lovely, to seal the bargain." The kiss was light and cherishing and then he backed deliberately away from her. "I don't want to disturb your delectable appearance," he said as he pulled the car back on to the road, "since we are very near our destination, and"—he checked the handsome Piaget watch on his arm—"if traffic doesn't hold us up, we shall make it on time."

"On time for what?" Susan asked as the sign for downtown Austin whizzed by.

"For the premiere of *The Best Little Whorehouse in Texas.*"

"What? Is that where we're going?"

"And why else would I dress up in a monkey suit?"

"I don't believe it!"

"Well, if you don't believe me, just look ahead as I round this corner." Floodlights spotted the sky and a police barricade blocked the street. Carlos eased up to the police line, pulled out what Susan recognized as a special invitation card and their car was permitted to slip through the blockade.

Susan was too thrilled and excited to speak as they stopped in front of the Paramount Theater and a uniformed attendant opened the car doors. Carlos slid his hand inside her elbow and guided her through the police line that held back a gawking mob of admirers and a retinue of cameras and media people.

"They think we're celebrities," Carlos shouted into her ear over the noisy crowd. Susan nodded in stunned silence as they reached the lobby where the fashionably dressed throng of socialites milled about. Susan clutched nervously at Carlos's arm as she recognized several famous stars and struggled desperately to maintain her composure. She envied Carlos's easy manner and self-assurance in the company of so many well-known figures. Tanya Tucker, Mel Tillis, and the Statler Brothers were introduced to her along with Austin's mayor and a host of other influential community figures. She couldn't help being impressed with how warmly they greeted Carlos and how he, in turn, knew them on such familiar terms. More introductions ensued until she thought her head would never stop spinning, and even the governor shook her hand with characteristic Texan hospitality. Then the roar of the crowd outdoors grew tumultuous announcing the arrival of Dolly Parton and Burt Reynolds.

"I'll introduce you to them after the show," Carlos promised as he escorted her to their seats in the auditorium. "It would be impossible now."

The Paramount was a beautiful theater, the pride of the city's cultural efforts. Originally built almost seventy years ago, it was one of the most precious historical landmarks in the state. Sarah Bernhardt had performed there and so had Caruso and the Juilliard String Quartet. For many years it was also a first run film theater and only recently it had become a national performing arts center. A tremendous restoration effort costing millions had returned the structure to its original luxury.

Tickets to this premiere showing were in keeping with the level of opulence the theatre sought to attain. Susan knew that prices started at one hundred and went as far as five hundred dollars each. The thought of that alone made her wonder what the forces were in her life that brought her here from a small rural community in northwestern Pennsylvania to this front-row box seat in Austin, Texas, sitting side by side with faces and figures that until now she could only know through her fantasies.

After the premiere the cavalcade of classic autos and limousines made its way to the Hyatt Regency for a party, a fabulous dinner and celebration held for all the patron ticket holders. It was a western-style black-tie and boots extravaganza that provided enough food and champagne to satisfy an entire Texas county. But the high point of the evening came for Susan when Burt Reynolds stopped at their table to speak to Carlos and she was introduced to him.

At first she felt shy, but Mr. Reynolds was warm, friendly, and very witty and soon had her at ease chatting merrily. Nevertheless, after he moved on, she found it difficult to grasp the reality of the whole experience.

It was a noisy, rollicking evening, immensely exciting and thoroughly interesting, leaving Susan on an emotional high. She snuggled against Carlos's arm as they drove through streets that appeared misty blue under the glow of the mercury lamps that lighted the city by night.

"I must say, Carlos, you travel in some pretty exalted company," Susan commented.

"Are you duly impressed?" His smile was self-mocking.

"I most certainly am. This has been one of the most exciting evenings of my entire life. I'll never forget it."

"But wait, it isn't over yet."

"Carlos, it's three o'clock in the morning."

"So? Should the hour determine our enjoyment? Remember I asked you to bring your swimsuit? Wouldn't you enjoy a relaxing moonlight swim?"

Susan eyed him suspiciously, but his invitation was too tantalizing to turn down. There was a hint of promise in his offer and she awaited the next surprise Carlos had in store for her. Surely he was one of the most unpredictable men she had ever encountered and perhaps that was why she was so fascinated by him.

On the outskirts of the city, Carlos guided the car through a pair of impressive wrought-iron gates and along a winding lane edged with rhododendrons and azaleas. They emerged before a terraced lawn and porticoed mansion that was hidden from the road. Carlos continued past the house to a gravel path and a second wooded area. Finally, they reached yet another clearing where a colorfully lighted deck, pool, and cabanas were revealed. He brought the car to a halt in front of a small cottage.

"Where are we?" Susan asked.

"It is the estate of Mr. and Mrs. Albert Torres, the banking family. You met them earlier this evening. Remember?"

"I met so many people."

"It doesn't really matter. They've given us the use of the cabana and pool for the remainder of the evening if we wish to use it." Seeing the wary look in her eyes he chuckled, "Of course, we will leave whenever you wish." Without another word he drew her closer to him and led her up a short flight of stone steps that brought them to a rustic-looking cabin. Once inside, he flicked a switch that lit up a room that boasted wooden beams and a huge fireplace. It gave Susan the feeling of a hunting lodge, informal and relaxing with leisurely furnishings and rich leather chairs. The slate floors, the animal trophies and varied assortment of hand weapons displayed on the walls created a strongly masculine environment. It crossed Susan's mind that she might very well be the prey in this setting, especially when Carlos provided her with a tour of the bedroom with its rich velvet drapes and heavy Spanish bed and chests. Did he expect her to share it with him? Most likely he did. But she wasn't sure she was ready to give herself to him.

Carlos was assessing the cautious look in her dark blue eyes and spoke deliberately to reassure her. "You can change in here *undisturbed* and I'll use the room next door. Unless," he said with a sly smile, "you prefer some company."

"No, I like the first arrangement just fine. But," she said, closing the door slowly, "if I need room service, I'll ring." Susan smirked at herself in the full-length mirror, satisfied with her retort and pleased too, with her lissome figure as she removed her evening dress and rummaged through her overnight bag for her swimsuit. Her lavender bikini was a good choice, she thought as she slipped into the flimsy garment that revealed her flat stomach and fit skin-tight around her youthful breasts. Standing there with her hands on her hips, she wondered whether things between the two of them were happening too fast. This was not her usual mode of behavior—throwing caution to the wind. Carlos was dangerous to her sense of balance, but he made her feel so jubilant, so carefree, so wonderful, that it was next to impossible to remain sensible and consider the risks of being exposed to such a magnetic male. And at the moment she didn't intend to. Grinning eagerly, she went in search of him.

Carlos was already in the pool, his bronzed body and black hair gleaming under the cabana lights. He swam with quick energetic movements, his figure silhouetted by the aquamarine lights of the kidney-shaped pool. Susan smiled and waved to him playfully as he stopped to view her curvaceous figure. Without speaking a word his eyes lingered on her approvingly and then roamed lustily along the contours of her body.

Susan sat at the edge of the pool and tested the water with her toes. Carlos climbed out of the water and onto the diving board. Her eyes were attracted first to his deeply tanned, well-shaped torso and then to the trim black European trunks hiding his maleness. Quickly she lowered her gaze to his firmly muscled legs as he stood poised on the board. *He's physically perfect,* she thought, as she watched him do a neat back flip into the pool. Surfacing beside her, his arm snaked around her small waist and he pulled her down beside him in the tepid water.

"That was superb." She applauded him gaily.

"Thank you," he bowed his head and kissed her shoulder. "Now it's your turn."

"I'd rather watch you." Her lips curved provocatively as he still held her.

"And I'd rather watch you," he countered and lifted her to the rim of the pool. His eyes seemed to drink in her loveliness and then she felt his hand touch her thigh and he planted a wet kiss on it. That triggered off a strange shudder along Susan's spine. The feeling disconcerted her and she rose hastily from where she sat and somewhat self-consciously proceeded to the diving board knowing he was watching her every move. She wanted to adjust the clinging suit but didn't dare attract any more attention to herself. Quickly she plunged into the pool and swam towards the opposite end, but before she reached her destination, two muscular arms seized her. Her natural instincts were to struggle from his grip, but Carlos pulled her resisting body more tightly into his arms and kissed her. She murmured something unintelligible in protest, and he smiled at her futile efforts. Lifting her into his arms, he strode to the cottage and directly into the bedroom.

Susan shuddered with a mixture of apprehension and anticipation as he silently removed her bra. She had known the question of sex would arise between them this evening, but it wasn't going to be easy for her. It had been some time since she had been with a man like this, desire churning inside with his every touch. Flashes of her ex-husband and the way their most treasured intimacies dissolved into ashes pierced her consciousness. Now what about this relationship? Where was she heading this time? Susan thought she had come to grips with love and sex, but this was the moment of truth.

There was no denying that his body next to hers set off a series of impulses that had been seeking release for some time. Carlos was clearly experienced at lovemaking and she marveled at how adroitly he aroused her senses and how quickly she responded to the delicate touch of his lips on her breast and his hands on her thigh. Then his mouth covered hers, first lightly, then with more force and passion, leaving her weak with desire.

"Your body was made to love," he uttered in that throaty voice. "Yet you seem to be tense. It is not natural for you to hold back, as I feel you are. Must I persuade you?"

"I . . . I'm sorry," she answered faintly. "Maybe I'm just not sure of myself and what I mean to you, Carlos . . . and where this relationship is heading."

"Don't let your legal training get in the way of your heart, my sweet." Her statement unsettled him. "Women

are not meant to be so rational and precise . . . especially
when it comes to love. Our desire to be one is all we need to
know about one another for now. Follow your emotions,
not courtroom logic, Susan."

"Courtroom logic! *Desire* is all we need to know!" The
words set off an alarm system in Susan's head. *Women not
meant to be rational.* That was all it took to annihilate any
lovemaking instincts he had aroused in her. It was all over
now. She knew it and so did he. It could never work out between them, not with that prehistoric, Castilian attitude
that he had embedded in his brain.

"What is it?" he demanded, bewildered, as she rose
abruptly from the bed and retrieved her lingerie from the
overnight case. Turning her back to him, she snapped her
bra in place.

"I just think that this was a mistake, that's all, Carlos."
Susan walked towards the bathroom with her clothing,
but before she could reach it Carlos had grasped her by the
arm and twisted her around to face him.

"What's that supposed to mean?" His eyes blazed angrily.

"Let me go, please!"

"Not until you tell me what kind of game you are
playing here!"

"It's not a game," she returned wrathfully. "I won't be
used by you. That's all."

"Used? You wanted me as much as I wanted you. Isn't
that so?"

"That might have been true, but I won't let any man
think of me merely as some sex object. And I know you do!"

"How do you know what I'm thinking?"

"It's your attitude. You don't see me as a person."

"How else should I see you"—he laughed—"but as a
lovely woman?"

"As an equal."

"Bah, that's just a slogan that's empty of meaning.
You're not worthy of such an uncritical acceptance of these
popularized fantasies. There are very real differences between men and women that no demonstration or law will
ever change." Then he gave her an appealing smile, "Be-

sides, how else would you expect me to act when I'm making love? Or," he said jokingly, "do you wish to assume the male role? Would you have preferred I let you carry me in here tonight?"

"I'm not going to be belittled in this manner." Susan folded her arms in front of her, refusing to see the humor in his remark.

"God damn it," he stormed. "You seem to be easily upset by my attitudes toward women, but have you examined your own recently? Free love is sanctioned by practically everyone in society today." He began pacing up and down like a caged panther. "So why this dramatic display from you? Are you planning to make every encounter between you and some man a forum for women's rights?"

"Of course not. Not all men treat women the way you do."

"I've never had any complaints until now. I'm at a loss to understand. What would you have me do?"

Susan felt they were on a merry-go-round getting nowhere. "Drive me back to San Antonio, or call me a cab so I can catch a bus from the station."

"I brought you and I will deliver you home," he said in a voice that was infuriatingly calm and collected. "No gentleman would think of doing otherwise."

A predictable stony silence enveloped them as they sped along in the predawn light back to San Antonio. Susan feigned sleep because it was easier that way. A perfectly beautiful evening had been destroyed and she reflected that perhaps she had won the battle but had lost the war in the process. It seemed absurd now, looking back on how it all happened, how it was triggered off so quickly by just a simple word or two, how it occurred without their volition, and finally how she wished she could say or do something right at this moment to clear the whole mess up. But she couldn't bring herself to think or say anything that would do any good at all. Instead, she just sat there mute and uncomfortable throughout an interminable drive until the car jerked to an abrupt stop outside of her apartment building.

True to form, Carlos got out to open her door in what

seemed almost a military fashion to Susan. His face was a blank mask.

"I . . ." she faltered. "I'm sorry it had to end this way."

"So am I. But there are no guarantees in this life." He shrugged and walked back to the car. "Good night. . . . Or should I say . . . good morning?" Before she could respond, he'd ducked into the car and driven away.

She was too tired now to think through all that had happened. All she knew was that if she had tumbled into bed with him without a better understanding between them, he probably would have thought less of her and within a few weeks would have discarded her for someone else.

With a man like Carlos it was the chase and conquest that counted. Although she didn't think she needed a lasting commitment at this time in her life, she didn't want a relationship in which she gave and he simply took. She wanted some kind of mutual understanding, but it was apparent she wouldn't get it from Carlos. As she climbed into bed, it was her rational side that told her it was probably better this way. But she remembered what he had said about the heart, too, and wondered if he hadn't made a more valid point than she originally thought.

Chapter Six

Monday morning Susan gladly returned to work. The pressures of her growing case load would help divert her attention away from Carlos and she was thankful for that.

But all day Sunday while she had read the papers, washed her lingerie and done some shopping, he seemed to intrude into her consciousness. And her adrenalin soared whenever the phone rang, lifting her hopes that Carlos would be at the other end of the line eager to see her again. But Carlos never did call, and Susan found herself thinking that perhaps it was best that way. Maybe she really didn't need or want the complications of a man in her life right now. Wasn't it enough to be free of all those smothering constraints of a dull marriage? Hadn't she learned one lesson already? Besides, her new job was complicated enough with its own set of demands and she realized that she had a great deal of personal pride invested in what she was doing.

The Maria Vargas case, in particular, had given Susan a real sense of purpose, but it had the potential to turn into a nightmare. Her worst fear was beginning to materialize. Reliable witnesses who could corroborate Maria's story had not come forth. But she had not given up. This very afternoon she was lunching with Margaret Peron, the account executive from the Haas Company who had consented to come and hear Susan out despite a great deal of reluctance.

She was a small, wiry woman with a determined chin and the forceful manner of a person who sells investments, an area of human endeavor traditionally the province of the male species. Watching her sip a martini and drag repetitively on a cork-tipped cigarette, Susan speculated that her counterpart was quite comfortable in the world of men and wondered whether she would be sympathetic to the plight of her client. She hoped she was.

"So you're Maria Vargas's friend."

"Attorney." Susan corrected with emphasis.

"Yes, all right. Well, I'm going to tell you exactly what I told Maria. 'Roll with the punches, kid, until you're in a position to fight back!' But I don't think Maria's in that position, Ms. Blaine."

It was evident that Margaret Peron was not going to be easily won over, but Susan intended to try.

"If I can obtain witnesses to support her case, she *will* be in a position to win. But I need *reliable* witnesses who want to see justice done. Are you willing to help me, Ms. Peron?" Susan's direct and sincere gaze seemed to have a mollifying effect on her companion.

"Well, I agreed to meet with you, Ms. Blaine. But I'm not sure I can give you the help you need. I know next to nothing about Maria and Harmon from direct personal experience."

"Let me be the judge of that. It's amazing sometimes how the smallest piece of information can unlock a whole warehouse of important facts and change the entire picture. Maria needs that break."

A waitress came to take their orders and brought their discussion to a temporary halt. Afterwards Margaret was the first to resume.

"I'm willing to help if I can, Ms. Blaine."

Susan heaved a sigh of relief and held out her hand. "Thank you. Witnesses have not been easy to come by."

"I know. Mrs. Hayes and the other secretary you tried to interview let it be known throughout the company where they stand. You can't blame them really. They're afraid of losing their jobs."

"What about you?" Susan asked pointedly.

"Sure I'm worried; that's why I resisted you at first. But to tell you the truth, I'm sick to death of the garbage Harmon's been getting away with all these years."

"And men like Harmon will continue to dish it out until we focus enough attention on cases like this one. It's important for women to stick together—"

"Whoa, wait a minute." Margaret held up her hand to clarify her position. "I'm not a women's libber, Ms. Blaine. I'm not interested in fighting other people's battles. I'm not into causes."

"I'm not going to ask you to organize a demonstration," Susan said lightly.

Although Margaret smiled she went on seriously, "This is for my friend Maria. A one-time thing. I'm not a crusader."

"It wouldn't be fair to ask you to lead a crusade in this situation. Maybe you'll want to do that later." Again Susan tried for the lighter touch. Then she went on resolutely, "But for now all Maria needs is the support of a credible witness who can offer valid and reliable testimony on her behalf. If you are willing to do that, you'll accomplish a lot more than most demonstrations will and you'll be helping a friend and perhaps most other women in similar situations as well." Susan stopped to see if she had her convinced.

Margaret toyed thoughtfully with her empty martini glass. "Well, what is it you want specifically to know about?"

That was the kind of opening Susan had been looking for. Feeling now that the ice had been broken, she felt free to bring out her note pad and begin questioning in earnest.

By the time she left the restaurant, Susan's spirits had risen considerably. Margaret Peron had been able to give her specific details and the address of Jane Connery, another possible witness. Unfortunately Ms. Connery was now living in Massachusetts. Would she be willing to fly to Texas for the trial? Susan intended to find out.

One of Owen's strategies for keeping on top of his staff's work was to call each individual into his office at least bi-weekly for a brief, informal review of their cases and an update on their progress. It was intended to be a non-threatening meeting, held over coffee, and Owen was usually very skillful in putting people at ease and helping them clarify and solve their problems. But this time, when he seated himself on the edge of his desk in front of Susan Blaine, she couldn't ward off a palpable agitation that seemed to first flutter inside and then tighten like an overwound spring. Maybe it was his characteristic self-assurance or was it his slick professionalism that somehow rattled her? Susan couldn't be sure what it was as she started to give a coherent accounting of herself.

"I thought this was going to be a pretty difficult case to get off the ground," he said sympathetically. "Tell me everything."

Susan glanced up at him and smiled. "Using your best attorney-client approach on me, Owen?" Her remark caught him totally off guard.

"Afraid you caught me out to lunch, Sue. I guess I'll have to monitor my approach a little more carefully. But why don't you tell me anyway. It looks like you need to ventilate a bit."

"God, you're right, Owen." Susan sprang from the chair and began pacing the room. "I'm having a devil of a time coming up with reliable witnesses."

"I thought you told me earlier in the week that Ms. Peron was willing—"

"She is, but so far she's the only one. I tried to get Jane Connery, but she's got too good an excuse. It's too far to travel. Everyone has some lame reason or other."

"You knew that would be the case before you started."

"I know." Susan threw her arms up in the air and then let them fall to her sides in exasperation.

"Are you giving up then?"

"No, damn it, I'm not!" Fire leapt into her eyes.

"Then are you looking for some advice?"

"Yes."

Owen came to her and propped up her chin with his long index finger. "Try Juarez. He has nothing to lose. He's re-tired. If necessary, hit him in his pride—defending the honor of Mexican-American womanhood."

His suggestion brought a rebellious glare to her eyes and Owen was quick to pick up the cue.

OPPOSITES ATTRACT

"Oh, I know, I know," he assured her. "That's the kind of thing you want to avoid as a modern woman. But you want to win, don't you? Then fight with every tool available to you. Don't worry about the niceties of how you do it. You need a victory. It will serve as a showcase in the future and this could be it. So go after it. I know you can do it, Sue." He grasped her shoulder and squeezed her lightly.

"Why, yes, of course, you're right, Owen. That's a good strategy. I'm going to tackle Juarez tomorrow. Thanks for the suggestion." She placed her hand on his. "I'm even ready to take on Harmon's lawyer, Tom Morley, even if he is one of the best in the country."

"Don't forget"—Owen pointed his index finger at her—"Morley approached you about an out-of-court settlement. It wasn't the other way around."

"That's true. If he were so confident of winning, he wouldn't have done that, would he?"

"Now," Owen cautioned, "don't jump to conclusions. Remember in a case like this, once the press and public get hold of it, even if Harmon wins, his reputation will suffer."

"Hmmmm, that's a good point. I hadn't thought of that. Even if I lose the case, I win. Right? Although I would prefer it the other way around," she joked.

Owen laughed and put his arm around her shoulder to give her an affectionate squeeze. "That's my girl. You can let me know how things went with Juarez over dinner at my place tomorrow night. That is, if you will come."

"I . . ." She paused, and Owen cocked his head at her hesitation.

"Yes?" he encouraged.

Letting out a nervous giggle, she went on to explain, "It just crossed my mind that if you were a different kind of man I could find myself in a situation similar to that of Maria Vargas."

"Good God, Susan!" Owen's eyebrows had shot up in astonishment. "Surely you never considered me in such a light?"

"No, no, of course not. But it has made me consider the pitfalls of an office romance."

"Yes, I'm aware of those hazards too. And personally I

65

think it's worth the risk." Taking her hands in his, he asked in a deep voice, "What do you think, Sùe?"

A small thrill of excitement ran along her spine. It was gratifying to know that he had considered the possible difficulties and still wanted her company. "Yes," she agreed enthusiastically. "Yes, I think it's worth it, Owen."

"I'm glad." He pressed her hands before releasing them. Then smiling, he added, "Now, all I have to hope is that my cooking is good enough to please you."

"Don't tell me you're doing the cooking?"

"Now who's being a chauvinist?" he chided.

Sue shook her head and chuckled. "Isn't it awful how we're all programmed?"

"That depends. There are some clichés about the sexes I wouldn't change for the world."

"Such as?" Susan challenged.

"Wait until tomorrow night. We can discuss them all then." Owen punctuated his sentence with a sly smile. "I'll expect you at about seven-thirty for cocktails."

"I'll be there."

As she stepped out of the elevator and started down the corridor towards Owen's apartment, Susan became aware of an anxious feeling that had been building in the pit of her stomach. This was a new experience for her. How should she act when calling on a man? It was a reversal of roles for her and she wasn't sure she could handle it without appearing foolish. Maybe the old custom was better after all, when men simply called on women and took care of all of the details. Certainly Carlos would never approve of this arrangement. Damn! Why did she have to think of him? She wasn't about to let him intrude upon her evening with Owen and spoil it. She pushed the doorbell to the apartment with a vengeful thrust of her finger, almost as if in retaliation for the thought about Carlos.

Owen greeted her wearing a tan pullover with an open neck and a pair of dark slacks that accented his lean, aristocratic look. Even when he was out of his familiar business suit, his informal clothes reflected good taste, on the conventional side, but definitely expensive. His apartment had the same kind of feeling. A black and white tiled foyer led into a spacious living room decorated mainly with Chinese furnishings although an eclectic motif was evident in his choices of sculpture, paintings, and accent pieces. Owen Forsythe definitely had the eye of the connoisseur.

"What a grand room."

"I'm glad you like it." Owen went immediately to a glass cart and selected a bottle. "Let's start with a drink. Is a Vouvray all right or would you prefer something else?"

"No, that will be fine." As she seated herself on the sofa, Susan realized she was still holding the bottle of brandy she'd brought for the occasion. Feeling slightly foolish, she held it out to him when he returned with their drinks.

"This is for you. I'm hoping your mother never told you not to accept gifts from strange women."

"Not exactly." He grinned. "But this is a first. Thank you, Sue. I'm glad you brought it for more than one reason. Not only will I enjoy drinking it, but it also gives me a good reason for kissing you."

"Do you need one?" she asked boldly.

"I hope not," he replied, bending his head to hers. Their lips met in a light lingering kiss. "Mmm, what a nice preview of things to come," he whispered. "Now while I check on dinner would you like to see the view from the balcony?" He opened the sliding doors and invited her to step outside while he disappeared momentarily.

San Antonio was a spectacular sight from twelve stories up. In the twilight, the city twinkled like a jewel and it captivated her attention for a long period of time.

"It's beautiful," she whispered when Owen stepped up behind her and encircled her waist.

"And you're beautiful, too." His lips pressed lightly against her ear and sent a tingling sensation up her arm and neck.

"I could stay here forever."

"We'll come back when the moon has risen. But right now dinner is served." He took her hand and led her to the table.

"What is it? It smells delicious."

*"Coq au vin—*I hope."

"It's hard to believe a corporate lawyer could also be a gourmet cook."

"Ah-ha, the chauvinist surfaces again!" he countered playfully and Susan stammered incoherently until he went on lightly, "But wait until you taste it. I must confess this is my first attempt."

"I have a sneaking suspicion," she said, recovering, "that whatever you do turns out a success."

"Thanks for the confidence, my dear. Now just let me turn on the tape deck and we can begin with our fruit cup."

It was a relaxing, intimate meal, and their conversation was light as Susan praised his culinary skill and suggested that she would be hard pressed to surpass his efforts when she prepared dinner for him.

"But the only other thing I cook is bacon and eggs," he confessed.

"Oh, well, that relieves the pressure on me," Susan teased as he placed peaches and ice cream in front of her.

It was only when the coffee had arrived that their conversation grew serious. Owen asked her how the interview with Juarez had gone and Susan explained that although Juarez had listened politely enough to her, he had not committed himself one way or the other. She was given the impression that Juarez was not very fond of Maria Vargas, so she had tried the chivalry angle suggested by Owen, although she hadn't liked using that ploy. It might have worked; at least Juarez had agreed to see her again.

Sitting here discussing the case with Owen brought back all her earlier misgivings about having dinner with him and getting involved in an office romance. Was any man really trustworthy? Wasn't Owen the boss? Couldn't he use his position against her if he so chose? As these thoughts crossed her mind, she rejected them as unfair to Owen.

Sensing her growing unease, Owen moved quickly to divert her attention from the Vargas case. He could understand her doubts about a personal relationship between them, but he had no intention of letting business spoil their evening together.

At a well-timed moment, Owen rose from the table and held out his hand to lead her from the table. It was a simple gesture, but it made Susan acutely aware of how easily he carried himself with such authority and confidence. She wondered how and where he had acquired those traits as she took his cue and placed her hand in his. Together they returned to the balcony while Chopin continued to play softly in the background. The after-dinner brandy left a warm glow, and Susan felt a sense of contentment as she rested her head against his shoulder while they watched the moon rising over the skyline. Slowly he turned her in his arms and kissed her deeply and meaningfully. It was the kind of kiss that made her want him to continue. But when he whispered the suggestion that they return to the living room, that broke the spell. Was this going to be the moment of truth between the two of them? Did she want Owen Forsythe to make love to her? As they passed the dining room table, she seized upon a delaying tactic. "Why don't you let me help you with these."

"No need. My butler will do them in the morning."

"What?" Susan came to a halt. "You fraud."

Owen's eyebrows shot up. "Why am I a fraud?"

"You gave me the impression you took care of everything yourself."

"Only on Alfred's days off or when I want to be alone with someone." He squeezed her hand gently, but Susan pulled away and walked towards the tape deck.

"Is something the matter, Susan?"

"No, of course not." She gave him a weak smile. "Do you have any Brahms?"

Owen didn't immediately reply and Susan waited tensely. "I'm glad you didn't ask for Tchiakovsky. Cigarette?"

Susan nodded and he brought the pack over to her, lighting one for each of them.

"Why not Tchiakovsky?" she asked after inhaling deeply.

"Too melodic. I like more contrapuntal scores."

"I like both. I guess I'm not as discriminating as you."

"As a lawyer I've learned to judge people accurately and

I happen to think you are very discriminating as well as clever."

"Oh, please don't flatter me, Owen."

"I'd never stoop to flattery," he stated with arrogance. "I hope you believe me when I say that you are special to me." His eyes held hers. Susan felt herself drawn to him but held back. She couldn't overcome her doubts about their association.

Realizing she had withdrawn from him, Owen led her to the sofa and sat down beside her. "Okay, Sue, let's have it. Something's troubling you and I know it's not the butler doing the dishes." He tried for a light touch, but she didn't respond.

"I don't think this is going to work after all, Owen."

"What's not going to work?"

"I think you know."

"You mean two brilliant lawyers enjoying an evening together?" He grinned, refusing to be daunted by her pessimism.

"No, I mean employer dates employee."

"Mmm, I suppose I could always fire you, but I doubt if that would improve our friendship," he chided mischievously before speaking seriously. "Why don't we take a look at the alternatives open to us?" Susan agreed and he explained, "As I see it there are two options open to us. One, we simply forget about seeing each other, or two, we maintain a professional relationship at the office and after hours we enjoy a personal . . . friendship."

"That's easier said than done."

"You surprise me, Susan, using that old cliché. Where's your sense of adventure?"

From under her eyelashes Susan studied him. Somehow she had expected Owen to be more cautious, more conservative, but instead he was being remarkably impetuous, and she found herself responding to it.

"What do you say, Sue?"

Gradually raising her eyes to his, she replied, "I suppose we could take it slowly." She waited for confirmation.

"Slowly," he agreed. His eyes continued to hold hers until she found herself capitulating.

Without conscious thought she found herself once again in his arms and instinctively she drew herself closer to his chest. Her hands found their way about his neck and into his soft hair. Warm, gentle kisses passed between them. And feather light caresses floated down her back and across her buttocks. Then he cradled her in his arms and she felt her mind go blank.

He was gentle in his lovemaking and his manner was so compelling that Susan craved more. She pressed against his taut body and his grip about her slender figure grew firmer. Then slowly he was releasing her, his fingers delicately massaging her neck. "You're a giving woman, Susan, besides being beautiful and discriminating." There was a sensuous smile as his mouth sought hers and his tongue slid delectably along her lips. "You know I want to make love to you, but only if you feel as I do."

Susan realized that he was leaving the decision up to her. *Do I want to love this man?* How different he was from Carlos. Abruptly she broke away from Owen, whose face took on a look of concern. But he said nothing and only waited. If she said yes to Owen would she be doing it to spite Carlos in some way? That wasn't fair to Owen or herself. When she gave herself to any man, it would have to be with genuine feelings for that person, not confused emotions masquerading as affection. She turned back to Owen, who had been watching her with questioning eyes. He was leaning against the fireplace mantel, a cigarette in his hand.

"I need more time, Owen. It's a lot for me to handle right now. The divorce from Jeff . . ." She realized she was making excuses, and giving him half-truths, so she stopped. "I hope you don't think I misled you." She paused momentarily and then continued, "I'd like you to ask me again sometime, after I've gotten my life's direction straightened out a little better." She waited for him to say something in response, something that would help both of them out of this awkward situation. "You're angry with me, aren't you?" she finally pressed.

"Angry . . . no. But disappointed . . . very. However, I understand about the scars of divorce. My ex left some deep ones of her own." He turned away from her and filled two brandy snifters.

"Do you miss her?" she asked as he handed her a glass. His face took on the look of someone who had just made a last payment on a bad debt.

"No, my dear, I do not miss 'Little Miss Gloria.' I am relieved to have her out of my life." He swirled the dark liquid in his snifter, studying its patterns carefully. "I suppose," he finally said, "that it is only fair to tell you. I have no intention of ever marrying again. Once for any man is enough."

"Or any woman," Susan countered.

Owen threw back his head and let out that peculiar kind of laugh that signals a realization about the limits of what life has to offer.

"Well, I'm happy to see that you and I can share the same attitudes toward the marital state . . . though we weren't able to share the same bed tonight."

He muttered the last part of his sentence with such feigned, overwhelming regret, that Susan couldn't hold back a laugh. Owen held up his brandy glass for a toast.

"Let's drink to our mutual freedom, shall we?"

Susan clinked her glass against his with a smile, happy that they were coming to a clearer understanding. But Owen sealed the pact with a throaty, playful warning.

"That doesn't mean that I'm going to stop making demands on that freedom in the future."

Susan remained steadfast. "I'm hoping you won't."

Chapter Seven

AFTER A WEEK of silence from Major Obregon, Susan discovered a bouquet of red roses at her desk. The card was signed "Carlos."

Although Carlos and Susan had parted with less than amicable feelings on the night of the movie premiere in Austin, Carlos could not allow her to slip away from him. She had captured his imagination and his desire to possess her had intensified, not diminished. Apparently he had decided to accept full blame for their differences, and from that day on Susan was constantly receiving reminders of his attention. If it weren't dozens of red roses at the office, it was a single nosegay of violets in her mailbox, or a book on horsemanship waiting on her desk, or a volume of poetry in her car. He even sent her a singing telegram over the phone and topped it all by hiring a trio of musicians to serenade her one Saturday night at three o'clock in the morning. Fortunately her neighbors thought it charming or hilarious depending on their age. And despite her chagrin, Susan was flattered. The night Carlos appeared at her door with his hat in his hand and an apology on his lips, she finally relented and gave him a drink before sending him away with a promise to attend the Air Show at Randolph.

Randolph Air Force Base opened its gates to the public one hot Sunday in late August for the annual Air Fiesta Show. It was the final day of a week-long open house and publicity blitz designed to win the support and good will of the civilian population who never failed to flood forth in the thousands for the air show.

San Antonio thrived on its military bases. There were

Alicia Meadows

three more Air Force installations in the area, as well as Fort Sam Houston, headquarters for the Fifth Army. But Randolph was the showplace with its picturesque Spanish architecture and photogenic "Taj Mahal." Pilot instructors who trained other Air Force pilots received their training at Randolph, and the cream of the crop were stationed there. Randolph was the "West Point of the Air Force."

"We've put together a spectacular show," Carlos told Susan and Vera Banks who were touring the grounds under his expert guidance. "Wings of Blue, the Air Force parachute team, will be dropping out of the sky and the Canadian Snowbirds are scheduled to perform later."

"Major Obregon, I don't mean to sound ungrateful, but couldn't we take a five-minute rest break in the shade somewhere before we continue our tour?" Vera expressed her woe with a rueful smile that was both pitiful and amusing.

It charmed Carlos into immediate contrition and compliance.

"You should have spoken sooner, Miss Banks. I forget that you aren't trained for the rigors of desert duty. How about a cool drink at the Officers' Club? It's just across the quadrangle."

"Major Obregon, you're a born leader," she cooed linking her arm in his, leaving Susan to follow behind. "Now if I can just teach you to call me Vera, I'm sure we will communicate beautifully." Vera turned her face up to Carlos who smiled charmingly down at her while turning very pointedly toward Susan. He grasped Susan's hand drawing her to his other side. His maneuver was not lost on either lady and succeeded in gathering the approval of both. Vera was not above making a play for a desirable male, and while she preferred to be the center of attention, she was not lost to Carlos's gentlemanly savoir faire.

They ordered drinks in a comfortable lounge where another of the Thunderbirds joined them. Captain Audley was a typical specimen of Thunderbird masculinity. He was tall, lean, and handsome. The young officer moved with grace and accepted introduction to Susan and Vera

74

with a style of alert appreciation that expressed intelligence and gallantry.

Vera was alight with animation. "Don't tell me you have to forgo strong spirits during training, gentlemen," she commented archly, observing that both men had chosen soft drinks.

"Only before flight-time, ma'am." Audley replied and added with a twinkle, "It's the only form of abstinence we are obliged to observe, I might add."

Susan merely smiled, but Vera caught the ball deftly.

"Gracious, what a relief! It would be an absolute sacrilege to sacrifice such gorgeous equipment," she retorted with a roguish ogle that elicited a burst of laughter from the others. "It's obvious that the Air Force is very choosy in selecting from the male species for the Thunderbird team."

Susan cast Vera a jaundiced glance. She was really pouring it on.

"That's very kind of you," Audley responded, giving Vera a warm look of regard which Susan and Carlos observed with mutual amusement. The sparks of magnetic attraction were flying fast. "Someday future Thunderbirds might be drawn from female ranks, as well," Audley suggested gallantly.

"Not while I'm flying the lead plane," Carlos interjected with mock horror.

"Major Obregon, what an unkind thing to say," Vera chided.

"If Carlos had his way, all women would be enclosed behind the walls of a harem," Susan joined in with just a touch of acid.

"I wouldn't mind a tour of duty behind the Major's wall," Vera suggested gaily with more than a hint of an offer.

"I can't speak for Obregon, but I have just rented a dandy harem site north of San Antonio. Could I interest you in an opening?"

"Wel-l-l, if I were to receive special privileges . . ." Vera teased. "Would I be number one concubine?"

"Vera Banks," Susan interjected with mock chagrin,

"where's that ardent libber I met at the Center a few short weeks ago? You surprise me with all this harem babble."

"Not at all, my pet. I never lose sight of the fundamentals," Vera advised condescendingly. Her attitude as wise sage annoyed Susan, and Vera's added platitude did nothing to mollify Susan's irritation. "Causes don't warm your bed on a cold winter night, honey."

"Tell you what"—Audley pulled his chair closer to Vera —"I like your politics, lady. Let's get down to particulars after the show. Why don't you meet me here later and we'll pursue this delightful prospect further."

"Audley's right. It's almost flight-time." Carlos turned to Susan. "Why don't you meet me here after the show, too. We'll make it a foursome, shall we?"

"Lovely," Vera responded.

"Fine with me," Susan replied and glanced to Vera with veiled contempt. Vera's blatant manhunting set her teeth on edge.

"Gentlemen, you're on," Vera chimed away, blithely ignoring her friend's chilly attitude.

The crowd heard the roar of the engines before the four planes swept over them. Coming from behind, the Thunderbirds shot out of the blue and passed overhead, their tails trailing smoke that lingered over the crowd. Major Obregon led his team through a loop, pulling over the top at about 6,500 feet above the ground and the planes passed overhead rolling and looping in and out of stunning patterns and maneuvers that left the crowd breathless.

Susan stood with Vera at the spectators' fence watching the T-38's soar into the burning sky above and felt fear for Carlos. Susan had done her homework and it did nothing for her peace of mind to know that pilots flying high-performance aircraft were subjected to G-forces that squeezed their bodies like a giant fist while the gases within them expanded like inflated balloons.

How could they stand it and still pilot the plane, she wondered, caught between emotions of fear and excitement. The dangers were staggering. Pilots had to overcome severe disorientation from the sudden course changes involving screaming dives and vertical ascents and still maintain a superhuman vigilance that allowed them to monitor computers and select targets. They had to avoid destruction by enemy craft as well when they were in actual combat.

The Talons were climbing in the diamond formation with their wing tips a bare ten feet apart.

"My God," Vera exclaimed. "Can you imagine what it must feel like to climb straight up like that!"

"It terrifies me," Susan cried. "Those planes reach speeds of over five hundred miles an hour."

"They're magnificent!" Vera shouted over the roar of the jet engines.

The crowd went crazy when the team performed the bomb-burst maneuver. Four men in the diamond formation were followed by Carlos as solo pilot, all climbing straight up into a vertical ascent. At the top the four diamonds suddenly broke formation, each veering off in a different direction while the solo pilot kept flying straight up and rolling his aircraft. The audience response was wild.

"What superb human beings!" Susan cried, enthralled with the spectacle presented by the soaring aircraft.

"Carlos is flying the solo plane, isn't he?" Vera asked as Susan nodded yes. "What a marvelous specimen of manhood that guy is. He can put his shoes under my bed any night of the week he chooses."

Susan cast a sudden sharp glance at Vera, barely controlling the urge to command her to keep her hands off, but bit back the impulse. Vera was a predator in the sexual arena and no doubt her charms were ample, but Susan understood instinctively that Carlos would not encourage a woman who was the aggressor. That was his role. And besides, Susan couldn't blame Vera if she entertained fantasies about Carlos. He really was a terrific man.

She felt a peculiar stab of pride in knowing that she was intimately involved with a man capable of such daring and mastery. In a sudden flash of intuition Susan perceived how wonderful it was to admire a man for his superior strength and skill. It was a joy to behold his perfection.

The feeling was almost mystical and yet passionate. God he was beautiful!

It was during the mock battle that the full implication of piloting a jet fighter made its devastating impression on the assembled crowd. Two Talons flew low over the crowd, then split apart and disappeared from view. Suddenly they loomed out of the firmament in a perilous head-on collision course. They were flying straight at one another, and it was only when their noses seemed inches apart that they crossed paths and zoomed away from each other.

It took a moment of breathless horror before the crowd absorbed the fact that the east-bound Talon was in trouble—that it wasn't a planned performance tactic which caused the plane to shudder and stall. In a timeless moment of silence, it fell, graceful and light, like a bird coasting on air, before it crashed to the ground and exploded in a sunburst of white light that quickly turned a furious orange-red.

Bedlam ensued. There were screams of spectators, the shouts of military personnel, the howl of fire trucks, ambulances, and emergency vehicles. People were running toward the wreck, away from the wreck—pushing, shoving, milling, and confused.

Vera and Susan did not move for a long time. They stood clutching one another, too horrified to act.

Susan drew her car up before the darkened portico of Hacienda Felicidad and rang the bell. Long moments passed while she struggled with the impulse to flee before she committed herself to a course of action that might lead her to consequences she did not fully desire. But she had to come. She had to erase the memory of that tortured gaze Carlos had cast so briefly upon her after the accident at Randolph. The pain of that memory cut her like a knife.

"Mrs. Blaine. You are good to come." Elena answered the door. "He is in the library." There was the unspoken recognition between them that Carlos needed her as she followed Elena down the darkened corridor to the library door.

Susan knocked but received no answer. She looked to

Elena, who indicated in a gesture that she should go in. Elena closed the door behind her.

The room was dark except for flickering light cast by a few burning logs in the fireplace. It took a moment for Susan to adjust her eyes and she could not locate Carlos. Then she saw him standing at the french doors which were opened to the soft summer night. Moonlight illuminated the outline of his body, and she perceived that his back was to her.

"Carlos," she called his name and he turned to her, but she could not see his face in the shadows. He didn't move. It was up to her. She hastened across the room and when she reached his side, he clasped her to his breast and held her so tightly that she could scarcely breathe.

"Querida, you have come," he whispered against her hair, holding her as if he would never let her go. And that was all she wanted at that moment—Carlos to hold her as if he would never let her go. She was pledging herself and was fiercely glad to do it.

They stood together not speaking for a long time. She could feel the tension draining from him as he relaxed his hold and she nestled more comfortably against his body.

"Why did it have to be Audley?" Susan heard his grief and wanted desperately to comfort him, but could find no words of solace.

"I don't know." She pressed a kiss against his neck and he stroked her hair.

"He was like a brother. We were together for years." There was another interim of silence. "Audley was the epitome of valor. There was nothing mean or small about him," Carlos whispered into her hair. "I really loved that guy."

Susan began to weep, and Carlos felt her tears against his skin. He touched her face with his fingers and was stirred into wonder.

"You are crying."

She pushed her face into his chest, but he took her head in his hands and tilted her face to the moonlight. He stared at her with eyes so deep and dark that she

trembled with the intensity of her emotions. She felt
tenderness pouring from him, drawing forth a torrent of
love from her heart.

"My God," he whispered, and kissed her yearning lips.
They locked together in an embrace of such intense passion that they were forced to draw apart in breathless surprise. They kissed again and again, covering each other's
faces with a rain of murmured endearments, while a tide
of desire swept through them stirring a physical need that
could not be denied.

Carlos lifted Susan and carried her to the rug in front of
the fireplace and opened the front of her blouse. He buried
his head against her breasts while Susan clasped him to
her bosom, at last finding the means of offering the comfort that her heart had yearned to give. He took her body
with such tenderness and devotion that the act of physical
union became a sacred rite. Never before had lovemaking
achieved the level of exaltation for Susan that she now discovered. They were joined together in mutual bliss and
their deep pleasure was heretofore an undiscovered delight for both of them. They gave each other love that
night.

Towards the end of the following week Susan found a letter waiting for her from Jeffrey when she returned home
from work. The sight of his precise handwriting struck her
with a shaft of guilt and she set aside the letter, choosing
to read it after dinner. But all the while she grilled her
small steak and tossed her green salad, her thoughts kept
circling the slim white envelope sitting on the hall table.
She felt as if she had been caught in an indiscretion, that a
judgment was about to be pronounced, that Jeffrey knew
about Carlos and would ridicule her.

But she forced herself to sit down and eat her meal
slowly before she finally slit open the letter and read its
contents.

Jeffrey was taking a sabbatical. He was joining a research team that was tracking a strain of deep reef coral in
the Red Sea that was thought to be a forerunner of the
Great Barrier Reef. Susan was amazed. Jeff had always

been so prosaic in his academics. She couldn't picture her button-down, pipe-smoking ex-spouse roughing it in the steaming desert heat of the Near East.

What was happening? Jeffrey absconding to the hinterlands; Susan falling in love with a Spanish conquistador.

Carlos Obregon. His dark visage surfaced in her mind. Don Carlos, master of a vast *estancia*, embodiment of a rigid, hierarchical culture totally out of sync with the twentieth century. An anachronism that belonged in history books.

But she thrilled to the memory of their lovemaking, her pulses racing and her reason abandoned.

During lunch the next day at the Fig Tree, Susan and Vera sipped daiquiris and discussed the men in their lives.

"Of course, Nelson is a dear thing. So eager to please, and quite good in bed . . . but I don't know. Something is missing." Vera's perplexity lent a wistful expression to her mobile features. She seemed rather downcast for a person who generally exhibited a lively demeanor.

"Do you ever get the feeling that women are pursuing a false god today?" Susan was in a pensive mood, too. Her involvement with Carlos was stirring latent yearnings that she thought she had shed with the achievement of maturity years ago.

"False gods. How's that?" Vera looked up from her drink, the light of interest in her green eyes.

"I wonder whether we're not sacrificing essential female instincts in order to compete with men in the marketplace."

"Oh, really, Susan, what on earth are you talking about?"

"I'm not sure I can attach appropriate names to the ideas I'm trying to describe. It's just a feeling I have."

"Well try. This ought to be interesting."

"Sometimes I wonder if the physical, biological differences between men and women don't have corresponding differences in the mental and emotional realm."

"You mean you buy that old myth about women lacking the smarts that men have?"

"No, I think women have as much brainpower as men, but maybe it's a different quality. You know, psychologists are finding that men are more right-sided and women more left-sided."

"So?"

"The right hemisphere of the brain is thought to be more logical and the left more intuitive."

"Hey listen, Susan, I can outthink and outsmart nine out of every ten men I meet."

"I don't doubt it, Vera. But what about that tenth man? What does he have?"

"And what about the tenth woman?"

Susan shrugged. "I'm not denying that there are brainy women—I'm only questioning what kind of brains women have. I think there's a difference. And I think it has something to do with feelings and intuitive capacities—that all this scrambling after power by women is destructive to the female psyche."

"You sound like a reverse Betty Friedan." Vera sipped her daiquiri and Susan remained silent. "Good grief, Susan. You're suggesting some kind of fertility code. Like hormones are destiny—"

"Well, aren't they?"

"Oh, bosh. How many drinks did you have before you met me here? Not tippling in the office, are you?"

Susan giggled self-consciously. "Oh, don't pay any attention to me. I don't know what I'm talking about. But you started it."

"I did?"

"Yes. You complained about Nelson and something being missing. I think men have lost their way because women are stealing their ecological niche away from them. Men don't know how to be men anymore."

"Well, I don't know about that. How about that gorgeous Obregon? He certainly hasn't lost his way. What a man!"

"That's precisely it, Vera. Don't you see? Carlos isn't like most modern men. He's so strong in his male identity."

"Oh, ho!" Vera lifted her eyebrows. "Now I understand what all this pseudopsychology is about. How far has it gone with you and the beautiful major?"

Susan blushed but made no reply.

"You lucky witch! What I wouldn't give to have a chance with the likes of him!" Vera twirled her drink, then lifted it to Susan. "Here's to you, sugar. Some gals have all the luck."

Chapter Eight

WHEN OWEN FORSYTHE first invited Susan to join him for the barbecue at the fashionable Triple L Ranch, she was noncommittal but as diplomatic as she could be. She wasn't at all certain of her feelings for Owen, and when she tried to analyze why, Susan couldn't find a concrete reason for any of them. Yes, they had had several pleasant evenings and afternoons together including a golfing date and dinner at her place. Yes, she felt very comfortable whenever she was with him. Yes, she enjoyed his company very much and found him highly attractive. But what was it about Owen that prevented her from giving herself to him?

The only honest answer that repeatedly rang true whenever she faced it coldly and objectively was simply that Carlos was the one who set off some kind of spark whenever they met. It wasn't something her legal training could help her corner with logic and reason. It just happened, that's all, and she couldn't be sure why. Maybe it was Carlos's overbearing boldness and daring which she both envied and hated at one and the same time. Maybe it was because he was simply _____ a yen for dangerous flair for the unusual and a yen for dangerous Often it seemed to Susan that Carlos represented everything that she was not and somehow that was the most appealing feature of all about the man. Up to now, life had taught her to value those traits that were safe, consistent, academic, and conventional. But here was a man who bore none of those qualities and yet there was some kind of magnetic attraction that seemed to envelop her whenever the two of them met. Susan flushed when she recalled how she had succumbed to the major after the air show. There was something passionate and undeniable in their relationship, but there were many pitfalls as well, especially his superior male ego and his condescending attitude toward Anglo-American women in general. That was a side to his character Susan found especially aggravating.

In truth, when those traits were tallied up in Susan's mind, a person like Owen looked like a much more manageable companion. Yes, Owen was sensible, sane, and stable, and she was glad to have him as a friend to rely on for help. But how far could she expect him to extend his friendship? Particularly when she knew where his intentions were heading. That gave her a twinge of guilt and she hoped he didn't suspect her of using him. She really didn't mean to do that, but when she discovered that Carlos would show up at the Triple L Ranch barbecue with "a friend," Susan called Owen to tell him that she had changed her mind and would love to go with him after all.

The barbecue was a big society function with most of San Antonio's elite loyally in attendance. It turned out to be an all-day gala with a wide variety of activities planned, including a trek on horseback to the hills. Susan talked Owen into foregoing the riding party. Instead, they came later when the affair was already in full swing.

A genuine western spectacle was what had been promised and Susan wasn't disappointed. From the start, it was Texas at its best. Their hosts, the Debroys, greeted them warmly and took great pains to make certain that Susan was introduced to a broad array of smiling faces. There was such an open air of hospitality and camaraderie about the gathering that Susan immediately felt welcome. She was getting quite accustomed to the good-natured banter and colorful drawl of the Texan socialite. Initially, it was a striking contrast to the reserved manner of northeasterners. But now she found it enjoyable and infectious.

The affair was sumptuously and hospitably catered. White tables were continually replenished with cocktails and interesting hors d'oeuvres. A surprisingly large number of people circulated throughout the sprawling Lshaped ranch house, then spilled out onto the enormous brick patio and rambled about the rolling green lawn to the open barbecue pit where an entire ox slowly turned on a spit. Everywhere, almost as far as the eye could see, the guests were involved in an endless number of activities.

"In Texas," Owen reminded Susan, "you come to a barbecue prepared for action. You can choose your own poison. What's it going to be? Tennis, horseshoes, badminton, swimming, bronco riding . . . ?"

"Anything but the last, please. Remember, I'm just an easterner," Susan pleaded, hoping for sympathy.

"Why, Owen, darling!"

Their path was interrupted by a low, feminine voice that murmured each syllable with an exaggerated drawl. Owen's face soured as he turned to face the woman who greeted him. It was his ex-wife.

"Why, Gloria. What are you doing here? I thought you were still on your honeymoon."

"Owen, you always were lousy when it came to dates." The green-eyed blonde paused to let her eyes roll in Susan's direction before she continued. "Never could remember birthdays, anniversaries or whatever . . . . We missed you at the wedding, darling," she said, with dripping sarcasm.

"Sorry. Had an important golf date."

"You bastard!"

"You bitch!" Owen retorted.

Susan winced and turned to leave, hoping not to be part of an ugly scene.

"Well, well, well. What have we here?" A booming voice broke in and a large, heavy-set man wearing a ten-gallon hat insinuated himself into the conversation just as it was about to end.

"Oh, Jack, my love, you must meet Owen's latest conquest." Gloria again paused for effect. "Susan Blaine— that's your name, isn't it, dear?"

"Owen always could pick 'em." Jack ogled Susan drunkenly. "Say, now. Why don't the two of us get better acquainted while these two have a family reunion?" He roared out loud and winked seductively as he tried to take Susan by the arm, but Gloria intervened.

"Jack, don't be an ass," she pouted, and wheeled off without another word. Sheepishly, her companion tipped his hat in a vain attempt at courtesy and followed his wife's retreating back.

Susan breathed a sigh of relief. "What a thoroughly unpleasant pair."

"They deserve one another," Owen said bitingly. Then slowly his anger subsided. "Look, let's forget them and enjoy ourselves. I see some friends of mine over there pitching horseshoes. Why don't we join them?"

It was an activity that helped change their moods very quickly, even though Sue had great difficulty in throwing the heavy metal shoes. Afterwards she and Owen matched their skills at badminton, a game she enjoyed much more. In fact, she took great relish in mowing down Owen in four out of the six games they played. Her opponent was duly impressed and wanted to know where she had learned the game so well.

"I was on the girls' badminton team in college," she explained modestly. "Haven't played for some time. I sure miss it."

"Well, I'd like the chance to get even," Owen said, "but why don't we go for a swim and cool off a bit? You weren't on the swimming team, too, were you?"

Susan laughed and shook her head negatively as they headed toward the pool. After a brief dip together, they settled back in some lawn chairs under an umbrella and ordered two vodka collinses. While they sipped their drinks and relaxed, the riding party was returning from the hills and Susan spotted Carlos immediately. At his arm was a lovely, dark-haired Spanish beauty who cut a striking figure in her riding jodhpurs, red silk blouse, and black riding sombrero.

Susan choked on her drink as she saw both of them heading toward their table. "Who's that with Carlos?"

"Margarita Contreras." Owen didn't hide his annoyance at Susan's obvious interest, but she was oblivious to his reaction. Her attention was riveted on the couple

headed in their direction. Susan really did want to meet
the woman and yet she was displeased with Carlos's au-
dacity in bringing her to their table. Polite greetings were
exchanged and before Susan realized what was happening,
Carlos and his friend were seated opposite them ordering
daiquiris. Susan gritted her teeth. It was all she could do to
keep her face averted from his. Conversation was halting
and restrained, but Carlos refused to be daunted. He was
incredibly brazen in his search for control of Susan's eyes
until finally she met his black, penetrating gaze only to be
struck by its intense mixture of anger and sensuality. It
made Susan terribly uncomfortable and she shifted uneasily in her chair, wishing that Owen would help her out of
this situation. But he did nothing.

Carlos's lovely companion focused all of her attention on
him, running her well-manicured fingers along the back of
his neck and along his shoulders as she whispered to him
in affectionate Spanish phrases. It all served to exclude
Owen and Susan completely, but Carlos seemed content to
let her purr and dote on him. Susan wanted to tell him that
he was being rude. Why was he doing this? It was embar-
rassing to watch that woman fawn all over him. Was it to
let Susan know that Margarita was Carlos's prospective
bride? There was no ring on her finger, but she was young,
of Spanish descent, and virginal—all the necessary qualities.

Margarita whispered something unintelligible to Carlos
who nodded and smiled back at her. "Let me ask Owen,"
she said. "You will come to the ranchero with Miss Blaine
on the twenty-first to see the horses, no? We have the best
horse ranch in all of Texas, Miss Blaine. You must come
see it," she said, turning in Susan's direction. She smiled
with the kind of superiority that only wealth can provide
and rolled her r's as she spoke. "The four of us shall ride
together."

I bet you'd like that, Susan thought, *so you can make me
look like a fool in the saddle.*

"That would be grand some other time," Susan hedged,
"but Owen and I already have plans to visit Padre Island
that weekend. Don't we, Owen?" She willed him not to fail

OPPOSITES ATTRACT

her as her eyes desperately locked on to his. The cue was clear and Owen nodded agreement.

"How unfortunate!" Margarita knitted her brows in disappointment. Susan breathed a sigh of relief but couldn't trust herself to meet Carlos' eyes.

Finally, Owen came to the rescue with a suggestion that they excuse themselves in order to change out of their swimsuits. As soon as they were out of earshot, he whispered in Susan's ear, "Are we, indeed, headed for Padre Island on the twenty-first?" His sardonic gaze swept over her.

"Thanks for saving me back there. I hope you didn't mind my using you that way, but I honestly didn't want to go riding with them."

"Have I missed something between you and Carlos that maybe I should know about, Sue?" Owen asked pointedly.

Her eyes fell when he asked the question. "Look, I—can we talk about this some other time?" she pleaded.

Susan needed more time to collect her thoughts. Anyway, did she really owe him an explanation? Probably not, but she wasn't completely convinced of that. He let her go with an understanding nod and she was relieved. At times like this she almost wished Owen weren't so big about everything.

After they changed, Owen was cornered by two of his clients and Sue gladly took the opportunity to wander off on her own for a few minutes. A sizable crowd had gathered at the corrals to watch some broncobusting, and she nudged her way up to the edge of the fence. Of course, she had seen movies of men trying to break untamed horses before, but this was the first time she saw it in reality and it was both exciting and awesome. She never realized the danger involved in trying to hold on to a fierce horse for only a matter of seconds.

Suddenly Sue recognized Carlos on the back of a wildly bucking stallion that snorted and stamped uncontrollably in the pen. A bell rang, the gate swung open and the horse charged out with Carlos' lean, muscular body rising and arching high into the air. The sight of him slamming up and down into the saddle terrified Susan and she found

89

herself screaming along with the crowd around her. The official clock ticked off the seconds while Carlos continued to hang on to the thrashing animal throughout a deadly rhythm of up and down jolts that surely must have punished his body. The pitch of the crowd rose higher as the second hand approached the time limit.

Just as the ten second point was reached, the crazed horse gave one, then two, violent upheavals and Carlos lost his grip. The animal bucked wildly away as Carlos was thrown into the air and came crashing to the ground with a dull thud. The crowd groaned in unison as he picked himself up and limped off, thoroughly disgusted.

Susan freed herself from the crowd and raced around the corral to the gate where Carlos was exiting, but she was stopped dead in her tracks. She had arrived just in time to see Margarita place her arms about his neck. Sue started to back away when Carlos spotted her. She turned abruptly and started jogging down a rutted track. The noise of the crowd receded behind her as she continued out into the open range of tall prairie grass. Finally, she stopped under a sprawling willow to take a deep breath. Leaning against the tree, Susan wondered what she had expected from Carlos anyway? Her musings were halted when she saw a man approaching her. At first she thought it was Carlos and she readied herself to leave. But when he came closer, she came face to face with Robert Harmon.

"Maria Vargas's lawyer, right?" He was sweating profusely, and he shifted about uncomfortably as he patted his brow with a handkerchief. A nervous smile twitched on his lips.

"Yes, I'm Susan Blaine." It was obvious he had seen her and followed her this far. But why? No possible good could come from an encounter with the opposition. "Sorry I can't talk with you, Mr. Harmon." Susan started to move but the large man blocked her way.

"Wait! I've got to speak with you."

"If it's about the case, you know that that's improper."

"Listen to me," he interrupted agitatedly, "you've got to

understand about Maria and me." There was a whining quality to his voice that repelled Susan.

"I don't think it's wise for you and me to be talking like this, Mr. Harmon. You have a lawyer who should carry out any negotiations in this case if there are to be any at all."

"Forget my lawyer! Look, I can't have this thing come to trial! It must not become a public spectacle. There's too much talk and speculation going on already. I don't deserve all this. I'm going to be dragged through the courts for what?"

"It's a little late to be worrying about that now. You should have thought about that before you treated Miss Vargas the way you did."

"I heard you were a hard-nosed bitch!" Harmon took a threatening step toward Susan, but she was prepared for it and sidestepped him with a nimble move.

"God damn it!" he swore in frustration, grabbing her arm in a clumsy attempt to overpower her.

With one swift, smooth, and well-executed turn of her body, Susan twisted his arm over her shoulder, locked her leg behind his and thrust her hip into his, sending her opponent reeling through the air to fall hard upon the ground. He gave out a loud groan and his eyes squinted in pain for an instant. Stunned, but embarrassed and enraged, he glared at the woman standing triumphantly over him before Susan turned and took off at a run. She looked back over her shoulder to see Harmon not far behind. Susan's leg muscles had tightened, slowing her pace. She heard his heavy footsteps pounding closer, and then strong arms unexpectedly grasped her by the shoulders. Susan wanted to scream but couldn't.

"Slow down! What's the matter? Hey! What happened?" It was Carlos and though Susan couldn't be more grateful, she was too short of breath and far too frightened to say anything. All she could do was point behind her towards Robert Harmon, who was lumbering in their direction. Roaring a stream of oaths, Carlos started toward her stalker. But Harmon had already sized up the situation

and had set off in another direction and Susan held on to
Carlos's arm.

"Don't! Let him go." She just wanted him to stay with
her right now.

"What happened? Why was he chasing you?"

"Well, we were talking for a few minutes and then he
started to threaten me. It was about him and my client in
the sexual harassment case. When he tried to manhandle
me, I flipped him."

"You did what?" Carlos was incredulous.

"I gave him a judo flip. Something I learned in a self-
defense course. It really helped out in this situation."

Carlos still couldn't believe it. Harmon was at least six
inches taller than Susan and close to twice her weight.
"Are you all right? He didn't hurt you, did he?" Carlos was
deeply concerned about her.

"No, I—I'm okay," she said, backing off as he put his
arms about her. He was studying her now with a serious-
ness that turned her knees weak. "Please . . . don't. I'm
just too upset right now."

But Carlos's fingers tightened their grip and his eyes
flashed that dangerous look she had come to know.

"I wouldn't do that if I were you unless you want to wind
up like Harmon did," she threatened.

"I would strongly advise you not to try it, *muchacha.* I
am not a Robert Harmon." Generations of Spanish hi-
dalgos spoke from his lips. Then, with amusement, he
added, "Besides, I have landed on my posterior once already today and that is quite enough for any man, don't
you think?"

"Perhaps that is a modest price to pay when you have a
pretty young companion to comfort you at your beck and
call."

"Oh! So that's it! You're angry that I brought a family
friend to this gathering, but you, *niña mia,* didn't even
mention that you were going to come with your friend Forsythe."

"Why should I? I'm free to come and go as I please," Susan retorted.

"Then I would hope that you would give me the same courtesy."

Susan really had no good reply and she didn't want to pursue the thorny conversation any further. "Owen's waiting for me. I must go." She turned to leave.

"The hell with Owen!" he stormed.

"And Margarita?" she demanded.

Carlos let out a long sigh. "Susan, Susan . . . on an occasion like this everyone is free to come and go as they please. Perhaps we both have to recognize that. Now let's stop this fencing with one another and take a little stroll, eh?"

Carlos took her hand and led her through the tall grass towards a quiet stream where willows, heavy with trailing green leaves, sheltered a sloping bank. Drawing her down next to him, he began to nuzzle her ear.

"Stop it, Carlos." Susan resisted his embrace, but it only tightened more and more and then his lips found hers and she felt herself succumbing. His lips roamed along her cheek and close to her ear where she heard him whisper, "I want you all the time, Susan."

It was the word *want* that brought her out of the spell that had been building. Was it only a physical need with Carlos? Was that all their relationship was going to mean? That night after the accident he had been so tender and the evening had been so full of promise, but now his blatant demands made her feel cheap and she jerked abruptly away from him.

"Tell me about Margarita, Carlos."

Susan's renewed attack stung Carlos. He sat up with a start and pointed a contemptuous finger. "No, you tell me about Forsythe instead. Are you sleeping with him?"

Susan turned away and scrambled to her feet. "You have no right to ask that!"

Carlos was sorry he had hurt her. Coming up behind her, he put his hands gently on her arms and murmured in her ear, "Oh, *chica*, I think I *must* have the right. I don't want to have my love portioned out with another man's love. Don't you understand that?"

She turned in his arms to face him. *"Niña mía,"* he said,

running his hand along her cheek. "My Spanish pride won't permit me to share you with Forsythe. You must tell him that you will not see him again."

"Oh, Carlos, how can you ask that? He's a good friend and don't forget, he's my boss, too." She paused and toyed with a button on his shirt. "If I did stop seeing him, can I expect the same from you where Margarita is concerned?"

A pensive look creased his face momentarily, but then Carlos smiled broadly and convincingly and opened his arms to her. "But of course. Of course," he said, and Susan rested her head against his shoulder for the moment, content with the thought that they had made an important pact together.

The klaxon ringing in the distance aroused the two of them out of their dreamy state. Susan reminded Carlos that they both had come with different partners and that they would now have to return out of politeness for the remainder of the evening's activities.

They linked arms and strolled back toward the gathering, where each went in search of their original partner. Susan found Owen with a group of people standing next to the bonfire that was being lighted in a kind of Indian ceremony. She didn't quite know whether she should start explaining her absence to him. Thankfully, Owen was in the midst of a conversation with a number of guests and several musicians and he merely nodded in her direction when she made an appearance. Shortly thereafter, he informed her that they were going to be seated at the Cranshaws' table. As they headed in that direction and the fire blazed in the sky, Susan read a very candid expression of disappointment on Owen's face and felt wretched. Throughout the lavish feast, Owen and Susan were constantly surrounded by so many people laughing, talking, buzzing amongst one another that it was impossible for them to have a moment alone together, and she was glad.

When supper was finished, there was square dancing and the infectious country music and energetic dancing helped to lift Susan's mood and she hoped it would do the same for Owen. She squeezed his hand and smiled brightly at him and that seemed all that was necessary to get him on the floor. The caller's lyrics, the fiddler's rhythm, and the compelling cadence of the dancers' footsteps brought smiles of delight to both of their faces. Late in the set, however, Carlos and Margarita made an appearance on the floor directly across from Susan and Owen. The caller's voice continued its chant commanding all of the dancers to "promenade, then form a star, make a grand right and a do-si-do." And then came the call to change partners and suddenly Carlos was beside Susan, holding her arm as they stepped in unison to the caller's refrain:

> "Swing her left and swing her right,
> Swing your honey all through the night.
> Swing her high, swing her low,
> Swing your honey, do the
> do-si-do."

Carlos obliged the director by encircling Susan's waist and lifting her high off the floor. Their set applauded appreciatively, but Susan didn't share their enthusiasm. The last thing she wanted was for her and Carlos to be the center of attention, especially with Owen and Margarita looking on.

When the set was over, Susan excused herself from Carlos and sought refuge in a ladies' room where she stalled for a long time, wondering how her life ever got to be so complicated. On her way out she came face to face with Margarita. Hurt and anger emanated from her black Spanish eyes.

"You are in love with *my* Carlos?"

"I didn't know he was *yours*," Susan countered.

"If you think he is not mine, you are mistaken."

Susan stood her ground. "Are you engaged? I don't see a ring."

"In our culture, it is customary for men to sow their wild oats before settling down. Spanish women have learned to be patient with their men. Carlos is no different. I know he has made conquest after conquest, but when he marries, he must marry a woman who understands him, a woman of his own blood."

Susan wanted none of this. "Begging your pardon," she said sarcastically, "but I do believe we are living in the twentieth century in the United States, not sixteenth-century Spain. It's not clear to me why you, a product of modern American society, feel compelled to wait for any man."

"It is a decent woman's place to be chaste and wait for her man." Margarita punctuated her sentence with a smug complacency that riled Susan.

"All right. While you wait, he's having a good time and you're unhappy. And there's no guarantee he will want you in the end anyway."

Susan's words momentarily nonplussed her opponent. "You're saying that because you hope to discourage me and take Carlos for yourself. But it will not work!"

"No, you're wrong, Margarita, I'm saying it because it's true. Look around you. Don't you see what's happening? Carlos is changing. And his sister Elena has already joined the twentieth century. . . . I'm afraid you'll have to do the same."

Margarita's lip trembled. "No! He will never be yours. You are nothing but an Anglo woman without virtue."

"Oh, really now, that's carrying things a bit far. An Anglo woman without virtue!" The characterization amused Susan and she laughed scornfully, serving only to antagonize her assailant even more. "But it's true! You will see. When Carlos wishes to marry and have children, it will not be you he chooses, but me!" Her defense complete, Margarita turned on her heels and swept away.

Susan wasn't so sure who she was more sorry for after that disturbing encounter—Margarita or herself? She walked back in the direction of the dance floor thoroughly unsettled.

"Hi." Owen held out a gin and tonic for her. "You look exhausted."

"It's been some day."

"Do you want to see the fireworks display that's coming up or do you want to leave?"

"If it's all the same to you, Owen, I'd be very grateful to leave right away."

By the time they reached his car and started driving down the mile long road to the exit gate, clusters of fire burst into sprays of color over their heads. *A fitting conclusion for this day,* Susan thought. It had been one bombshell after another with only a few moments of quiet in between provided by Owen. She was in a war all right, a war with herself, and she didn't know where to turn next for the answers.

Chapter Nine

S USAN ACCEPTED CARLOS'S invitation to attend his cous-
in's wedding with more trepidation than anticipation,
but she wanted to test herself in his world. There was a
mystique involving the Spanish heritage and culture that
was indelibly etched into Carlos's persona that she had to
confront in order to discover her true feelings. She approached the event as a soldier facing his first bout of combat. She was frightened to her bones.

Carlos was alarmingly handsome when he appeared at
her door. He looked like a subject in a Renaissance paint-
ing. The white ruffled silk shirt and impeccable black dinner jacket fit to perfection. His taut, dark skin, the fine
bones of his face, his burning black eyes and white porce-
lain teeth, all were too perfect. Yet he greeted Susan with
an utter unself-consciousness that was totally disarming.
His eyes proclaimed her beauty and he voiced his admiration earnestly.

"*Querida,* you take my breath away!" He raised her
hand to his lips in an old world gesture that was irresisti-
bly romantic. Never had she felt more womanly than she
did now as her amber chiffon skirt swirled about her slim
legs and she linked her hand through his arm and sailed
down the stairs to his waiting Jaguar.

And never had she felt more intimidated than she did as
they passed through the gates of another sprawling *estancia* and alighted before the heavily timbered doors of the
Morales's palatial *casa.*

"Does all your family live like kings?" Susan asked with
a touch of disapproval brought on by her insecurity.

"Is that how we live?" Carlos replied complacently. "It doesn't seem that way to me."

But it did to Susan. It was very difficult not to feel intimidated by the opulence and lavish display. The house seemed a velvet and brocade museum with heavily carved furniture and cool, tiled floors leading through arcaded corridors and across vast interiors. Manuel Morales and his bride Maria greeted their guests with a simple graciousness born of generations of aristocratic breeding. The newlyweds stood on a vast stone balcony beneath a silk canopy festooned with roses and lilies. The bride was radiant and demure with magnificent black eyes and an ivory complexion of unblemished purity. She wore a tight-fitting lace cap studded with jewels over her dark hair from which descended a profusion of sheer illusion surrounding her in a cloud of filmy white. Her gown was heavy with lace and in her slim hands she held her bouquet of white roses and lilies that cascaded to the hem of her satin slippers. Her groom was handsome and adoring. They were a storybook couple.

"Mrs. Blaine, may I introduce you to Leo and Valery Serrano." The mother of the groom led Susan away from Carlos to a group chatting near a marble fountain with an alabaster mermaid pouring an urn of sparkling water into a shallow basin.

Somewhere a stringed ensemble was playing delicate chamber music. Susan recognized the lovely Canon in D of Pachelbel. Waiters passed among the throngs of well-wishers bearing silver trays of champagne and delicacies. Susan lifted a glass of champagne to her lips and forced a friendly smile to her face.

"How do you do," she greeted the group with composure.

"Mrs. Blaine is an attorney with the Forsythes," Mrs. Morales explained brightly while the others smiled and sipped and studied the stranger in their midst.

"Do you really practice law?" one dark-haired girl in the group questioned with genuine amazement. "I mean in the courtroom before a judge and jury?"

"Yes, I do," Susan answered blandly, masking her own

99

incredulity that a modern young woman should express such naiveté.

"And I'm sure she does a very good job if Owen Forsythe has taken her aboard," Leo Serrano gallantly offered.

"I must hope so," Susan returned graciously.

"Have you been long in San Antonio?" Juan Sebastian asked conversationally.

"No, I'm afraid I am a comparative newcomer. But I'm fast becoming a loyal supporter of San Antonio." Susan took a sip of champagne and decided it was time to turn the conversation onto another track. "The bride and groom are a handsome couple. Are they planning a wedding trip somewhere?"

"They are traveling to Venezuela where the bride has relatives and then to Madrid to visit some of the groom's family," another young woman named Joanna replied.

"Ugh, all that family," the dark-haired Lisa grimaced. "That's not for me, I can tell you."

"Ah, but Manuelo is worth it." Joanna rolled her dark eyes appreciatively. "He's so handsome."

"Yes, but soon Maria will be home raising the babies while Manuelo, well, you know." The group laughed conspiratorially in recognition of a common understanding, but Susan felt uncomfortable with the chauvinist values implied.

"Do you have any children, Mrs. Blaine?" Valery Serrano asked.

"No, I don't. I've been so busy establishing my career."

"Oh, what a shame," Lisa commented.

"Not at all," Susan retorted. "I'm not so sure I want children."

"Not want children?" Lisa was shocked, and Susan was glad.

"Lisa, *chiquita*, don't be such a simpleton. Anglo women are raised differently from ours," Juan intervened. "It is perfectly respectable for them to work and compete with men in the business world."

"Indeed it is. And so it should be for the *Latinas* as well."

Elena Obregon had joined the group and seized the opportunity to mount her favorite soapbox.

"Spare us the polemics, Elena *mía*," Juan pleaded. "This is a wedding celebration, not a liberationist rally."

"Indeed, Elena, do you never give up?" Lisa sniped.

"Dios, you're all hopeless," Elena exclaimed but not without humor. "Come with me, Susan. I want you to meet some friends who are actually living in the twentieth century and not stuck in the mud of the past," she flung smartly at the group.

"Taking her to meet your *inglesados,*" Joanna taunted sarcastically.

As they moved away, Susan asked Elena, "What's an *inglesado?*"

"Oh, it's someone who defects to Anglo values," Elena replied. "Don't pay any attention to that bunch. They prefer to live in the past," and she steered Susan across the lawn to meet friends who were largely young university students and, as Elena had characterized them, very much into the twentieth century.

Just when Susan was beginning to relax, Carlos appeared at her side and took her away to meet his mother.

Señora Obregon was a diminutive Spanish autocrat in jade green holding court among a coterie of stylish matrons who obviously deferred to the Obregon matriarch as the person of senior eminence. Her dark, observant eyes matched her dark tresses, which revealed no trace of the gray that might be expected in one of her mature years. Her lips welcomed Susan, but her eyes did not.

"How do you do, Mrs. Blaine." She smiled frostily, a mere lift of the corners of her unmadeup mouth, and fastened her eyes to Susan's face in a relentless examination of the Anglo girl her son presented to her. Costanza Obregon had already heard much about this intruder of whom she disapproved on general principles. Susan Blaine was not to her taste simply because she was a member of that unacceptable class, the Anglo-Americans. Carlos left Susan to his mother's tender mercies.

"I hope you are enjoying the wedding celebration," Mrs. Obregon suggested.

"Everything is so beautiful," Susan replied, striving to sound natural and normal while inwardly struggling against the discomfort of knowing herself to be under scrutiny. Her fingers clutched her glass too tightly and her mouth felt dry. *Damn!* she thought. *I hate this.*

"This is a proud occasion for the Morales family," one of the ladies commented. "The marriage has been planned since Manuel and Maria were children."

"You mean it was arranged?" Susan questioned baldly, her surprise and worse—her distaste—communicating itself forcibly to the group.

"Why not?" Mrs. Obregon replied haughtily. "We do not leave such important matters to the whims of youthful passions. Marriage is for a lifetime, is it not?"

Oh God, Susan thought. *Here it comes. Damn you, Carlos, for subjecting me to this.*

"Your husband, Mrs. Blaine, he is a lawyer, too?" Polite inquiry from one of the ladies.

"No. . . . My husband was, I mean . . . I have no husband." Susan cast a nervous glance in search of Carlos.

"Ah, how sad to be widowed so young," Mrs. Obregon commiserated.

"No," Susan exclaimed almost angrily and stared into the smiling faces surrounding her. "I'm not widowed. I'm divorced."

"I see." Costanza Obregon allowed a moment of silence to pass before resuming the conversation. "That too is a tragedy. One fears for society these days. There are so many temptations for the young to overcome."

Susan could not believe she was being forced to add her silent assent to a consensus that clearly condemned her. What gall! But she could think of nothing to say in her defense under the circumstances, and her pride burned bitterly.

"Ah, there is Margarita." Another of the ladies nodded toward the young woman headed in their direction.

"Margarita, *ven aqui,*" Mrs. Obregon called. "Have you met my son's betrothed?" Carlos's mother questioned Susan innocently.

Well, I guess I'm getting the full treatment, Susan told

herself philosophically. *Go ahead, ladies. Do your worst.* "Indeed I have. Lovely girl." Susan suddenly felt like laughing. Somewhere the orchestra which had switched to modern tunes was playing "Send in the Clowns."

Margarita came up dutifully and greeted the ladies happily, exuding the confidence of one who feels herself among her supporters. Unaccountably, Susan pitied her. Human beings were so pathetic in their alliances and allegiances. Susan wanted to go home, but there stretched many hours ahead before she would be allowed to retreat. She reached for another glass of champagne from a tray passing by in the hands of a solemn-faced waiter.

Susan's inquisition was cut short by Elena's rescue once again. The girl knew what her mother was up to and was too fond of Susan to allow the sport to continue. Carlos was heartless to have delivered the Anglo into her mother's cruel clutches. From the look on Susan's face Elena knew that Susan was most definitely of the same opinion. Carlos was in trouble with this lady.

"You must pay no attention to my mother, Susan. She inhabits another time zone." Elena tried to make peace. "You can easily see how it is with this world." Elena nodded toward the festive ranks of beautifully garbed and polished people making a charming picture on the green lawns of the Morales estate. Music, laughter, flowers, and smiles—all contributed to the image of a traditional ritual faithfully observed.

"I'm beginning to see, although I'm not altogether sure of my own reaction. It's all rather overwhelming." Susan held back some of her harsher observations.

"I'm sure it is for someone new to our life-style."

Susan heard Elena's unconscious identification with the people she believed herself to be in conflict with and smiled. "There is much to admire here. I can feel the solidarity and tradition that binds people together."

"Of course. But there is much that is suffocating, too." Elena shrugged her shoulders fatalistically and grabbed Susan's hand. "Look, there's Carlos. Let's go get him, the *diablo.*"

As dusk settled over the party hundreds of tiny white

Alicia Meadows

lights which were threaded among the shrubs and trees were lighted, and colored lanterns strung over the dancing pavilion were turned on, casting pools of soft colors upon the partners swaying to the romantic melodies of a bygone era.

Carlos claimed Susan for the first dance and did not release her when it was over, but kept his arm protectively around her until the next tune was struck. Susan forgot her earlier distress in the joy of being held close to Carlos's heart as they danced through a succession of love songs that wove a spell of magic and amorousness between them. From time to time they would look into each other's eyes, and the undisguised emotion between them was perceived by many an onlooker. The strength of Carlos's arms and the power of his thighs brushing hers as he guided them effortlessly across the floor were intoxicating and heightened Susan's physical awareness of Carlos to a painful degree.

But the spell was broken abruptly. One of Carlos's relatives sought a dance with Susan and Carlos reluctantly turned her over to Johnnie Castanedo, a suave charmer who had had his eyes fastened on Susan more than once during the afternoon. He held Susan too close and she tried in vain to force a few inches between them, but he laughed with a gleaming display of perfect white teeth and pressed her even more tightly to his chest. Susan was ready to struggle further until she spied Carlos twirling past them with Margarita gazing adoringly at him. The sight of that pair stung her with a shaft of sharp jealousy and she let Johnnie whirl her around to his satisfaction.

From that dance there followed another and then another with several young cavaliers equally ardent in their pursuit and equally sure of their masculine charm. Susan couldn't see Carlos anywhere and her jealousy turned to injured pride. *Damn him!* He was too mercurial for her peace of mind. Just too damned elusive. What did he mean by openly revealing himself her devoted slave one minute and then pouring himself out just as lavishly on the next handy female? She didn't understand what to make of his behavior, and she didn't enjoy the emotional seesaw he created.

The highlight of the evening occurred just before the bride and groom were to depart on their honeymoon. The newlyweds performed the wedding quadrille before the assembled crowd to the thrilling strains of several classic guitars. The dance was a slow moving saraband in which the couple started far apart and moved through a set of formal patterns that brought them very close without ever actually touching. It was very demure and at the same time very sexual. Everyone was captivated by the ritual seduction, and when it was finished the groom carried off his bride.

Carlos had come up behind Susan during the wedding dance and led her onto the dance floor once more where he proceeded to guide her through the provocative steps of a tango to the accompaniment of the throbbing Spanish rhythm of "Jealousy."

"Just follow me, sweetheart," Carlos commanded.

Susan was surprised by her ability to keep up with the changing patterns, but she gave herself to the vibrating music and Carlos's expert control, and suddenly she was dancing with assurance as her excitement increased to match the demands of the dance and Carlos's blazing eyes urging her on.

"Let's show them how," Carlos whispered.

And did they dance! Side by side, they stepped together down the dance floor with arched precision, their arms raised above their heads in haughty hidalgo style; then they turned sharply and lacing their legs between one another, they whirled with mounting speed around the floor, dipping and swaying as the pulsating music intensified to a feverish crescendo. A reckless sensuality sent fire through Susan's veins and she wanted Carlos to make love to her. They ended the dance with a flamboyant dip as Carlos bent low over Susan's arched body and murmured ardently, *"Mi corazón, te adoro."*

"Carlos," Susan cried softly, and for one heady moment the world exploded with splendor and Susan understood the glory of a man and a woman. She wanted to hold the moment still, but time flowed on, moving them out of their enchanted sphere. They left the pavilion arm in arm, and the evening might have ended a success if Carlos had taken her home then, but Johnnie Castanedo spoiled it.

Carlos and Susan were strolling together across the lawn and enjoying the soft night air.

"Would you like something to drink, sweetheart?" Carlos suggested.

"Oh, yes, something cool and nonalcoholic. As a matter of fact, I would love a glass of ice water right now."

"Water," Carlos teased. "You have no soul."

"Truly, Carlos, cold water sounds like nectar to me."

"Then cold water you shall have. Wait here and I'll hurry right back."

Susan sat on a stone bench beside a leafy birch tree and waited for Carlos. It was a lovely warm evening.

"Well, what is Miss Muffett doing out here all by herself?" Johnnie came out of the shadows and sat down beside Susan.

"I'm waiting for Carlos to—"

He didn't allow her to finish. "Has that cad run off and left you for Margarita again?"

"He went for refreshments," Susan replied haughtily.

"Sure he has." Johnnie laughed. "Call it what you will." Then Johnnie slipped his arm around Susan's waist and began nibbling her ear.

"Please, Johnnie. Stop it."

"That's right, honey. Play hard to get. But I saw you on the dance floor."

Susan tried to push Johnnie away and stand up but he clamped his other arm around her and kissed her hard on the mouth. She could smell the alcohol on his breath and began to struggle against his assault but he only forced himself on her more brazenly.

"Let me go," she hissed, all the while fearing to create a scene, and fearing even more Carlos's wrath should he come upon them. "Carlos will be back any minute."

"I'm not afraid of—" Johnnie never finished his boast.

Carlos was suddenly lunging at him, cursing him for a dog, and the two began throwing punches at one another.

"I'll teach you how to treat a lady, you gutter hound," Carlos blazed, and swung at Johnnie who dodged deftly and laughed.

"What's the big act for?" Johnnie taunted. "She's only an Anglo bitch."

"Sangre de Dios!" Carlos growled menacingly. "You'll regret the day you were given a tongue to speak," and he slammed his fist into Johnnie's jaw, not missing his target this time.

Blood spurted from Johnnie's mouth and Susan screamed, "Stop it! Stop it!"

But Johnnie was enraged now also. He realized that Carlos meant to murder him for the insult he had given to Susan and therefore to Carlos.

Susan drew back in horror. The sound of their fists smashing into each other's faces sickened her, and the sudden gathering crowd was a humiliation too awful to endure. Carlos was killing Johnnie. He had him down on the ground and was pummeling Johnnie with a rain of murderous blows. It took three men to pull Carlos off Johnnie, but Susan didn't wait to see the outcome. She had never personally witnessed human violence before and she was trembling with shock. The sight of blood and the grunts of pain were seared into her consciousness and the whole scene filled her with revulsion and disgust. Susan fled back to the Morales mansion seeking a corner to hide in or a means of escape altogether.

It came to her with awful clarity that she did not belong in this world of powerful emotions and fierce pride. Despite the surface propriety of formality and custom, there was a cruel, almost primitive undercurrent of raw, human passion in the Spanish culture that frightened Susan. Her upbringing within the restraints of WASP mores and her training in law were a conditioning too far removed from the cultural traditions of the people she had observed at the Morales estate. A message had been relayed to the hidden layers of her consciousness by the experiences she had undergone throughout the afternoon and evening, and the

message had finally reached the surface of her conscious
mind. Carlos was wrong for her. The very essence of his
appeal—that basic male dominance which so clearly de-
fined the female identity—was threatening and dangerous. She would lose herself and all she had achieved were
she to capitulate to his masculine allure.

Once again Elena was Susan's avenue of retreat. The
girl had been sent by Carlos to find Susan while he was
cleaning himself up after the brawl with Johnnie. Elena
perceived the depths of Susan's distress and allowed herself to be urged to drive Susan home without contacting
Carlos first.

"Please, Elena. Don't say anything to Carlos. Just take
me home."

"But, Susan, my brother will be very worried about you.
He will be very angry with me."

"I know. I'm putting you in an awful spot, Elena, but I
can't face Carlos right now. I need time to think. I must be
alone. I couldn't stand any more fireworks. Do you understand?"

Elena studied Susan for a moment. "Yes, I do. I'll take
you home. Come with me. We'll go out the back way and no
one will see us, *por Dios.*"

On the way back into town, Susan urged Elena to convince Carlos not to follow her home that night—that the
best thing he could do was give them some breathing space
and time to assess their thoughts and feelings.

Elena was dubious, but she promised to try.

"I know I'm asking an awful lot of you. But still I'm
relying on you to be my emissary to your brother. Tell him
I will contact him when I'm ready to talk. Will you do that,
Elena? Please? I will be greatly in your debt."

"I will try, *amiga.* I really will. But you know Carlos. He
is very impatient."

"Yes, I know Carlos. At last I'm beginning to understand him and his *modus operandi.*"

Elena must have taken her mission seriously. Carlos did
not come to Susan's door that night, but even so Susan
didn't sleep. She was unable to quiet her fears. Her brain
and heart were in a turmoil, but uppermost was a sense of

flight. She was suffering from a kind of claustrophobia; Carlos and his entire background were too much to handle. Thoughts of Jeffrey rose to the surface of her mind. She had run from him to find a new meaning in life and having found it was seeking to flee it as well. What kind of person was she becoming? Susan was tormented by her own behavior. What did she really want?

Owen was the most comforting element in her life, she told herself. Perhaps with him she could find the safe harbor she was seeking.

A few nights later Susan had Vera Banks over for dinner and girl-talk. She needed a confidante and a friend. Vera was wearing her red hair in a longer style and for a while they discussed fashion and beauty before settling into the topic of the men in their lives. Vera was seeing a new man, a stockbroker engaged in some rather dubious financial schemes and whose tastes in the realm of sex bordered on the bizarre.

"I honestly don't know what to make of him," Vera admitted. "I really don't go for that kinky stuff. What's wrong with simple, straightforward sex?"

"Maybe you're more old-fashioned than you think you are," Susan suggested.

"Mmm," Vera considered. "You're right, you know. What's the matter with men these days? Why can't they pull their act together?"

"Sounds like a talk we had once before, remember? I said then that maybe the trouble was women trying to move in on the men."

"That's right, you did say something like that," Vera agreed, "but I'm not so sure I go along with that notion either." Vera took a gulp of her wine and kicked off her shoes. "Shucks, honey, don't tell me you'd trade your law books and the courtroom for a full-time stint in an apron in front of a kitchen sink."

"Lord, no. I can't argue with you on that, Vera. Domestic I'm definitely not." Susan too drank her wine and curled her feet under her.

"Then what's the answer, do you suppose," Vera yawned comfortably.

"That's the sixty-four-thousand-dollar question, my friend." They paused momentarily, pursuing their own train of thoughts. "Did I ever tell you about the macho-man that almost cornered me in a bar when I was traveling through Louisiana?"

"No, you did not. Tell all," Vera urged. "Did you spend the night with him?"

"God, no. He was an ape. He scared the hell out of me."

"What'd he do?"

"Nothing really. But only because I didn't give him the chance. He was a typical red-neck. All brawn and no brains."

"Doesn't sound too romantic. What made you think of him?" Vera questioned.

"I'm not sure. But there's something trying to come through to me." Susan unwound her feet and sat forward in her chair. "I had another scare recently—with Carlos . . ."

"Oh, baby, don't tell me you ran away from him?"

"Yes, I did."

"You gotta be crazy."

Susan made a rueful grimace. "You may be right. I'm getting a little worried about myself."

"Why don't you tell mama all about it."

"I'm not sure I can. But I'm beginning to wonder. I ran from Jeff because he was too staid and dull, and I ran from Carlos because he's too fiery and volatile. And because he has some of that macho mentality—like that guy in the bar."

"Aw, come on, Sue, you're not telling me that Carlos is some kind of apeman, are you?"

Susan stood up. "My God, that's true. He's *not* an ape. You just made me realize it. Carlos is powerful and all man, but he's gentle and refined. At least most of the time he is. I was making the either-or kind of mistake. Either a man is a civilized bore or an uncivilized caveman."

"Nothing in life is so clear-cut."

"That eases my mind a little. But not much. I really think Carlos is too much for me to handle."

"Well, anytime you want to send him packing, just be sure you give him my address."

"Carlos is free to go where his fancy leads him, you know," Susan said.

"Yeah, so you say. But you don't mean it. Anyway, that kind of he-man is definitely my style. And I bet there's no kinky stuff in his sexual handbook either."

Susan was very quiet. *My God,* she was thinking, *how true.* Carlos didn't need the bizarre to make sex intense and thrilling. She had discovered that the night at his home after the Thunderbird disaster. Never had she felt herself more of a woman than she had in loving Carlos and receiving his love in return.

"And what about Owen?" Vera was asking. "Yoo-hoo, Susan. Are you there?"

"Oh . . . Owen? I don't know about Owen. It's true that I feel so good about myself when I'm with him. He's very much a man, and yet so very different from Carlos."

"I don't know whether to laugh or cry, Susan Blaine. How come you have all the luck? Not one, but two prime candidates. I am one jealous female."

Chapter Ten

SUSAN AND ELENA had made a lunch date before the Morales wedding, but now that the day had arrived Susan actually was fearful of seeing her. It was only a week after the fiasco with Carlos and just looking at his sister immediately conjured up the Major's image. The resemblance between the two was unmistakable. Their dark, liquid eyes, the proud chin, the warm, absolutely enchanting smile—all bore the stamp of that regal family.

Damn it! Susan swore to herself as she placed a pitcher of iced tea in the refrigerator and slammed the door shut. If only she could have avoided her guest today. But that wish was quickly erased with the sound of the doorbell, and Susan reluctantly strode to the door to deal with the inevitable. After all, she reflected, she owed the girl a debt of gratitude for her assistance at the wedding and in keeping Carlos away.

"I hope you don't mind that I am early." Elena smiled nervously. She made her entrée carrying a small leather valise. "Do you mind if I change out of this?" She was wearing a full-skirted silk print. "I came directly from mass, and I did not want to return to the hacienda to change," Elena continued to explain as Susan led her down the hall to the bedroom. A few moments later, Susan's guest rejoined her in the kitchen. Now she was wearing a pair of tight-fitting aquamarine designer jeans with a colorful matching top.

"May I help?" she asked, observing Susan attempting to close the refrigerator with her hip while balancing two plates and the pitcher of iced tea in her hands.

"If you'll take the napkins and the silverware, we can go

out on the patio," Susan said over her shoulder as she continued to juggle her way in that direction.

"Just as long as you don't expect me to prepare the meal," Elena said in a self-mocking tone.

"Don't you like to cook?"

"Well, to tell you the truth, I am not as good at it as I suppose I should be. You know, of course, that all Mexican-American women are expected to make that skill their number one priority in life. That is because it is taken for granted that they must please their husbands."

Susan pondered the statement of the raven-haired beauty now seated across from her. "Something seems strange to me about you and Margarita Contreras," Susan observed. "You both are of the same generation, you're both from the same background. But whereas she embraces her heritage, you seem to rebel against it."

"You may be correct in what you say, but it is not really so odd. After all, Margarita loves my brother and wishes to marry him and—" Susan's expression made her stop in mid-sentence. "Did I . . . say something that—I mean, I didn't want to—"

"No, no," Susan tried to ward off her guest's inquiring gaze with a tight smile. "Your brother and I have no claim on each other."

"That I am not so sure about," Elena conjectured. "I see how my brother looks at you. He does not look at Margarita the same way. You see it, too?"

"Why don't you help yourself to something to eat, Elena?" Susan busied herself in an obvious attempt to avoid the question. Knowing Carlos's attitude toward women, Susan wasn't so sure that his sister's innocent remark should be taken as a compliment or not, and she certainly did not want to discuss it at length with Carlos' sister.

Susan poured a glass of tea for her guest and offered her sliced avocado from a plate. "Let's not discuss Carlos and me, Elena. Let's talk about you. You seem to be the renegade of the clan. I wonder why?"

"It is many things, I guess. How could one live in these times and not be aware of what is happening to women?

113

My world is one in the midst of many opposing forces. You saw how it was at the wedding. If you ask me to explain why I am a renegade, I honestly can't tell you because it's much too complicated. On some things I do rebel openly, but on others I feel that I still cling to my roots and traditions. I have been exposed to the Anglo world and I don't want to live in the past. And above all else I have met Brett Sinclair."

"Ah, the young man with bright hair and a red sports car?"

"Yes," Elena said adoringly. "And that is why I have come to you."

"Oh?" Susan replied. "And what would you want from me?"

"I need . . . an experienced woman's advice."

Susan couldn't hold back the laughter that was prompted by her guest's choice of words. "Experienced woman? Well, if that's what you're looking for, I doubt very much that you've come to the right place, my dear."

"But you are a successful woman. A career woman. And I hope you don't mind my saying that you have also been married and divorced. You are aware of the difficulties that all women must face. You are also quite liberated . . . and you know men and their ways."

The catalog of qualities Elena had selected made Susan blanch. Had she just been given a compliment or an insult? Just who and what did Elena think she was? To compensate for her silence, Susan poured herself more tea.

"I do hope that I haven't offended you by what I have said. That would be the last thing that I would want to do. You see, you should know that I admire you very, very much and that is why I came here today."

"Oh dear! Elena, I think I'd better explain some things about myself to you before you become misled in some way. I certainly appreciate the compliment you have just given me, but I think you should know that I'm just a very ordinary woman living what I consider a very ordinary life. I'm not so sure that I should receive any awards for my accomplishments thus far, nor do I feel I deserve any one else's admiration. Like most people, I've made my fair share of mistakes, and there are times when I am quite confused and uncertain about my own life, how I am managing it, and the direction I'm heading. As far as being a liberated woman . . . well, yes, I suppose that I am. But that doesn't mean that I don't ever have doubts, or that sometimes I wish I had a man to lean or depend on. I don't know if that's what you wanted to hear, but I'm trying to be as honest and helpful as I can."

At that moment, Elena looked taken aback. Her face revealed an expression suggesting she wasn't being told what she wanted to hear. As Susan gathered their plates and began to make her way to the kitchen Elena rose to help her. "But you are a woman who has become totally independent," the younger woman said. "You're not being held back from being what you want to be simply because of ties from family, ties from tradition and *raza*, obligations that are superficial and arbitrarily imposed. That's what I want to be rid of. I don't care about family, position, or tradition. I want to be independent, too. I want a career, too. And nobody in my life seems to understand that except perhaps Brett."

"Oh? We're back to Brett again, are we?"

"Yes, yes. I'm in love with him. But can you possibly see my family, especially my mother and brother, accepting him as a future son-in-law?"

Frankly, Susan did not, any more than the clan had been willing to accept her in their midst, but she tactfully avoided agreeing with Elena. Susan wondered whether the girl was really in love or whether she was somehow manufacturing some image that she felt she had to assume.

"My mother has already chosen a husband for me," Elena announced bitterly when the women had settled themselves on the living room couch with their drinks.

"You mean your family has *arranged* a marriage for you too?" Susan asked incredulously.

"Oh, nothing so old-fashioned as that," Elena sighed. "I simply was informed how pleased both families would be if Marco and I were to wed. That would be uniting two descendants of the original land-grant families. You understand. And then my sole function in life would be to raise babies instead of raising issues." Elena gritted her teeth and said defiantly, "Well, I'm not going to do it! I will not submit. I know what I should do. I should just go ahead and live openly with Brett!"

Susan shook her head in disagreement. "You ought to think twice about that. Frankly, I think that you would only succeed in creating a major catastrophe with that tactic."

"Maybe you're right," Elena agreed. "You know my family, especially my brother. Good grief, there would be murder."

"There must be another way. . . ." Susan was tapping her glass lightly as she thought out loud.

"That's why I have come to you, Susan. You have a logical way of looking at things. You've got to help Brett and me."

"I suppose you and Brett have already discussed the possibility of marriage?"

"We do not wish marriage at this time," Elena said after some hesitation. "We both have several years of education and then, of course, we must concentrate some time on developing our careers. Besides . . . Brett's father has forbidden him to marry until he has completely finished his schooling. If he does, he will be disinherited."

So much for Brett's commitment to a marriage with Elena, Susan thought, but dared not voice it aloud. She offered her companion some cautious advice. "Maybe you just need to give yourself more time, Elena. Since you both have at least a few years of studies, there really is no rush to make a decision on this right away, is there?"

"Brett is tired of waiting," Elena replied, downcast.

"But have you explained the situation to him? Have you made him look at the options you're facing?"

"He thinks I exaggerate."

"Hmmm. Then he hasn't met Carlos," Susan said with perfect understanding of her friend's dilemma.

"Carlos refuses to meet or talk with him."

Such stubbornness, Susan thought. Such unreasonable-ness! How could he be like that? And what right did he have to control her life in the first place? Why didn't he realize what he was doing to these two young people? Didn't he know that the more he tried to divide the two of them, the more they would be determined to remain together even if it meant doing something drastic? Susan knew, of course, that no amount of reasoning would change Carlos's mind. If the situation were to be saved in some way, it was Elena who had to do it—wisely, cautiously. Somehow, she had to be made to see that.

"Let me ask you this question, Elena. Do you approve of men and women living together without being married to one another?"

"*¡Madre de Dios!* That is my dilemma! I can say quite easily with my mind, yes. But my heart, my emotions, my guilt-ridden conscience, say no." She shook her head, struggling for a solution. "Tell me, Susan, what would you do if you were me."

"But that's just it, Elena. I'm not you. Our backgrounds are totally different. What may be right for me may be completely wrong for you. All I can do is tell you to weigh your decision carefully. I know that's not much help, but let me also say this. It is a decision that could possibly affect the rest of your life. And you will have to live with that decision. Don't let anyone else make it for you. Do it yourself. Don't let anyone push you—not your family, not Brett—into taking a step you'll later regret. If Brett really loves you as you say he does, then he'll want to do what is best for you, and he'll also be willing to wait until you are sure you know what this is."

There were tears in Elena's eyes when Susan stopped speaking. Almost by instinct, the younger girl put her head against her confidante's shoulder. "Promise me that you won't do anything rash," Susan pleaded.

The sound of the doorbell precluded any response from Elena. When Susan answered it, Elena sat up with a start hearing a familiar voice. It was Brett! Elena was almost in a panic to make herself look presentable after her emotional outburst.

Brett was a good-looking young man, lean and attractive with a thick mane of hair and an infectious smile that easily charmed a woman. Susan immediately saw why Elena was so vulnerable where he was concerned. Brett's light and breezy manner was in sharp contrast to Elena's more serious nature and fiery temperament. But Susan felt they were somehow good for one another, capable of finding each other's strengths and nurturing them, and by the time the two of them had excused themselves and gone, she found herself rooting out loud for them to make it together and on their own. An enviable adventure, Susan reflected.

A few tranquil days on a spectacular stretch of sandy white beach with gently lapping waves and glorious sunsets appealed strongly to Susan's psyche after her recent experiences with the Obregon family and the mounting pressures of the Vargas case. So when Owen Forsythe suggested an escape weekend to Padre Island, it couldn't have come at a better time. But the images she had conjured up were at odds with the reality when they arrived at Port Isabel and crossed the causeway. The view of the beach was obstructed by high-rise hotels and hundred-thousand-dollar condos, expensive restaurants and fast-food places rising stridently above the sliver of sand.

"My God, this isn't Miami Beach, is it?" Susan exclaimed.

"Them's fighting words to a Texan, ma'am," Owen said, using a ridiculous drawl.

"Oh, I didn't mean to imply that it's an imitation of Miami. It's just that I expected . . . well, something more deserted with lots of stretches of lonely beach."

"That's what you'll see in the northern part of Padre Island. We'll visit there later. That's where you'll be able to find some interesting driftwood along the shore and maybe some pieces of an old wrecked shrimp boat."

"You mean the romance is all at the other end of the island?" she asked, rolling her eyes playfully in his direction.

"That's something you'll have to decide for yourself." Owen winked in response to her ploy as he brought the car to a halt in front of a garage door attached to an attractive pink stucco beach house.

"Hmmm!" Susan hummed in admiration. "Is this yours?"

"My father and I own it jointly." Owen continued to talk as he got out of the gray Mercedes and pulled their luggage out of the trunk. "We've been coming to the island since I was a boy. It's been a family tradition for as long as I can remember, long before it began the tremendous commercial buildup you saw. We're inveterate fishermen, you know. By the way, do you like to fish?"

"Me? Fish? With worms? Ugh!" Susan made a face and Owen laughed. "I'm better at collecting shells."

"You can take the girl out of the city, but you can't take the city out of the girl . . . or something like that." Owen's quip brought a smile to her lips as they entered a tiled entrance hall that was cleverly cluttered with flower-filled planters, huge ferns, and attractive vases. Susan wondered who took care of the large number of plants that obviously required a great deal of attention. They passed on to a spacious living room with colorful, comfortable rattan furniture. Owen beckoned her to the sliding glass doors that opened on to a slate terrace where a gentle sea breeze mingled with a brilliant sunlight. Putting his arm about her shoulders, he guided her out for a view of the Gulf waters. The ocean air had a tang to it when she took a deep breath, and the golden sun on her skin had a soothing, relaxing effect on her.

"Mmm," Susan purred appreciatively. "I'm awfully glad you suggested this idea. I really needed a change of scenery and this fits the bill exactly."

"Wait until you see the surf," Owen said enthusiastically. "It's absolutely gorgeous."

"I can't wait!"

"Well, let's get going then. Let's change and get down there."

Owen showed Susan to a white bedroom with wicker furniture and then he went off to his own room. When they met outside a few minutes later, his hands were full of beach gear—blankets, towels, and a radio. As he juggled all of the necessities, his eyes came level with Susan's shapely legs when she stepped out on the porch. The hip-high cuts of her one-piece midnight blue swimsuit seemed to beckon his attention almost maddeningly, and Owen decided that he was not going to mask his interest.

Keenly aware of his admiring glance, Susan felt a modest blush come to her face, then staved off the intimate moment by daring Owen with a race to the shore. Before he realized what was happening, Susan had jumped from the deck, let out an undignified screech as her toes hit the hot sand, and then taken off at a dead run. Her lithe and supple body moved quickly and gracefully over the burning beach. Small puffs of sand kicked up from under her feet as she raced ahead with Owen responding to her challenge in hot pursuit. The race ended at the water's edge with Susan declaring herself the proud winner just seconds ahead of Owen who paused just long enough to drop the blanket, towels, and other equipment in a heap. Ignoring her fatuous proclamations of victory, he scooped her up bodily in his arms and raced directly into the water, plunging both of them into the turquoise surf. Susan shrieked as she felt the shock of the cold salt water sweep over her body, then she struck out ahead for a swim into the waves. Owen quickly joined her, pleased with his manly display, and they swam side by side, bobbing, weaving, then drifting with the tide.

After a thirty-minute swim, they established a beachhead for lazing under the late afternoon sun. They relaxed on their blanket and munched a snack of nectarines and potato chips and watched swooping sea gulls doing their aerial acrobatics.

"Mmm, this has got to be the closest thing to heaven," Susan murmured as she sat up and stretched her arms high above her head. "I haven't felt this relaxed in months. I mean, not a care in the world. It's really a great feeling."

"You bet," Owen agreed. Then he rolled over and stood up, examining his shoulders. "But we might have one thing to worry about pretty soon if we don't get out of this sun for a while. It's easy to get burned out here."

Susan used a hand cupped as a visor over her eyes as she looked up at Owen standing over her offering his hand. It was impossible to avoid noticing his firm body with a mat of curling hair that wandered over his chest, ran downwards to his navel and disappeared under his trunks. Her senses mysteriously quickened as she reached for his hand and he helped her up.

"Oh, look! Somebody's water-skiing." She pointed towards the water, acutely aware of Owen staring at her and quite conscious of the fact that she was using a ploy to avoid meeting his eyes. But they never left her face. She met his intense gaze momentarily and smiled under the electricity of meaning that was being communicated between the two of them. Susan knew then and there that the true depths of her feelings for Owen were at a critical point in their relationship. This weekend would have something very important to tell her about what she really felt for him.

Early in the evening they dined at a terraced restaurant that overlooked the Gulf. Colorful umbrellas shielded the tables from the sinking sun as they both sipped white wine and ate lobster tails while a quiet trio played some moody South American rhythms in the background. After dessert and brandy, Owen suggested a walk along the shore to watch the sun's final descent. Streaks of pink and gold lingered in the sky and were reflected in the water as they walked barefoot along the sandy shore and the foamy surf swirled back and forth around their feet. The last rays of the purple twilight dwindled magically into darkness and a silhouette of a distant ocean steamer drifted into view along the horizon, then disappeared slowly. That lonely image remained imbedded in Susan's memory long after it was completely out of sight, stirring up feelings and longings that somehow she couldn't explain.

Languorously the two of them strayed, arm in arm, towards the beach house. At the porch steps, Owen brought Susan into his arms and kissed her with a long, tender, awakening kiss. He murmured softly in her ear, "I've been wanting to make love to you for a very, very long time." His lips grazed her ear lobe maddeningly as he whispered, sending a wild and exciting impulse of sensation along her neck and down her arm. "Now, check me if I'm wrong, but I think you want me, too."

She couldn't answer him directly. Instead she lay her head against his warm chest and let the sea breeze waft lightly about them. It was inevitable. She knew all along this would happen the instant she agreed to come here for the weekend with him. And it made her wonder why she had put Owen off for so long, especially when he had been so patient in the first place and so understanding. Really, he had willingly given her so much—the kind of friendship and support that a woman should expect from a man. If, of course, that man were truly interested in her. Most of all, he didn't make unreasonable demands, didn't smother her with just his own needs. That was something she had never experienced with Carlos who often left her with a battered ego. Oh, no! No! He was not going to intrude on this moment or on this night again; she swore it to herself.

Susan turned in Owen's arms to face him, then ran both hands behind his neck and along his face and brought them to rest on his chest. She looked at him directly. Here was the man who had shown her compassion as her boss and listened intently to her troubles with her cases and had given her good advice in her career. Owen was able to make her laugh at his silly jokes and help her to develop a sense of humor about her own shortcomings. He was really a likable guy, but even now her feelings for him, or for that matter, any other man were not entirely clear. No bells were ringing, no rockets were flying. Just what was it she wanted from a man in her life anyway? And, damn it, why was Carlos still there nagging in her subconscious?

"I didn't hear you say yes," Owen pressed.

Susan shrugged off the inner conflict, angry with herself. At this moment she needed and wanted Owen and that was that.

"Why, whatever made you think you had to ask?" she said, hoping that her reply wasn't too long in coming.

Owen slid back the glass doors that led from the deck to his room. Against the sound of crashing waves and only the light of the moon to guide him, Owen slowly undressed her, then loosened her black lace bra and her bikini pants. As his hands slid up her back and then down the length of her body, his lips found their way along her neck, setting off an uncontrollable tingling sensation. Now his body was firmly against hers and she felt his masculine passion throbbing dangerously near. An undulating movement locked their bodies in an erotic dance of desire. His nakedness was hot against hers, and her passions inched upward slowly in eager anticipation of a sweet and swooning ascent. And then she heard him give off a low moan and her body shuddered in response.

Owen drifted off to sleep almost immediately, but Susan found herself unable to unwind the giant spring that was lodged deep within. Tossing nervously, but as lightly as she could, she hoped not to awaken him. Along with her thoughts in the darkness, she had to admit to herself that this episode was not all that she had wished it could have been. Quite simply, he had left her unfulfilled and she wondered whether or not he realized it. As her hand brushed back her hair, she noticed her forehead damp with perspiration.

Carefully, quietly, she slipped out of bed, picked up her robe and went out onto the deck for a cigarette. A cool ocean breeze gently touched her mane of hair, unkempt from lovemaking. Standing there in just a light silk robe, a chill came over her but she just folded her arms tightly to provide herself with some protection. A low, melancholy feeling was coming on. No matter how hard she tried to sidestep it, Carlos's image appeared and re-appeared stubbornly. Why couldn't he let her be? Waves were dashing relentlessly against the darkened shore. They were tumultuous waves—as tumultuous as her own inner thoughts. Carlos was a better lover. *Admit it*, she told herself. Didn't every woman deep down fantasize about a lover that was masterful, sensual, virile, somebody that inspired her with something out of the ordinary, a man that generated excitement and imagination in a relationship? Carlos could do that.

On the other hand, that wasn't enough! She wasn't

about to be relegated to second place in any man's life and end up catering to his male ego until he tired of her or, as in Carlos' case, until he finally ended up marrying Margarita. No, it would be better not to get involved at all, better to end it now before the pain of separation became too much to bear.

That's the way it always seems to be with men in my life, Susan reflected. *Always a lot of ups and downs, a lot of highs and lows, a lot of good times and an awful lot of soul searching. But then again, maybe that's what love is always about in every woman's life.*

Actually, as far as Owen was concerned, Susan couldn't really point to a single trait that she could honestly say was a big obstacle for her to accept. He was a good-looking man, and he was a bright person, a competent and respected professional. He was easy to get along with and she was sure that he would never demand a total commitment from her. From what she knew of him after all of their hours together, Owen would recognize her need to be free and to be her own person, to have her own goals and aspirations and to pursue them without feeling guilty about some trifling male demands. Susan speculated that neither of them would ever be deeply hurt should there ever be a point in their relationship when they would have to call it quits.

Susan took one long drag on her cigarette and flipped it out into the darkness. Funny, she thought, just a moment ago nothing seemed to make any sense. Now she found herself leaning back again towards Owen. It was a safer road to travel, a more manageable relationship, one that seemed to make the most sense right now.

Satisfied that she had come to a wise decision, Susan opened the glass doors and slipped back inside. Only then did she realize how chilled she had become. Removing her robe, she sought the warmth under the covers and found Owen awake and waiting. He slid a warm arm underneath and around her shivering body.

"You were away for a long time out there. Have you wrestled it all out now?"

It was a pointed question that she hadn't expected and

she marveled at how in tune he was with her inner thoughts. She couldn't say anything, but just nodded against his chest and snuggled up close to him.

"Good. I'm glad." Owen had waited for her to come to grips with her dilemma and reach her own decision. If she returned to his bed, he knew he had won, but if she hadn't, well, then it would probably have ended abruptly right then and there. "Mmm, you're cold. Let me warm you up," he murmured, bringing her body close to his once again.

The remainder of the weekend was wonderfully pleasant and flew by quickly, filled with walks along the shore and more magnificent sunsets they agreed they would never forget. Owen cajoled her into doing some fishing too, but Susan preferred a ride through the secluded campsites and bask in the sun. There were lots of memorable moments and images from that weekend that passed through her mind as they drove back home, and she found herself recounting them during quiet moments alone in the days that followed. But it was that decision she had made on the deck about Owen that remained fixed in her mind.

It wasn't easy returning to work Monday morning after the splendid weekend at Padre Island, but her tight schedule and increasing case load soon had her back in the swing of things. The first item on her agenda was a contract she was drawing up between two young men who were going into the sporting goods business together. After that came the case involving two young women who owned a house jointly. Their problem stemmed from the fact that one of the women was planning to remarry and each woman was demanding the house for herself. Susan arranged to meet with the other lawyer in the case, hoping for an out-of-court settlement.

Susan had set the afternoon aside for the Vargas case which was shortly to come to trial. Having received the name of another possible witness, Susan dialed the number of a Mrs. Ruth Logan. When Mrs. Logan answered, Susan briefly explained the reason for her phone call.

"I don't know who gave you my name and number, but

they're wrong. Dead wrong!" The woman was defensive and belligerent, and Susan could see another witness slipping out of her grasp.

"If I could come over to your home and speak to you, Mrs. Logan—"

"Don't you come around here! Do you want to ruin my marriage?" There was real fear in the woman's voice.

"No, of course not. I just want to talk to you and see if you can help my client prove her case." Susan tried to soothe the woman but nothing seemed to work.

"Look, you," Ruth Logan screamed angrily, "you keep away from me! I have nothing to say to you or to tell you. Absolutely nothing!"

"Mrs. Logan, another woman has been sexually harassed. . . ."

"I don't care! You try to involve me and I'll have you arrested for . . . *harassment.* You get the message?" Suddenly the receiver slammed down, reverberating against Susan's eardrum. Seething with emotion, she held the dead phone for several seconds before dropping it back into place. This was one of those moments when she didn't like her job very much. Unsteadily, she reached for her pack of cigarettes, lit one, and inhaled. Calming down, she slowly crossed Mrs. Logan's name off her note pad. A hostile witness would be no help to Maria Vargas.

Chapter Eleven

"SO I HAVE FOUND you at last."

Susan whirled with the soapy sponge in her hand and would have run if her dignity had permitted her to follow her instincts. "Carlos, where did you come from?" she asked breathlessly.

"From my car across the street just now. Or, if you prefer, the caverns of hell these past weeks." The look he cast upon Susan was touched with pain. *"Querida,* why did you not call me?"

"I meant to, Carlos, but . . . I didn't know what to say." Her mind was a whirlwind of conflicting, half-formed thoughts and desires. Carlos looked so handsome, it was so good to see him, but Owen and Padre Island . . . oh, God, what a mess! And here she was in dirty jeans and a torn shirt washing her car. "I must look a sight." She raised a soapy hand to her hair, trying to smooth it against the slight breeze that was tousling it into further disorder.

"You look enchanting. Like a little girl." Carlos took a step closer then stopped. They stood watching each other while the afternoon sun warmed them and they relaxed their guard. They were glad to see each other. An unexpressed yearning was satisfied when they were together.

"Well, don't just stand there and let me do all the work. Here." Susan tossed Carlos another sponge. "Get to work. Or are you afraid of messing that pretty white shirt?" She teased playfully.

"Step aside, lady, and let a man show you how it's done. No Obregon lets such a challenge pass without action."

"So I've noticed." Susan smiled and the two of them began to laugh, as much from eased tension as from fun.

They had a good time washing and polishing Susan's blue Datsun. At one point, Carlos removed his shoes and socks and rolled up his pant legs and the two of them slopped around in the water from the hose, splashing and spraying one another. An easy feeling of camaraderie rose between them and they rubbed and scrubbed at Susan's car until it gleamed in the golden afternoon light.

By five o'clock they were both tired and hungry and Carlos suggested they go out to eat.

"No, Carlos. I'm too tired and lazy to bother dressing. Why don't you come in with me and we'll have some eggs or a sandwich. What do you think?"

"I think that's the best idea I ever heard fall from your beautiful lips. Lead on, *chiquita*, and I will follow." Carlos seemed to be hinting at something.

"Well, I didn't think I was proposing a solution to the nuclear arms race. It's only a quick meal I'm suggesting. Nothing more," Susan returned lightly but meaningfully.

"Nothing but a quick meal. I understand."

To Susan's delight, Carlos insisted on preparing their sandwiches and making coffee while she took time to have a quick shower. She came back into the kitchen fifteen minutes later dressed in clean slacks and a blouse and discovered Carlos setting the table and bare to the waist. The sight of his tanned torso thrilled and frightened her. Carlos caught the alarm on her face and reached for his damp shirt.

"I was merely letting it dry in the sunlight, Susan," he explained while he pulled it back on even though it was still damp.

Susan ignored the issue. "That coffee smells heavenly, Carlos. I'm starved. How about you?"

"Same. Let's eat."

The awkward moment passed; they sat down together and chatted comfortably as they ate their sandwiches.

"This is delicious coffee," Susan said when they had finished eating. "I can't believe you made it."

"Why not?" Carlos demanded haughtily. "I can cook a damned fine dinner when I put my mind to it."

"I bet you can," Susan replied with a touch of dismay. "It's just that I never expected you to know the oven from the sink."

"What kind of a man do you think I am, Susan? I'm just an ordinary guy."

"No, you're not, Carlos Obregon. Ordinary is the last word I would use to describe you."

"Hmm. What word would you use?"

"Uh-uh. That's a topic I refuse to engage in." Susan smiled impishly and rose to clear the table.

"Why don't you just sit still and let me pick up in here," Carlos offered.

"Enough is enough, *señor*. You go sit in the living room. I'll just stack these two and a half dishes, and be right in. Now get!" she commanded.

Carlos jumped up and saluted, and they both broke into laughter again. They were really having fun together.

When Susan joined Carlos, he was sitting back in the recliner and had turned on the radio to some soft classical music.

"Well, don't you look comfortable."

"I am." He sighed deeply to emphasize his contentment. Susan sat on the couch opposite Carlos and was just the slightest bit piqued at his remaining so far from her. She had actually been priming herself to face some amorous advances from him.

They sat quietly, relaxing and listening to Chopin as shadows filled the room, imperceptibly transforming the companionable silence into intimacy.

"I love that second movement," Susan whispered as the delicate piano notes trembled into stillness.

"Chopin speaks of love with a touch of sadness," Carlos added to Susan's thought.

"I wonder why sadness seems to make love more meaningful," Susan murmured.

"That is a very revealing observation to come from you," Carlos commented.

"How is that?" Susan sensed that she might not want to follow the subject to its conclusion.

"I know I shouldn't say this, but I don't think modern women deal with the full spectrum of emotion where love is concerned."

"That's typically arrogant of you, but I'm curious. Just what is the 'full spectrum' of love and what portion do modern women exclude?" Susan questioned crisply, her female defenses fully alerted.

"*Querida,* don't be so quick to take offense. I am not criticizing."

"Yes, you are, Carlos, but okay, I'll relax. Now tell me more of this notion you have about modern women."

"Let's change the subject, sweetheart."

"No, Carlos, please. Explain what you meant."

"Very well, but I beg your indulgence. It is not something I have thought out. It is just an impression I have gathered through experience."

"Which is extensive, no doubt."

Carlos merely raised his hands and let them drop. "It seems to me," he hesitated, "that there is a lot of selfishness among women today and a seeking after pleasure only. Very little willingness to endure the pain and hurt of love. No tolerance for suffering."

"And men have such a tolerance, I suppose."

"Indeed, no. But if women do not maintain the tenacity to endure then love never has time to sink its roots and grow. It is continually stunted and aborted."

"Very fine sentiments which neatly relieve the male of any obligation."

"I don't think so, Susan. I happen to believe that women are made of better stuff and must teach men how to reach higher. Men have the capacity, but women have to show the way."

"That still sounds like an old-fashioned cop-out to me. It's time men were made to grow up."

"Perhaps you are right," Carlos agreed conciliatingly, "but do you see much growing up anywhere today?"

"And women are to blame," Susan said drily.

"I don't know. Sometimes I think so."

"Let me ask you, Carlos. Are you prepared to endure pain for the sake of love?"

He smiled ruefully, "Damned right I am. Especially after this last two weeks." He paused. "Susan, why didn't you call me? You told Elena you would."

Carlos had maneuvered the conversation skillfully. "I know, Carlos, but I . . . wasn't sure I should."

"Why not?"

"Carlos, I don't think I'm ready to discuss this with you yet. Why don't we have a drink and call it a night? I'm really very tired and my most important case opens in court tomorrow."

"Susan, at least let me apologize for the embarrassment I caused you at the wedding. I need to hear your forgiveness." He was so earnest. "I tried waiting until I couldn't stand it anymore."

"You don't have to apologize, Carlos. You were following a code of behavior I don't understand. We—our values are very different." God, this was terrible.

"Susan, don't say such things. We're not so different. Give me another chance to prove I can be the kind of man you want."

"Carlos, life is difficult enough without trying to overcome such deep cultural differences."

"Susan, you make my heart hurt." He came over to her and drew her to her feet. *"Mi corazón,* I love you," he whispered and kissed her passionately. Susan could not stop her response. She wanted Carlos to kiss her again and again. "I knew it," Carlos whispered exultantly. "You do care."

"Oh, Carlos, please. You have no idea how difficult you are making life for me."

"But that is life, *mi amor.*"

"I can't handle this right now. I need all my energy for the case I'm bringing to court."

"All right, Susan. I won't pressure you tonight. Just say you will see me again."

"Okay, Carlos. Fine. Now you must go."

"Geza Anda is playing Chopin with the San Antonio Symphony next Friday. Will you go with me?"

"I can't. I'm sorry, but I'm busy."

"Then Saturday night. Dinner?"

"No, I can't. If you must know, I'll be out of town next weekend."

Carlos sensed her guilt. "Do you mind telling me where you're going?"

"You have no right to ask that question. It's none of your business," Susan retorted.

"Yes, it is. You *are* my business." The male supremacy of generations of Spanish grandees blazed from his dark eyes.

"There you see! It's just what we've been talking about. All right, *Señor* Obregon, let's just see what you make of this! I'm going to attend the National Conference on Municipal and Corporate Law in New York City with Owen Forsythe."

"You mean you are traveling to New York alone with your employer?" Carlos demanded.

"Yes, I am."

"By God, Susan, that's not right."

"Maybe not by your standards, Carlos, but it's all right by mine."

Carlos was trying to control his anger, but it radiated from him in nearly palpable waves of violent emotion. He turned from Susan and took a few steps before facing her again. "You will be staying at the same hotel?"

Susan felt like a child caught playing hooky. The situation was preposterous. Why was she allowing this intimidation? "Yes, we will." She took a deep breath to forestall the next question. God, what would he say if he knew about Padre Island? "Carlos, this has gone far enough. I can't allow you to badger me like this. I think you should leave now before you say something foolish."

"Foolish?" Carlos stormed. "Is a woman's honor foolish?"

"Carlos, this is hopeless. We inhabit two different worlds. I simply don't share your Latin sentiments."

Carlos grasped Susan's shoulders painfully. "You can't go to New York with Owen Forsythe."

"I most certainly can. And I most certainly will." Susan was burning with anger.

"I won't let you do it, Susan," Carlos exclaimed through clenched teeth, clutching her shoulders tighter.

"Carlos, this is ridiculous. Let me go."

"Not until you say you won't go to New York with Owen."

"Listen here, Carlos Obregon. I am going to a professional conference with a colleague. And in any case you're not my master. No man is. I'll go where I please. When I please. With whom I please. Do I make myself clear?"

"How many pleases are enough to satisfy you?" he sneered.

"Who's to say?" she taunted brazenly.

Carlos almost crushed the bones in her arms. "Johnnie was right. You're just an Anglo bitch!" He flung her onto the couch and stormed out, slamming the door so hard that a vase on the mantel fell to the floor with a crash.

Susan sat on the couch and cried, brushing the tears angrily from her face and rubbing her arms. *So long, Carlos. And good riddance.*

Susan's arms bore the marks of Carlos's fierce handling the next day, but the long sleeves of her tan oxford shirt covered the telltale signs of their encounter, and the pressing concerns of the court case successfully squelched the memory of that episode from her consciousness. The Vargas case was in possible jeopardy from an early motion filed by the respondents, which were Robert Harmon and the Haas Company as joint defendants. There were indications that the case might become entangled in a technicality. The Haas Company's attorney, Quentin Ruggers, a crafty veteran of the courts, argued that the Human Relations Commission's findings were inadmissible because the amendment to the San Antonio City ordinance of 1976 which altered the ordinance of 1954 to include discrimination on the basis of sex had not been properly published and further that discrimination because of sex did not include the concept of sexual harassment. If the judge found either point to be correctly taken, the case could be dismissed and Susan would have to file an exception and start all over again. She trembled with anxiety at the thought and tried to suppress her fears in order to remain alert to the testimony being given.

The courtroom was filled with interested spectators. The subject of sex in any of its various aspects was an irresistible lure to the public. Any case with sexual ramifications was sure to draw a crowd. Many hopefuls had been turned away at the doors to courtroom number ten that morning and members of the press were in attendance in force.

Susan wanted desperately to win this case. So much depended on it. Not only was it a showcase for her legal talents to the community at large, but more importantly, it was her chance to prove to Owen that his trust in her was well placed. No one could ask for a better employer. Owen had stood behind her every inch of the way in the Vargas case. Not many women had a boss whose support went without strings or intrusions into her professional choices. He never crowded Susan's freedom to operate according to her own perceptions and preferences. And despite his romantic aspirations, when it came to their working relationship, Owen was a model of professional honor. He was warm and supportive but kept his hands off her and her cases. She had to do well to justify the respect he had accorded her.

Susan studied the judge's impassive countenance searching for a clue to his sentiments but found no revelation in his stolid features. The jury seated to the left listened attentively, but court personnel seated up front revealed more boredom than interest, having reached saturation levels long ago in cases far steamier and sensational than the present dispute.

Susan was relieved that they had reached a jury trial. Her goal was to bring the focus of public attention to bear on the problem as much as to win the case. And when Susan learned that Judge Drizer was to preside, she was doubly relieved that a jury was acting. Conservatism was his middle name. It would be a rare day in jurisprudence that a feminist case received an unbiased decision in his hands if he were left to his own devices.

As Susan studied the judge, memories of her father intruded into her concentration. Her father had often presented that same stern visage when he was weighing matters of moral import. It disturbed her to remember that her father, too, had been an arch conservative and that his judgments, once reached, were irreversible. She forced her attention back to the court proceedings.

Harmon was the most notably uncomfortable individual in the room. The case was costing him heavily in personal reputation and public esteem. Susan's encounter with him at the Triple L Ranch was an humiliating adjunct to a situation already brimming with disgrace. The look he cast on Susan and Maria was filled with bitter hatred. Unless serious doubts could be raised about Maria's veracity or morality, he would leave the arena a damaged man. So far neither Morley nor Ruggers had succeeded in eliciting testimony harmful to Maria Vargas. Their best hope lay in the question of the interpretation of the amendment to the city ordinance and the issue of its having been properly published.

The courtroom had warmed uncomfortably by early afternoon despite the air-conditioning. Sun streamed in from tall windows lining the west wall and a sheriff's deputy interrupted proceedings when he attempted to draw the vertical blinds to cut the glare. One set jammed and there was a clatter that halted testimony from Billie Turner, the mail clerk at the Haas Company.

Susan resumed her questioning when the disturbance settled down.

"Was it customary, Mr. Turner, for the interoffice mail system to be used for delivery of personal mail between office employees?"

"Not usually."

"In your service as mail clerk at Howard Haas for the past two years, just how many times were you individually called upon to deliver packages or correspondence of a personal nature between employees?"

"Three times."

"And who were the parties requesting your service?"

"Robert Harmon."

"Anyone else?"

"No. Only Mr. Harmon."

"And to whom were the deliveries made?"

"Maria Vargas."

Susan took a step closer to the witness. "And did you know the contents of any of those deliveries?"

"Well, once Mr. Harmon showed me a picture and asked me if I didn't think the . . . person looked like Maria Vargas."

"The person in the picture that Robert Harmon showed you, did she look like Ms. Vargas?"

"Sort of." Susan waited for Billie to continue. "She had dark hair like Maria."

"Anything else?"

"I suppose she resembled her. I don't know. She didn't have any clothes on."

"It was a picture of a naked woman?"

"It sure was. She was the centerfold from *Playboy* magazine."

"I see."

Amused titters from the spectators were silenced by the bailiff and Susan resumed her examination. When she questioned Billie about the other two deliveries he explained that he knew nothing more than that one was a letter-size envelope and the other was a box of candy. Susan then turned her witness over to counsel for the respondent, Thomas Morley.

"Now Mr. Turner, I want you to turn your mind back to the day you delivered the *Playboy* picture to Ms. Vargas."

"Yes, sir."

"Can you recall what conversation passed between you and Mr. Harmon?"

"Not exactly."

"I'm sure you can if you try. After all, it was a *Playboy*

nude. Didn't you wonder why Mr. Harmon was sending it to Ms. Vargas?"

"I told you he thought she looked like Maria."

"Didn't you wonder what the reason was for sending it to her?" Morley insisted.

"Mr. Harmon said it was the kind of thing Maria liked . . . that she was proud to display her charms to admirers."

"Anything else?"

"Well, that she, uh, knew how to make the most of her equipment."

Susan looked to Maria whose face was livid with anger. Maria whispered in Susan's ear.

When Morley was finished, Susan approached Billie again on redirect. "Just one more question if you please, Mr. Turner. What happened when you delivered that picture to Ms. Vargas?"

"She freaked out."

"Would you elucidate, please?"

"She tore the picture into a million pieces and threw them in the trash."

"And what did she say?"

"I'm not certain. But she was plenty mad."

"How do you know?"

"It sounded like she was swearing, but it was all in Spanish."

"Thank you. You may step down."

Susan called Margaret Peron to the stand. Margaret Peron's testimony was persuasive. She replied to questions put to her by Susan in a straightforward manner that was credible and precise. When she was asked about her personal experience of Harmon's techniques with female employees, she readily admitted to having been a former target of Harmon's sexual advances.

"He made it perfectly clear that the position of account executive was mine for the granting of sexual favors."

"What was your response to those terms?"

"I went to bed with Robert Harmon on three separate occasions." Margaret didn't bat an eye. She was a cool customer.

"Can you provide any proof that these assignations did occur?"

"If you check the registry at the Camino Real Motel for the month of January 1981, you'll find the dates of our assignations duly entered there. I received my promotion on January 27, 1981—which can also be verified by company records."

Susan handed over certified copies of the registry and employment records to the County Clerk.

"And you have not dated Mr. Harmon since?"

"No. I paid my dues. Besides, he had turned his sights onto Maria Vargas."

"How did you know that?"

"The office grapevine. Robert's campaigns were common knowledge."

Morley cut short his cross-examination when it became apparent that Margaret Peron could not be discredited. She was a very convincing witness on Maria's behalf.

The increasing heat from the glaring afternoon sun raised beads of perspiration on foreheads and stirred physical discomfort. Spectators shifted, jurists fanned themselves, and attorneys loosed their ties. Judge Drizer leaned to the bailiff and whispered for a moment.

"There will be a twenty-minute recess," the bailiff announced. "All rise."

The judge left by a door behind his chair. People wandered into the hall to smoke and speculate. Susan turned to the law clerk from Forsythe's and sent him to the clerk's office for a copy of City Ordinance Amendment 495-A of 1976. She wanted to examine that document tonight to discover for herself just how serious a threat it raised to the validity of their position.

"How is it going?" Owen Forsythe had come in an hour ago, unnoticed by Susan.

"Owen, am I glad to see you! I just sent Jim to the clerk's office for—"

"I know. Don't look so worried, darling. That amendment was published in timely fashion."

"But what if it weren't? All this could be for nothing." She cast a glance around the courtroom.

Owen reached out a finger and smoothed the crease between Susan's worried blue eyes. "You've done all you could, Sue. Your case is developing solidly. The groundwork has been thorough and complete. The jury is on your side."

"Do you think so? Oh, Owen, I needed to hear that." She heaved a deep sigh. "You're right. I've covered every possible avenue." She smiled. "Did you hear the Peron testimony?"

"Indeed I did. Boffo! No one has any doubts about Harmon after that."

"She was good, wasn't she?" Owen nodded. "Still, I want to read that amendment for myself."

"Sure you do." Owen studied Susan's serious face and smiled encouragingly. "You're doing a great job. Keep it up." The tipstaff came in. "I have to leave for the Dallas meeting in an hour. I'll call you tonight."

"Please do. And Owen"—Susan reached out and touched his hand—"thanks a million. You always say the right thing."

"Just don't forget it when you're rich and famous."

Susan laughed and felt ready to face the remainder of the afternoon. How kind of Owen to come and cheer her on. She was so lucky to have been hired by the Forsythes and taken into their firm. Under Owen's wing, her self-confidence had burgeoned. In his steady approval she saw reflected an image of herself as both a competent attorney and a desirable woman.

From the looks of things, Maria wouldn't be called to the stand until tomorrow. A lot depended on the jury's perception of Maria's character. Susan forced some misgivings she felt about her client to the back of her mind. Maria, like Margaret Peron, was a tough cookie. It was subtle priming from Susan that guided Maria's choice of a demure navy dress with a white collar and cuffs and sensible low pumps over the flashy pink print and strappy sandals that were Maria's first selection for her courtroom debut. Susan had coached the woman on how to respond to her questions, but there was no preventing Maria's natural

Alicia Meadows

style from intruding itself during the cross-examination. Oh, well, no use borrowing trouble.

Susan called Thomas Juarez to the stand, and while he didn't greatly help Maria's case, he didn't harm it either. Mr. Juarez was dignified and pedantic. He phrased his responses in a slow, roundabout way, but he made it clear that Maria Vargas was competent and reliable and that was enough for their cause. The opposition spent little time with Juarez and Judge Drizer adjourned after the gentleman had given his testimony.

Susan was sitting at her desk at home studying the San Antonio Community Relations Ordinance of 1954 which addressed itself to discrimination on the basis of race, color, religion, national origin, and ancestry. The amendment of 1976 added the words handicap, age, and sex to the list. The issue between discrimination and harassment was cloudy at best. No doubt Harmon and Haas would try to prove that Maria's demotion was the result of her inadequacy on the job, but Susan's careful research had revealed no foundation for such a charge. Maria's job evaluations had ranged from good to excellent and there seemed no one at the company who could prove incompetency.

Still, Susan herself had warned Maria in the early days that federal law was unclear about sexual harassment and discrimination.

The telephone rang and Susan answered it. "Owen, it's so good of you to call. How are things in Dallas?"

"Smooth sailing all the way. How about you?"

"Nothing eventful happened after you left. Judge Drizer adjourned after Juarez gave testimony."

"Harmon is going to lose. He has nothing going for him."

"God, I hope you're right. I've been reading the Community Relations Ordinance and it does leave a lot of room for argument."

"It's not the best written law to come down the pike—which gives you as much leeway as it does Harmon."

140

"I suppose you're right. But there's Judge Drizer. I don't trust him. You know what a conservative he is."

"That's true. But the jury is the one to decide the case. Not Judge Drizer. What about the press? Did the reporters hassle you?"

"Oh, I almost forgot. Be sure to get a copy of the *Express* tomorrow. Wanda Troyer did an interview on Maria, and you know Wanda will be sympathetic. Feminism is her bag."

"Terrific! You're on the road to victory, Sue. I'll be back to celebrate Friday night. We'll drink champagne."

"I'll keep that in mind." Susan paused. "Owen, I don't know what I'd do without you."

"Don't even try to find out."

"I won't."

But instead of Owen, Carlos claimed Susan's thoughts for the remainder of the night. The look of angry pain on his face before he had slammed the door last night burned in her mind with disturbing clarity.

Leave me alone, Carlos Obregon, she thought angrily and punched her pillow trying to force herself into a comfortable position and to the unconsciousness of sleep.

The next morning Judge Drizer called the attorneys into his chambers.

"There has been a new obstacle raised in this case," he announced and Susan's heart fell. *Here it comes,* she thought. "I have here"—the judge lifted a court document —"a duly filed notice of objection to the amendment to City Ordinance 475-A of 1954."

"May I see it?" Quentin Ruggers exclaimed with unconcealed excitement.

"One moment," Judge Drizer remarked and continued his discourse. "Apparently a Josephine Billings on behalf of the South Texas League of Christian Women for Decency, a Baptist organization, requested a hearing to raise objection to the proposed amendment. No hearing was ever held. As you know, the San Antonio Code of Municipal Incorporation provides for notice and opportunity to be heard to individuals or groups wishing to raise objections to proposed ordinances or amendments." Judge Drizer handed the document to Ruggers while watching Susan thoughtfully. "I have no choice but to dismiss this hearing. The amendment, as it stands, is invalid."

Susan didn't hear any more. The judge issued a decree nisi dismissing the plaintiff's complaint and providing ten days to file exceptions. She turned to Maria Vargas and fought bravely to keep her expression under control. But inside she was crying.

Later, over coffee with Maria, she discussed the collapse of their case and both agreed to take a few days to recover from the blow and decide their course of action.

God, she needed Owen. The trip to New York was a blessing. She had to get away from San Antonio and her world in disarray.

Chapter Twelve

IN SPITE OF everything that had happened in the past few weeks to fill her life with confusion and turmoil, Susan's spirits were on a major turnaround when the taxi door opened to drop her and Owen off at the St. Regis Hotel. It was shortly after six o'clock on a lovely fall evening in New York, the city that always spelled automatic excitement to her; and she was looking forward to the long weekend that they had planned.

"Ready?" Owen smiled after registering at the desk. He took her by the arm and they followed the bellhop with their luggage to the elevator. "We have adjoining rooms on the twelfth floor . . . as you requested," Owen whispered on their ride up. Susan nodded self-consciously. She had made it clear that she did not want Owen to reserve one room for the two of them. Strange as it might have seemed to him or anyone else, she intended to remain independent. She felt that it was a matter of integrity. And when the doors were opened onto her elaborately appointed room, she was not sorry to have it all to herself; as a matter of fact she was completely satisfied with her decision.

After they had each taken a few minutes to get organized, he rapped on the adjoining door. "I've arranged for dinner at Alfredo's at eight-thirty. That should give us plenty of time to relax and change. Okay?"

"Sounds fine to me," she answered absently while examining her new cranberry-colored cocktail dress with a critical eye. "It's not wrinkled. Miracle of miracles!"

"That's good. One less thing to worry about," Owen smiled as he came up behind her and planted a kiss on her

neck. It caught her off guard in a sensitive spot and she
whirled around immediately to face him. Draping her
arms around his neck, she met his lips with a warm, affectionate kiss.

"Mmmm," Owen muttered appreciatively. "Maybe I
should cancel those reservations . . . ?"

"Oh, no, you're not going to get off that easy." Susan
pushed playfully at his chest to release herself from his
arms. "You raved about Alfredo's all the way into town
from the airport, and I intend to find out for myself first-
hand about the fabulous food it has to offer. Now while
you're readying yourself for this feast," she said, ushering
him out of her room, "I'm going to pretty myself for the occasion, too."

The dinner turned out to be everything Owen had promised. It began with an extraordinary antipasto which was
followed by the legendary fettucini Alfredo and then veal
Marsala. After dessert, Susan raised her tiny glass of Ben-
edictine and brandy in a salute to her companion's good
taste.

"Utterly sinful! That meal absolutely bordered on the
obscene, and it probably sentenced me to two whole
weeks on the Scarsdale diet, but it was worth it. If we
don't come here again the next time we're in New York,
I'm going to be very disappointed." The final sip of B
and B drifted warmly inside and Susan felt just a little
light-headed.

"I'll remember that," Owen assured her, helping her out
of her chair.

When they left the restaurant, she held tightly to his
arm and confided that she was feeling just a little bit
merry. "After the wine and the B and B, I think I need the
support of your arm."

Owen smiled with amusement. He had never seen her in
a situation where she was slightly out of control. "Why
don't we just take a nice brisk walk for a few minutes to
clear our heads before we go back to the hotel?"

Susan nodded and giggled in an uncharacteristic way
that triggered laughter from Owen. They continued in this

way until they found themselves walking down the street in a kind of burlesque promenade.

"You know something?" he said. "You're even more fun when you've had a few drinks." He wouldn't admit it, but he was feeling a little tipsy, too.

"Well, I rather like the state I'm in right now to be perfectly honest. What happens to me is that I have two reactions. The first one is that I get kind of silly and I guess you could see that already."

"Yeah, and I think it's quite becoming," he said with a grin. "What's the other reaction?"

"The other reaction is that I lose all of my inhibitions. I'm just a sucker for mad and passionate love when my brain becomes slightly addled."

"Really? I can't imagine any girl from proper Massachusetts losing her inhibitions for very long. Tell me, how long does this feeling usually last?"

"Well, let's see." Susan looked at her watch and bit her lip in an attempt to hold back a smirk. "If we're not in bed within the next five minutes, you may end up reading a good novel in your own room tonight."

"In that case . . ." Owen didn't need to finish his statement. Instead, he left her standing on the sidewalk and ran out into the street to flag down a cab. "With a little bit of luck," he said, as he slid beside her and closed the door behind him, "we'll be able to get the fairy princess back in time before the magic spell is broken."

The liquor had indeed relieved Susan of any inhibitions, and she gazed up eagerly at Owen's trim elegant form as he divested himself of shirt and pants and came across the room to the bed where she lay upon the yellow sheets clothed only in her black lace chemise.

"You're beautiful, Susan," he rasped as he sat down beside her and bent his head to hers. They exchanged light, persuasive kisses that deepened and explored until their breathing became as one.

She felt his warm caressing hands arousing, stimulating, and weaving a hypnotic spell of pleasure over her until her own arms and legs tightened around his body drawing him closer, closer while she moved tantalizingly beneath him murmuring his name.

Desire mesmerized them until their trembling bodies reached fulfillment.

Afterwards Susan snuggled next to Owen, happy and relaxed. As she drifted off to sleep, Susan thought that perhaps at last she had found contentment.

In the morning after a quick breakfast, Owen was off to Columbia University to ready himself for a lecture on corporate law he was giving later that day. And Susan headed for Fifth Avenue to browse for some dresses at Saks and Bergdorf Goodman. That was something she couldn't resist doing, even though she knew it was going to break her budget. Some of the price tags really made her flinch and also made her think about how her life had changed since going to Texas. Both Carlos and Owen lived in a world of wealth and privilege, and it hadn't taken her long to adapt to that environment. It was an enjoyable experience for her, however long it lasted, even with some of its bittersweet pitfalls. And there were a number of them, she would be the first to admit. But the biggest pitfall facing her this morning, she suddenly realized, was how to pay for the gown she just selected for the gala event that was to be held the following night at the St. Regis ballroom. It was a simple but elegant garment, made of black crepe and trimmed at the neck with sequins. It was just too tempting to pass by, even though when she mentally added its cost to the hotel bill and the conference, it made her wonder if she would end up having to defend herself in a personal bankruptcy case.

With a shrug of her shoulders, Susan pulled out her credit card from her wallet and handed it to the obliging clerk. "When in Rome . . ." she mumbled to the woman who paused in the midst of writing out her sales slip.

"I beg your pardon?" the salesgirl asked.

"Oh, nothing," she chortled to herself.

When she returned to the hotel, Susan realized that she was now running late and decided to forego lunch in order to get back to the conference. At the registration table for the symposium, she heard her name being called and turned to see a familiar face. It was Ted Updike, a chum from law school. They stopped to reminisce for a few minutes, and while they did, he seemed to be looking around for someone until finally he asked whether Jeff was attending the conference with her.

"I guess you haven't heard, Ted. Jeff and I are divorced now."

"Hey, that's tough."

"Not really. It was for the best. I'm sure of that."

"Super!" A mischievous grin came to Ted's lips. "I always did want to ask you out, but with Jeff always around I never could get the ball into my court. I hope my chances are a lot better now."

Susan put him off with a congenial laugh. Ted Updike was not exactly her type with his mod clothes and trendy talk. He was always just a little too Machiavellian in law school, and he seemed to be playing too many different roles to suit her. "Listen, I can't talk now. I'm on my way to a lecture and I'm late already. Maybe we could meet during the coffee break. There is someone I'd like to introduce you to."

"Oh, oh, that doesn't sound too promising. Looks like someone's already ahead of me, but okay, I'll look for you."

Susan nodded and hurried off to the lecture hall where Owen was speaking. Embarrassed to be late, she slipped into the back of the auditorium and slid into an empty seat. He was a good speaker, blessed with a firm and resonant voice, articulate in his delivery, charming in his ability to hold his audience's interest. At the conclusion of his speech, he received a strong round of applause, and then the forum opened for a question and answer session. As it turned out, the session lasted a lot longer than she had anticipated, and when it concluded Owen rushed her on to another lecture. Ted Updike and the coffee break were forgotten.

The next session was unbearably dull and when her stomach began to growl from hunger, that was all the motivation she needed to leave in search of something to eat.

As soon as she left the amphitheater, she found Ted Updike on her heels. Apparently, he, too, had been in the same session and shared her judgment about its level of interest.

"Hey, I've got a great idea, Sue. Let's go get something to eat. I've looked over the remaining lectures and discussion groups scheduled for the rest of the afternoon, and I can guarantee you that you'll never stay awake through all of them. Besides, we can get something a lot more interesting to eat than what they're going to offer you tonight in the cafeteria. What do you say to that?"

He was probably right on both counts and she could feel her stomach growling again, almost goading her to say yes. And as far as Owen was concerned, it was unlikely that he would be missing her. He was so wrapped up in conference proceedings that he'd practically ignored her ever since her arrival.

"Okay, Ted. If you're buying, you've got a deal."

Traffic was slow and so were the waiters in the restaurant that Ted had selected in midtown Manhattan. When they had finally been served, Susan looked at her wristwatch and then double-checked it. It was after seven o'clock!

"My God, Ted, where did the time go?" She grabbed her handbag and jacket and got up to leave.

"Hey, hold on. What's the hurry?" Ted was still munching on a sandwich. "Anyway, by the time we get back to Columbia everything's going to be all over. Sit down and relax. You didn't even finish your meal."

"Yes, I know, but—"

"Hey, do you have to check in with this guy or something? That's what's got you bugged, right?"

"Well, I did come to the conference with him and he certainly will expect to—"

"Wait a minute, wait a minute. Is this fair to me? I wanted to spend a little time with you and you're worrying yourself silly over him. Is he going to miss you because you had a date for tonight?"

"Well, no . . . not exactly."

"Fine. I'm asking you out for the evening then. Look,

let's do this. Let's finish this meal in a nice, slow, civilized manner and then why don't we head down to the Village afterwards? I know a club that puts on a fabulous show that I'm sure you'll love. Hey, how about giving your old colleague and friend a little courtesy here, huh?"

Ted was like that. Always using a favor to his advantage, and making you feel like a jerk if you didn't go along with him. The invitation was interesting because the Village always held a fascination for her—at least it had during her college days. There had been some wild and exciting times down there, and she was sorely tempted to take a fresh new look at the place through the eyes of maturity.

"Hey, listen," Ted argued, "by the time we get back from this place, the university's going to be deserted anyway."

"I guess you're right," Susan acquiesced, wondering what Owen would think. If only there were some way to call. But there wasn't and that was all there was to it. He would just have to go it alone tonight, she thought, but she couldn't help feeling a twinge of guilt about it.

Ted talked her into it, and for the sake of being polite, their little trek into the bowels of the Village cost her four more hours in his company, something that became more of an ordeal with every passing hour. When they finally pulled up in a taxi in front of the St. Regis, Susan recalled the title of one of her favorite books: *You Can't Go Home Again*. How aptly it applied to her return to her former haunts. It would have been better if it had all been left locked in the inner recesses of her imperfect memory because dimly lit basements, close quarters, and smoke-filled rooms featuring off-the-wall comedians no longer held the appeal to her that they once did. And she had had enough, too, of Ted Updike who apparently felt that his generosity gave him the right to paw her in a dingy club and again during the ride uptown.

"Good night, Ted," Sue said coolly as she climbed out of the cab.

"Hey, aren't you going to invite me up for a nightcap?" he asked in the manner of a whimpering puppy dog.

"No, I'm sorry, Ted," she said, her patience right at its edge. "This isn't my apartment. It's a hotel."

"So? They've got liquor and beds, don't they?" A lecherous glint came to his eyes.

"Sorry, Ted. I'm with a friend," she answered before thinking that his comment deserved no reply whatsoever.

"Hey, that's okay. A *menage à trois* sounds terribly exciting."

Susan swung on her heels without another word, leaving him with a doltish and uncomprehending look on his face. She was more angry with herself than she was with him. What an intolerable boor Ted had turned out to be! But her own behavior tonight had been absolutely foolish. Running down to the Village and wasting time with a half-wit like him whose company she never really cared for certainly wasn't the brightest thing she had done in recent history. On the way up in the elevator to her room, she wondered what she had hoped to accomplish. Was she trying to test Owen in some way? Would he be angry with her? He had every right to be. After all, one of the assumed reasons for coming to the conference was to be together.

Once inside her room, she threw her handbag on the bed, kicked off her shoes and went directly to the adjoining bedroom door. After rapping lightly and receiving no answer, she opened it and peered in to see Owen stretched out on the bed. She called his name softly, but there was no reply and she quietly eased the door shut. For one long minute she speculated on the possibility that he really was awake but simply was ignoring her. Maybe she deserved it, if that was what he was doing, but it was not a pleasant prospect to contemplate. Then Susan rejected the idea outright because she didn't see Owen as that kind of man. Her apology would just have to wait until morning, she decided, and went to bed.

But her agitated state wouldn't permit her to sleep. After a restless night of tossing and turning, Susan found it almost impossible to get up the next morning. She knew, though, that Owen was an early riser and she forced herself out of bed so that there would be time to talk before they left for the university.

Owen's greeting was noticeably indifferent across the breakfast table when she joined him in the hotel restaurant. He had come down without her and ordered some poached eggs alone. After Susan sat down, he picked up the newspaper he had been reading and buried his face behind it.

"Owen," Susan called over the paper to him. "I'd like to talk to you about last night."

The paper lowered and his steel gray eyes seemed stern. "Last night?"

"Yes. I—I thought you'd probably want some kind of explanation. . . ."

He studied her solemnly for a tense moment. "It seems to me that we agreed that we would make no claims on one another. And so, I'm not going to renege on my part of the bargain."

"But this is different. We came here together."

Owen's eyebrows arched upwards in that superior way of his as he reminded her pointedly, "I wasn't the one who forgot."

Sue's face flamed. "I did come to your room last night."

"Oh?"

"Yes. I did. But you were asleep. I came to apologize."

"Okay. Apology accepted. Now let's have some breakfast. These eggs look like they're getting cold."

He was using his best trial lawyer techniques on her now, and she wanted to strike him for it. That wasn't a game she wanted to get drawn into. "Well, I can see that this conversation has come to an end." Susan flung her napkin down on the table and returned to the room.

Owen did not immediately come after her, and just as she decided that she would leave for the conference without him, he appeared at her side and they shared the taxi ride uptown.

After an agonizing interval of silence, he was the first to

speak. "I'm at a loss to understand, why you should be angry with me, Susan. Haven't we said right along that we should be free to come and go as we please? That we wouldn't smother one another by interfering with each other's individual freedom to do what we wanted to do? So, to be perfectly frank, I felt that I just might be overstepping my boundaries by questioning you about where the *hell* you had gotten to last night. I'm merely trying to stay true to that agreement."

"All right," Susan agreed. "You're correct. I suppose we did agree to that arrangement and I guess I shouldn't have made such a fuss. But do you want to know something honestly? I would have been glad if you had demanded some kind of explanation. I mean you're so damned concerned about maintaining our mutual rights and freedoms, it seems like you're working another corporate contract instead of some kind of human relationship." Susan put her face into her hand and rubbed her forehead in frustration.

"Look," she continued without glancing up at him, "forget about what I just said. I—I don't have any right to do that. I was the one who was at fault and I should be willing to accept the blame. It's just me, I guess. How strange! Now that I have a relationship with no strings attached, I seem to be looking for them."

Susan wanted to get Owen's reaction to her thoughts, but their taxi pulled up in front of the university and the general discussion came to a halt. But at least the air had been cleared somewhat, although not entirely to her satisfaction, and when she and Owen went their separate ways once again in order to attend the seminars they had registered for, Susan wished their little talk hadn't ended so suddenly. There was a lot more they had to talk about, and that point seemed never to leave her mind as she sat through what seemed like an endless procession of speakers.

A dinner-dance was being held that evening at the St. Regis for all of the conferees and by that time, the two of them seemed in a much better frame of mind. When Susan emerged from her bedroom in her evening dress, Owen held out a dainty corsage of two white gardenias tied with a white satin bow and offered it to her with a broad smile on his face.

"Why, that was thoughtful of you," Susan exclaimed, taking the flowers from him and pinning them at her waist. "When on earth did you find time to get them? You were at the conference all day today and—"

"Well, most of the day." A sheepish grin came across his face. "I have to confess that I slipped out to a shop during the seminar on correct trends in corporate litigation. Anyway, the people I talked to afterwards told me that I really didn't miss much. And besides, I thought the corsage would go nicely with your black dress. I must say, you're looking quite lovely in it tonight." He stood back, admiring her at length.

"Well, I'm so happy you took notice," she said.

Owen came up behind her and breathed deeply. "Mmm! You know something else? You're giving off a scent, too, that's pretty heady stuff. Terribly distracting ammunition you're carrying with you tonight." Susan turned to laugh, then went willingly into his arms for a cherishing kiss before they left for the party.

The ballroom was a grand and stately vision to behold with its green and apricot colors, its gilt chandeliers and long latticed windows draped with magnificent velvet curtains. Each table was flawlessly decorated for dinner with crystal stemware and crisp linens. Elegantly dressed waiters poured wine in a silent but efficient manner, and an exceptional banquet meal began of snapper soup and avocado salad, a tomato supreme and a steak Diane with mint-glazed carrots and potato puffs. When the whipped ice cream cake and coffee finally arrived, violinists appeared to make their rounds at each table.

After dinner there was dancing and Owen swept an eager Susan on to the floor. Their bodies swayed gracefully together in time to the sweet strains of the music. Close to her now, the captivating fragrance of her perfume once again flooded his senses, and he molded her body dangerously close to his. They continued their dance, oblivious to everyone else on the floor, until the set came to an end.

For one long moment, they remained there, still in each other's arms, not wanting the music to stop, quite conscious of the physical urges that were beginning to emerge.

When the floor had cleared and the musicians had gone for a break, Owen and Susan drifted in search of some refreshments and soon found themselves in a conversation with the Carberrys, some personal friends of Owen's. This was a congenial but hard-drinking couple who insisted that everyone at their table join them for an impromptu party as soon as the dinner was concluded. Owen found it difficult to say no and soon he and Susan found themselves at the Carberrys' Park Avenue penthouse, where a large and noisy crowd had arrived.

"Just a little impromptu party, as I said," the now slightly inebriated host said as he greeted them at the door. "C'mon, let me get you a cocktail." Before he did, a tall, willowy blonde sidled up next to him and the last Susan saw of the two of them they were wandering off in the direction of the bedrooms.

"Hmmm, I wonder what Mrs. Carberry will have to say about that." Susan nodded at the disappearing couple.

"I doubt very much whether she'll even notice," Owen said. "They have your garden variety open marriage circa latter-day enlightened twentieth century."

"You mean everybody knows about it?"

"Yes, including themselves. They've worked out an arrangement that apparently suits them just fine. Both of them talk about it quite openly. They really seem to like one another and like to live with one another, but have no qualms at all about seeking out, shall we say, sexual variety."

"Interesting pastime," Susan observed laconically as she sipped her drink. "I'm sure the whole gang will live happily ever after."

"Hey, Owen, who's your little friend here? Aren't you going to introduce me?" A diminutive middle-aged man with a pencil mustache insinuated himself on their private conversation.

"Oh, hi, Maury. This is Susan. Where have you been recently? Haven't seen you in a long time."

"And you're not going to while that beautiful music is playing and this lovely female is here ready to dance. What do you say, Susan?"

He was like a human dynamo, this aggressive little dandy who immediately gave the impression that he was grasping hungrily for every single pleasure he could get out of life regardless of who might get in his way. Not even waiting for her answer, he pulled Susan in a surprisingly rough manner toward the other side of the room where someone was playing "Memories" on the piano. It happened so quickly that Owen was left standing there alone without another word said, and Susan was caught totally off guard by the stranger's whirlwind manner.

A temporary dance area was designated near the piano where there was a hardwood floor and several couples moved silently about. Maury had strong coarse hands that gripped her so tightly that he was actually causing her discomfort. Once on the dance floor, he held her unbearably close and breathed heavily into her ear. Angered, Susan found herself actually struggling to free herself of this thoroughly disagreeable character, but she did not want to create a scene. It was intolerable but she suffered through one dance which was then extended into a medley of songs. And when it finally did come to an end, she escaped from this unbelievably annoying stranger without so much as a word and milled through the crowd in search of Owen.

Furious over his failure to help her or even warn her about his lecherous little friend, Susan spotted him halfway across the room holding what appeared to be a rather intimate conversation with a seductive-looking auburn-haired nymph. Not caring at all what was going on, Susan marched right to his side and broke up their tête-à-tête. "Owen, I'd like to speak with you, please."

"Oh, Sue, listen, I want you to meet Beverly."

"So, you're the reason I haven't seen anything of Owen this time around," warbled the nymph archly.

"Beverly!" Owen was clearly annoyed. "You know there's nothing between us."

"Maybe not this time, sweetheart, but don't you remember the last time you came to the Big Apple for a conference? Hmmm? It was a little different then, wasn't it?"

Owen looked as though he wanted to kill, but Beverly continued to smile provocatively as her red-enameled nails glided down his arm. "Oh, well, there's always next season." Blowing a kiss in his direction, Beverly drifted off.

Owen eyed Susan, frustration written all over his face. "I don't want to talk about it."

"Neither do I, quite frankly. Look, let's just go, okay?"

"Gladly." There was a note of relief in his voice as he led her towards the door.

"Hey, Sue." It was a familiar and unwelcome voice. A grinning Ted Updike with a raised glass in his hand halted their progress.

"Listen, about last night—"

"Forget it, Ted," Susan said curtly, cutting him off in mid-sentence. She wanted to keep right on moving, but there just was nowhere to go. Ted had already turned his gaze from her to Owen and thrust out his hand.

"I think I know you. Mr. Forsythe, right? Remember me? I was Mr. Bower's assistant on the Colman-Hartford and Lerox Corporation case, the computer company merger?"

"Why, yes, I do remember you, Mr. Updike. How is Les? I haven't seen him for years." Owen could see Susan gritting her teeth over the fact that he stopped to talk to Ted.

"Oh, yeah, Les is okay," Ted droned on. "You know, I left Bowers and Bowers to strike out on my own about ten months ago. Got tired of doing all the legwork. I frankly have my sights set a lot higher, you know, if you get what I mean."

"I think I do," Owen said without masking his disdain. "I hope you realize that you've managed to leave one of the best firms on the East Coast."

"That might have been true some time ago, but not anymore. No, I'm doing much better on my own."

"Glad to hear it." Owen looked in Sue's direction. "We must talk about it again some time, but right now we're in a bit of a hurry."

Ted nodded, but as Owen led the way through the cluster of guests, Ted grabbed Susan's arm. "Hey, Susie. That bozo reminds me of Jeff, you know? Just another one of them arrogant know-it-all bastards. You like that type, huh?"

Susan glared back with contempt at Ted who gave off a mock salute before disappearing into the crowd. She looked around to find Owen edging his way toward her with their coats under his arm.

"You all right?" he asked, leading her out to the hallway and into the elevator.

"Yes, I . . . I'm all right. I'm just happy to get out of that place, that's all. I think I've had about all of the humanity that I can bear for one evening."

But Ted's words kept repeating in her mind even though she was sure he was wrong. The similarities between her ex-husband and Owen were merely superficial, except that it was strange that she had never considered them before. But that was because she knew both men intimately and their differences were more obvious to her. Owen was an aggressive businessman and lawyer while Jeff was a more or less staid professor with little ambition. The elevator came to a jolting halt and the door opened out on to the lobby, distracting her from making any further analyses.

As Susan and Owen stepped out of the elevator, they came face to face with Mrs. Carberry and a well-dressed youngish man who was at her side.

"Owen, darling, are you leaving so soon?" she queried as she passed into the elevator with her companion.

"Afraid so. We have an early plane to catch."

"Oh, too bad. Don't forget to look us up the next time you're in town." The doors of the elevator closed before he was able to promise to do so. Spontaneously, Susan and

Owen turned to look at each other, then broke out into laughter.

"I don't know why you're laughing," Susan said, "but I know why I am."

"Why's that?"

"Because that was just about the most pathetic sight I think I've ever seen. I don't just mean those two, but the entire scene up there."

"Why?"

"Why? Need you ask? Isn't it perfectly obvious what's going on up there? It reminded me of some scene from an absurdist play with all of those madcap characters drifting about from one person to the next in some kind of aimless pursuit of love and happiness."

"But isn't that what most people are searching for in one way or another?" Owen helped her into a cab outside the apartment house and Susan resumed the point she was making when they drove away.

"Yes, I suppose so, but there seems to be something very different about the way this modern game is being played. What I saw there tonight and what I guess I'm just beginning to realize, naive girl that I am, is that there's little that seems to be meaningful in all of those hot pursuits. It's almost like a dog chasing its own tail and not even realizing what he's actually doing. I'm seeing a lot of people having relationships but not having any romance in their lives. I'm seeing a lot of people bedding down with one another but not really loving one another, and I'm wondering where all of the joy is in that?"

"Maybe you're taking all this a little too seriously, Susan. Those puritanical days are all past us, you know, and you probably would resent the strictures that that kind of thinking used to place on women. Besides, what's wrong with having some fun?"

"I'm not against fun. That's not the issue," she said, ignoring his attempt to kid her out of her suddenly sober mood. "What I'm saying is that all everyone seems to be concerned with is a physical relationship, and although I hear a lot of talk about love, it's pretty hard to find people who are after a caring commitment to one another."

"Whoa! Now let me get this straight. Aren't you the same woman who only a few months ago was talking about the importance of freedom and no commitments whatsoever?"

"Yes, maybe I did," Sue admitted. "But I'm starting to change my thinking on the whole thing. Maybe I'm confused like everybody else, but something is telling me that the heart and soul of all of those glamorous relationships just seem to have vanished somehow. When the veneer is rubbed away, all that's left are many superficial, selfish ego trips. To me, that gets less and less attractive the more I witness it."

Owen remained silent for a long moment before he replied. "All right, Susan. I can see this is something that's on your mind and is really bothering you. I realized it this morning and maybe it's time we cleared the air on it, because as I see it, while you're speaking in generalities, you really are talking about the two of us. And what you're saying is that we, you and I, have no commitment. We, too, fit the mold that you've suddenly begun to recognize and find so unattractive. We're one of those modern couples that you've just been dissecting, isn't that right? And isn't that what we said we expected from one another right at the outset? So where are we now?"

Susan stared out at the traffic going by. "I—I'm not sure," she mumbled. "I haven't thought it through." Dismally, she sank back into the corner of the seat, wondering how this conversation had reached this point. A few more words in this vein, and it would be all over. Certainly Owen had been an important part of her life recently, but sooner or later she had to ask herself just how loving their relationship really was. There was an undeniable spark missing, but would it come in time? Or was she just kidding herself like everyone else? And would she end up drifting along from man to man like those tragicomic figures she found so strange and unappealing? Would she, in time, become too jaded to ever recognize her soul mate, her Mr. Right, if he did come her way?

The unbidden image of Carlos intruded itself in her consciousness with an answer she wasn't willing to accept.

She remembered quite vividly how he could make her spirits soar, but she wondered why their entanglements always seemed so stormy while Owen, who seemed compatible in most ways, managed only to leave her senses intact.

Susan decided not to say another word to provoke a larger breach between Owen and herself. But he, too, was reflecting on what had been said between them. When they returned to the hotel room, he attempted to make love to her, but she turned away. Then Owen knew. If he wanted Susan Blaine, the price was going to be a commitment, and that was something he had promised himself never to do again.

Chapter Thirteen

Ever since her return from New York, Susan found herself repeatedly awakened early in the predawn darkness, unable to sleep. This was one of those mornings. Once again she found herself staring silently at her ceiling, thoughts racing in her head as she listened to rain drops that pelted against the windows and waited restlessly for the light of day.

Owen had withdrawn behind a shield of cool, businesslike demeanor at the office ever since their revealing conversation the night before they left New York City. Just as she expected, he had made no attempt to see her after working hours either, and it hurt her more than she cared to admit. Yet she couldn't bring herself to plot any calculated lures that might rekindle his interest in her. It just wouldn't make sense. Not after their last discussion concerning the two of them. And definitely not until she came to grips with the issue of what she wanted—from a man, from her career—and the idea of a commitment—to what and to whom? When she thought about it clearly, her career was very important to her. But somewhere, too, she was aware of wanting eventually to marry and be a mother and have a family and, of course, share a life of love with one man. Yet it seemed incongruous for her, as a successful lawyer, to be contemplating those options. While everyone else was looking for freedom, flexibility, and mobility, she was still toying around with the old-fashioned ideas of marriage, commitment, and stability. Why did she have to be different? Didn't the obvious solution lie somewhere in between? Wasn't it possible to maintain a career and have the kind of durability that came from a marriage? The men in her life at present just didn't seem ready to entertain all of these possibilities in a woman. Back to square one, she sighed, as she rose at last to face the day. Even though it was Saturday she decided she couldn't lie awake another minute.

It wasn't yet seven o'clock in the morning as Susan sat down to her usual breakfast of tea, toast, and grapefruit. The unexpected ringing of her doorbell jarred her out of her typical leisurely pace. Just a little apprehensive over a caller at this hour of the morning, she went to the door cautiously and asked who it was. The voice of Elena Obregon answered her. When the door was opened, Susan knew something was wrong. Elena's deathly pale face and tearful eyes were enough to make it clear that she was almost in a state of panic.

"My God, Elena, what is it? Is something wrong?" Susan couldn't imagine her coming here without it being an outright emergency. "Is it Carlos? Did something happen to him?"

"No, no. It is not Carlos." Elena brushed back her disheveled hair and looked as though she were about to break down and cry.

"Come on in," Susan said, taking her by the arm. "I can see you're upset about something important."

Elena couldn't speak. She just nodded, fighting back her tears valiantly.

"Look, Elena," Susan said, trying to make her feel comfortable, "I'm right in the midst of some breakfast. How about having something with me? Okay?" Susan guided her visitor into the kitchen and sat her down. "Now, how about some tea?"

"You must help me, Susan," Elena said in a pathetic whisper.

"Of course, of course, Elena." Susan slid a cup of hot tea in front of her guest. "Here, drink this first and then let's talk about it."

Susan watched her take several sips in silence trying to regain her composure.

"Have you had anything to eat this morning? You look starved to me. I'll make you some toast and eggs." Susan didn't wait for an answer and busied herself with preparing some scrambled eggs in a skillet. Occasionally she looked over her shoulder at Elena who made no attempt at conversation. Instead, she just stared into space. Finally, after the eggs were served and Susan thought she had calmed her caller down, she broached the question of the reason for her visit.

"Do you want to tell me what's troubling you, Elena?"

Elena bowed her head and mumbled, "It's Brett . . ." and stopped, but Susan, thinking she understood, encouraged her.

"Have you had a lover's quarrel with Brett? Is that why you came here this morning?"

"Yes. No. . . . I'm afraid it's much . . . worse than that." There was a note of desperation in Elena's reply.

"Why, what is it, Elena?" Susan placed a comforting hand on her shoulder.

"He . . . he has . . . left me . . . deserted me."

"Oh, that's awful. I am really sorry to hear that, Elena."

"There's more, though. That's not all. I wouldn't come here just to tell you that . . ." Tears welled up in Elena's eyes. "I don't know how to tell you . . ."

Susan's stomach muscles tightened with apprehension, but she tried not to show any anxiety as she spoke. "I'm your friend, Elena. I'm not going to be your judge. I'll just try to help if I can."

"I've been such a fool, Susan. Just a blind, silly fool. Brett swore he loved me . . . but it wasn't true. Now all I have to show for it is disgrace. Instead of happiness, which is all that I wanted, I end up in disgrace."

Susan suddenly knew what Elena was about to tell her and hoped it was not true.

"I am carrying his child."

"Are you sure of that? Have you seen a physician?" Elena was weeping and only nodded her head affirmatively. "And Brett? What about him? Does he know about this, too?"

Again Elena nodded to indicate that he did.

"What happened, Elena? What did he say when you told him?"

"He said he did not want to get involved in marriage because of this. He thought it would be a poor reason for getting married and that we would regret it later. Instead, he suggested that I get an abortion. An abortion! Me! With my Catholic upbringing. I told him absolutely not."

"And then what did he do?"

"Nothing. He just walked out."

"How long ago was that?" Susan hoped that if it were just a matter of a few hours, he might return after he had had a change of heart.

"Two days I have been waiting for a call from him. Two terribly long days. And nothing. Then I called his fraternity house and they told me he left early for the Thanksgiving holidays."

"Well, then, he will be returning soon," Susan offered the possibility of some hope.

"The landlord told me that Brett has not paid the bill on the rooms we rented together secretly, and if I wanted to stay there any longer I must pay the rent."

"That's got to be the lowest—"

"No," Elena said in his defense. "Don't blame him. He always told me that he could not marry me until he finished his education."

"That doesn't excuse him for this kind of treatment of you. After all, he has some part to play in all of this. It seems to me that he has some kind of obligation to you. It may not be marriage, but he can't just walk out and wash his hands of the whole affair as if it never happened at all, as if he never heard of you before in his life."

Susan's blunt appraisal of his behavior brought more tears to Elena's eyes, and Susan could have kicked herself for having thrown more fuel on the fire. "Don't worry, Elena. We'll think of something. We'll work this thing out together. There are some legal points to consider here. Maybe he can be made to see he has an obligation to you."

"Oh, no!" Elena cried. "I will not make him marry me. I

would never force any man to do that. That could only result in a lifetime of resentment."

Susan had to agree with that point, and for a space of time the two sat in contemplative silence until Elena admitted, "Quite honestly my most immediate concern is the prospect of telling my family and how they will react to all this. I must tell them. I have to. There's no avoiding it. And yet I don't know how to."

Susan's heart skipped a beat in sympathy for her friend. She knew it would not be an easy task, to say the least. All she could think of was Carlos's reaction to such an announcement. He would be blind with rage when he heard about this, and that was a prospect that Susan would like to avoid at all costs.

"Susan," Elena pleaded, "I don't think I can do this by myself. I need your help. Will you come with me?"

Susan had hoped Elena would not ask this of her, and even though she felt indebted to Elena for helping her out of a difficult situation with Carlos, this was not the way she wished to repay the favor. "Elena," she said, "I hate to say no to you, I really do. But I don't think it's my place. Can you understand that it's just too awkward a situation? It would put me in the role of an intruder."

"Susan," Elena sounded on the verge of panic, "I can't face this problem alone. You must help me! Please! You are able to handle my brother better than anyone else I know."

When Susan rolled her eyes disdainfully, Elena continued her plea. "You are a professional lawyer and I need to be defended. You would not refuse a client in a case such as mine, would you? How could you refuse a friend? I need your help, Susan. You must realize this. I have no other person on earth to turn to."

Susan finally relented. After all, any woman could find herself in the same position. And poor Elena having to face Carlos just made the problem all that much worse.

Susan gritted her teeth as soon as she agreed to help her friend. Wasn't it ironic, she thought, that life would play this perverse little joke on her, allowing her to get trapped into defending Carlos's sister for something she knew he could never accept? The more she thought about it, the more she was convinced that it would be certain to end up in disaster. Well, that would be the *coup de grace*. No more Carlos, no more Owen. Just what benefit could she hope to gain from this mission, she wondered?

That question was still in the forefront of her thoughts as she drove up to the Obregon hacienda with Elena trembling with fear at her side. Susan had wanted to rehearse their strategy one more time before encountering the family, but as soon as they pulled up in front of the portico, Carlos strode out to meet them, a black scowl on his face. Even so, Susan felt the strange magnetism that emanated from his physical presence. It occurred to her that their last encounter had ended in open hostility, but that couldn't stop the quickening of her heartbeat at the sight of him. Somehow she sensed that while his outward focus was on Elena, his innermost thoughts were on her.

"Madre de Dios, Elena, where have you been?" he demanded in that powerful voice. "Mother is beside herself with worry over you. Do you realize the grief you have caused her?"

Elena did not reply and only put her head down as he led the two of them into the house. "Susan, I apologize for my manners, and I thank you for bringing my thoughtless sister home." His smile was warm, making Susan regret all the more that she had accepted this suicidal mission. "Will you wait for me in the library while I take Elena to see my mother? I'll try not to be too long. You and I have a great deal to discuss. I'm so glad you're here." He paused before the heavy wooden library door and regarded her with a look of intimacy, Susan thought. Oh, how she wanted to clear the air between the two of them! But one glance at Elena's doleful face and she knew that it just wasn't possible.

"I'm afraid that I can't, Carlos. You see, I'm here on Elena's behalf."

His black eyes changed expression and stared searchingly from one face to another. "Excuse me. You should understand that this is a private family matter, so you see there is really no need for you to . . ."

"Elena has asked me to be present," Susan interrupted.

Carlos turned abruptly to his sister, fury in his eyes. "What is the meaning of this nonsense, Elena? Since when does it become necessary for you to come home with a lawyer to defend you?"

"Please, Carlos," Elena begged, "I want Susan present. I have asked her to come here as a favor to me. She has come only at my insistence, and if she is not going to be permitted to stay, I will leave."

"What kind of ridiculous plot are you females cooking up here?" he roared, seizing her by the arm. Elena cried out as she tried to wrench herself free of his grip.

"Carlos," Susan intervened in as calm a voice as she could muster, "let me speak to you. I'd like to explain what this is all about before this gets completely out of hand. Please."

"Yes, Carlos, listen to what Susan has to say." Impatient for an answer, he released Elena and Susan suggested that the girl go to her room while the two of them talked alone. When she did, he remained there with his hands on his hips almost menacingly, waiting for some explanation, until Susan led the way into the library. As she was about to speak, her mind was suddenly diverted by the memory of them making love for the first time in this very room. Those images of him were so vivid that she directed a loving gaze at him and met a warm glow in his eyes letting her know he too was recalling that union. But she could see he was quickly suppressing it as his expression hardened, and she found herself straining to bring all of her lawyer's instincts to bear to face him squarely.

"Very well, Susan," he spoke sternly, folding his arms in front of his chest as he sat on the edge of the desk. "Now perhaps you can shed some light on all this and give me some reason why you seem so compelled to take part in this little family drama."

"First of all, let me say that I came here with great reluctance. Even now I'm sure that I probably would have been better off never getting involved with this whole matter. But you have to understand, Carlos, that your sister asked me to help her. If I didn't think it was serious I wouldn't be here."

"What is this serious matter?" His eyes narrowed suspiciously.

Instead of answering his question, Susan asked one of her own. "How often have you sat down and talked to Elena of late?"

"What kind of a question is that? Of course, I talk to her all the time."

"No, I mean *listen* and ask *questions* and try to understand what your sister was thinking and truly feeling."

Carlos shifted uncomfortably; nevertheless, he scoffed, "I listen as well as any brother listens to the nonsense that fills a young girl's head."

"I'm afraid that attitude has helped place Elena where she is today. You've ignored the fact that she is a modern young woman, capable of passion, and desirable to young men."

"What are you telling me?" His appearance grew suddenly savage. Since the moment Susan had insisted on accompanying them to see his mother, a nagging suspicion that he had refused to acknowledge during these past forty-eight hours finally exploded inside him. A helpless rage choked him and then burst, like a broken dam. He roared unintelligibly and pounded his fist on the table. "She's been with one of those worthless college lowlifes, isn't it?" He pounded his fist once more. "Isn't it?" He turned and strode towards the door, but Susan tried to bar his way.

"Wait, Carlos. Please wait and listen to me!"

"Who was it?" His fingers dug into her shoulders as he grasped her roughly, but she remained mute. "Never mind. She'll tell me." He started to step by her, but she held her ground bravely.

"Carlos, don't hurt her any more than she already has been hurt. You have to realize that she needs you and your support now more than ever."

"Just answer one question for me," he demanded with a jutting jaw. "Has she so disgraced herself that there is no longer a place for her in this family?"

"You're not going to tell me that you could be so unfeeling that you would disown her outright? Only because she's made an understandable mistake?"

"So the worst is true, is it?" He sank into a chair and ran an agitated hand across his brow, his anger subsiding momentarily into resignation. "You're telling me that she's pregnant, is that it?"

Susan nodded. "But it shouldn't have to be looked upon as though it were the end of the world. We're not living in the Dark Ages anymore, you know."

"*¡Dios!*" he muttered angrily, rising from the chair. "It is exactly that kind of glamorized liberal thinking and propaganda that has brought dishonor to women. How tempting those terms are—freedom! independence! career! How eager everyone is to trade away their natural gifts for those shoddy dime-store promises. And where does it all lead? Look at the results. Look at what liberated women like yourself are now responsible for creating—allowing innocents like Elena to believe that anything her impulses tell her to do is all right, that she's foolish for not taking everything she can get without giving in return. I hope you're not coming here now to tell me that I have to swallow all of this and then support it, too? Why? Why should I be expected to?"

Susan had been waiting patiently for an opening, but a light knock on the door prevented her from responding. She feared that it might be Elena, but when Carlos opened it, Mrs. Obregon stepped into the room. "*Mamacita,*" Carlos said, his wrath subsided noticeably as he led her to a chair, "I thought you were resting."

"I heard Elena and Mrs. Blaine arrive." The regal matron looked pale and anguished. "I've just finished talking with Elena . . ." She paused. "A revealing discussion."

"You . . . know then?" Carlos said.

"Yes, I know. Undoubtedly Mrs. Blaine has been good enough to inform you." A glacial stare was deliberately directed at Susan.

Carlos put a protective arm around his mother. "Don't worry, Mama. I'll find out who the young man is that is responsible for this and see to it that they are married at once."

"That may be your wish, Carlos, but I have no intention of allowing Elena to remain in my home until that time. In fact, I do not wish to see her again."

"But, Mrs. Obregon, you must be reasonable!" Susan interjected.

"Reasonable, *Mrs.* Blaine?" Mrs. Obregon put special emphasis on *Mrs.* as if to communicate her contempt for Susan. "I do not find it necessary to share your ideas about what is reasonable and what is not. Although you seem intent on making this your concern, I must assure you that it is not." With that, the diminutive but imperious woman rose and started across the room. Carlos, however, stopped her with a cautionary finger that he pointed at her.

"Just a minute, Mother." He was speaking reflectively now and ran his fingers along his chin with a pensive expression in his eyes. "It will do us no good to attack Mrs. Blaine. After all, I believe that she has come here solely to offer her help in some way. We are free to accept or reject whatever advice she may offer us. Unfortunately, it is too late to prevent what has happened to Elena. Nothing can undo that. And in the end it will be up to me to determine what Elena must do."

His unexpected words of defense both surprised and mollified Susan and at the same time annoyed his mother. "Very well, my son," Mrs. Obregon said coldly, "the decision is yours to make. I ask only that when you make it, you will do it with discretion and honor." She turned toward the door to leave and Carlos opened it for her.

"I will take care of all the arrangements," Susan heard him whisper as she disappeared from the room.

"May I ask how you are going to handle this?" Susan asked when they were alone.

"Elena will simply be sent away for a while until the matter takes care of itself."

"What? You can't be serious."

"I am serious. Very serious. And that is exactly what I intend to do because it will be best for all concerned if she does not remain here."

"Best for whom? Surely not Elena."

Carlos poured himself and Susan drinks from a decanter. Swirling the liquid in his glass, he began pacing the library. A mixture of annoyance and exasperation furrowed his brow. "You must remember that it would be pure hell for Elena to remain here with my mother and have to be reminded every minute of every day that she is disgraced. Don't you understand that?"

Susan wanted to say that she couldn't but decided against that. Instead, she just bit her lip and uttered an audible "Oh" to indicate her recognition of the problem. But while she didn't want to antagonize him any further on this issue, she wasn't about to say she agreed with him. No more appeasing the male ego just to preserve peace.

"I must assume responsibility for finding an appropriate solution for both my mother and sister," Carlos continued. "I need your help. Until other arrangements can be made, may I ask that Elena stay with you?"

Susan agreed without hesitation and Carlos was relieved. Then she wondered if that were a wise thing to do, especially in light of the cool reception accorded her by *Señora* Obregon. Under the present circumstances and especially for Elena's sake, it was just impossible to say no.

Carlos slipped into his Air Force jacket and readied himself to leave. "I'll be back to see her tomorrow when I'm off duty."

"Don't you think you should talk to her now before you leave?" Susan ventured.

"No!" he exploded. "Do you have any idea how this whole thing is tearing me up inside? How could this happen to my sister? If I see her now I might do something rash or say something that I'll later regret. No, I need more time to sort all this out." He paused at the door and looked at Susan as though he just remembered who she was. "You know, when you walked in here today, I'd hoped that we could once and for all smooth out all those differences between us. Somehow it seems that we're never able to do that. It just makes me wonder why it's always so damn difficult. Why is it that we're always at opposite ends of the pole? Instead of you being on my side there's always some kind of conflict that manages to come between us."

"I'm afraid it often does seem that way, Carlos," she answered bleakly. "I wish it weren't."

He shook his head in acknowledgment and they exchanged a long glance that revealed a sense of yearning and regret mutually felt. And then he was gone, leaving Susan alone, the traces of that meaningful glance lingering in her mind. Damn him! What was the answer to it all anyway? Why were they always drawn to one another when so much separated them? How could he have the gall to ask for her help and then just take her for granted?

Susan was still muttering under her breath as she went in search of Elena. She found her packing two suitcases in her bedroom, her eyes damp with tears.

"She told me to go! My own mother! Just when I need her help!"

Susan put her arm around Elena's shoulder and gave her a squeeze. "I know, Elena. Listen, you're going to come and stay with me for a while."

"Thank God for you, Susan. I promise I'll try not to be a burden to you."

"Don't worry. You're no burden. You're a friend and you'll be company for me. Here, let me help you pack."

"Where's Carlos?"

"He's gone now, but he said he'll see you tomorrow at my place."

"I see. He doesn't want to have anything to do with me either."

"No, I don't think that's true. I just think he has a lot of things that are closing in on him right at the moment and he needs to mull them over a little bit. That's all. Besides, he was due at the base. And he asked me to look after you until he could come speak with you."

"Susan, I want you to know that I'm very grateful for your help. You've been very kind to me."

"Well, Elena, I know what it's like to be all alone with

no one to turn to. But I know you're going to come out of this okay. And you'll probably be a better person for it because crises like yours help us learn a lot about life that we never realized before. You've got to hang in there and see it all through. It'll be all right."

"Perhaps," Elena said, shrugging her shoulders as she closed one of her suitcases on the bed. "Do you remember when I came to you this summer and you told me I was a renegade? That I was rebelling against my heritage? And I said then that there were certain beliefs I still embraced even though I rejected many others? Well, I have to tell you that one thing I really do believe in is that children need both a mother and father. It is just not right that I should have a child and not have a husband. That's what is hurting me the most about all this. I can live with the disgrace, but I can't live with that thought constantly in my mind."

"But many women are doing just that today," Susan argued.

"I'm not that kind of woman. It just won't wash with me." Elena snapped the last suitcase shut, lifted it from the bed and started down the hallway. Following her out to the car, Susan worried about her new roommate and about how she would be able to stand up to the pressures of the coming weeks. Elena was much more traditional in her thinking than she had ever been willing to admit.

On the way back from the hacienda, the girls made several stops, one for some groceries, another for a prescription refill, and a last stop to pick up some of Elena's things from the apartment she had shared with Brett. When they reached Susan's place, it was late afternoon and by the time they got Elena settled in and had dinner, the two were ready to call it a day. The emotional upheavals of the day had been exhausting, and as soon as Susan's head hit the pillow, she fell into a deep sleep that was troubled with bizarre dreams involving Carlos, Elena, and their mother.

When she awakened the next morning, Susan made breakfast and rapped at Elena's door to see if she were up. Receiving no answer, she cautiously edged open the door and peeked into the room. To her surprise, the bed had been made and Elena was gone. Elena's remarks about not wanting to be a burden to Susan suddenly crossed her mind. How serious a threat was that? Susan quickly checked the closet and drawers to see if Elena's clothing was still there. That meant that she probably intended to return, Susan reasoned. Or did it? Another more frightening prospect surfaced, one that she did not want to contemplate. Susan rubbed her brow nervously and then heard a key in the lock of the apartment door.

"Elena!" Susan cried out her name so excitedly that she startled the younger woman. "Where were you?"

"Oh, did I worry you? I was at mass. It's Sunday, you know."

"Oh, yes, of course. I forgot." Susan tried to hide her sheepish look but Elena knew she was concerned.

"You were afraid that I might do something foolish, weren't you, Susan?"

"No, not really," Susan lied. "I just couldn't figure out where you had gone. There wasn't any message and I didn't know what had happened."

Elena placed a hand on Susan's arm to reassure her. "Look, you don't have to worry about me. I may be unhappy and I may be frightened a little bit, but I promise that I'm not going to do something rash." Elena lifted her head proudly and new-found strength seemed to emerge from her eyes. "Besides," she went on, "if I am not about to take the life of my own child, is it likely that I should take my own life?"

"Elena, I'm sorry. I guess you thought that I didn't trust you."

"For a woman who's supposed to be a tough lawyer, you sure have a soft heart, Susan." Elena Obregon was smiling for the first time since she'd come to her and Susan breathed much easier. They hugged each other and laughed.

For the rest of that morning and most of the afternoon, too, they put their heads together and talked about the plans to be made for Elena and the coming child. Late in the afternoon, Carlos appeared and their enjoyable chatter came to a halt. Immediately, he was on the offensive with Elena, demanding to know the name of his sister's lover.

"You never cared to know who he was before. Why should it be necessary for me to tell you now?" Elena retorted.

"I didn't come here to play games with you, Elena," Carlos said, his black eyes flashing threateningly. "I am in no mood for any of that. I want the name of that worthless bum in the red sports car!"

"There is nothing you can do, Carlos." Elena's heart was pounding wildly over the thought of what her brother might do. "It is too late."

"Yes, it is too late. Too late to protect your honor. And I blame myself for that. I should have known where you were headed."

His harsh words stung her and Susan saw her blanch.

"Listen to me, Elena, I've given this a lot of thought and there's only one thing that can be done to get this thing straightened out. You've got to marry this fool and that's all there is to it."

"But don't you understand?" Elena pleaded, her lips quivering. "He doesn't want to marry me! What would be the point?"

"The point is that the two of you are responsible for what has happened here, and now you both have to pay the price. When I think of it all, I could kill that lousy bastard!" Carlos pounded his open hand with his fist.

"Why don't you just kill me instead? I'm the one who has disgraced the family. I defied you. Just do away with me, and then you'll be able to walk the streets with your head up high. Do it! Do it now!"

Tears streamed down Elena's face as she screamed defiantly at her brother. Susan came to her side, afraid that Carlos, if baited long enough, might oblige her request. Recognizing the need to separate the two of them, Susan led her out of the room giving Carlos some time alone to cool off. When she rejoined him, she spoke in a hushed but stern voice.

"I never would have let you in here had I known you were going to upset Elena the way you just did."

"Did you expect me to handle her with kid gloves? I am beside myself with anger and frustration over this whole thing. Here I am trying to help her out of the most serious crisis in her life and my hands are being tied. You must help me get the name from her."

"Oh, Carlos," Susan clutched her head and gave a desperate sigh. "Don't ask me to get involved in this, please. I can't tell you his name. Elena doesn't wish this to go any further than it has already. Can't you see that? What good would it do even if you could force him to marry her? What kind of a marriage would that be?"

"So you would rather see her disgraced in the eyes of her family and friends? You know that she can never return home again if she has this child out of wedlock?"

"Fine. If her friends and family are so quick to desert her when she needs them the most, then maybe she's better off without them."

Carlos looked stunned and pushed his fingers through his hair. "You just won't understand, will you? You won't even try to understand my point of view, my family's point of view, our heritage. Well, if you won't help me save her from her own foolishness, then I'll just have to do it alone. And when I find that bum I'm going to give him a thrashing he'll never forget."

As he turned to leave, Susan placed her hand on his arm. "Carlos," she said, trying to soften him with a reasonable voice, "this isn't getting us anywhere and it isn't solving the problem for Elena. Let's let Elena handle it. She's very unhappy right now, but she's also a strong person and capable of making her own decisions. The situation is tough, but she's coming to grips with it the best way that she can. There is another alternative, you know, that you haven't considered, but she has. Elena is thinking of giving up the baby for adoption. There are many childless couples who would love to take her child and give it all of the love and affection it would need. Then she could finish law school—"

"You're not seriously suggesting that as a reasonable alternative, are you? I just don't believe my ears! You put that in her head, didn't you?" He was glaring angrily once again and pointing a menacing finger for emphasis as he spoke. "You know something? I'm beginning to think that you're almost enjoying this—seeing Elena challenge everything my family stands for. Does seeing me humiliated like this satisfy your liberated ego in some way?"

That was the last straw for Susan. She backed from him and pointed toward the door. "Okay, I can see the accusations are getting hot and heavy and much too personal at this point and there's no use discussing it any further. Just get out of here, Carlos, and don't come back!"

Without another word, Carlos stormed out of the apartment and slammed the door so hard Susan thought it was going to fall off its hinges. She sank down on the sofa and buried her face in her hands. Well, that was it! she thought. If ever there were a grand finale performance to a romantic relationship, that had to take first place for high drama in her life. How dare he make those remarks about her? What unbelievable nerve! Susan groaned out loud in utter frustration and when she reopened her eyes, she was face to face with Elena.

"My brother! I don't blame you for being angry with him. I'm so furious with him, I would love to slap his arrogant face!"

"That makes two of us," Susan agreed.

"I'm completely convinced that he's totally hopeless."

"So am I, Elena, but I don't want to talk about him anymore today or tomorrow or the day after that or maybe for the next century or two. About all I want to do is just sit down, read the Sunday paper or maybe watch a funny movie on TV. I need some time to get these problems off my mind. And you do, too."

The two of them made a pact not to talk about anything relating to Elena's difficulties for the rest of that evening. It was a welcome agreement. Both of them needed a respite from all of the problems that the men in their lives seemed to generate. With those topics officially off limits and this being the week of Thanksgiving, Susan and Elena decided to have an all-female party and invite Carol, Vera, and a few of Elena's university friends for a turkey dinner.

It turned out to be a better day than either of them had anticipated. Preparing for the dinner helped both of them take their minds off their troubles and soon their senses of humor reappeared. For Elena it was a learning experience and Susan enjoyed showing the step-by-step process she had been taught by her mother. And as they washed, cut, stuffed, and tied the bird, Susan drew many hilarious parallels with the human male species and what she often yearned to do to them. Elena was appreciative of her ludicrous analogies and the more she laughed at each of them, the more Susan was able to concoct them.

Somehow through all of their chattering the bird was ready for roasting. "Let's see. A twelve-pound turkey, twenty to twenty-five minutes per pound, between four and five hours cooking time," Susan estimated out loud as she finally placed it in the oven. "Now that that's out of the way, we still have to ready the potatoes, the salad, the cranberries, and the dessert. The dessert! Oh, what am I going to do about that?

"Oh, let me help you with that," Elena volunteered. "I can make you a fantastic German Chocolate cake in no time at all."

"Go to it," Susan said, looking at her watch. "Time's flying right by."

By the time their guests arrived, the table was set, the wine was chilled and the cake was iced. It was a chatty, amiable group that sat down to dinner together, and there was no problem keeping a conversation flowing. At first the discussion centered mostly around the dinner itself, and Susan's excellent mushroom stuffing received a generous number of compliments. When the main course was finished, talk turned to politics, and soon Vera was dwelling on one of her familiar topics, the plight of the modern woman. Fearing that Elena's problem might easily be drawn to everyone's attention, Susan diverted discussion by rising from the table to prepare everyone for the grand finale to the meal.

"Coffee and dessert, everyone?" There were some weak

protests raised about the number of calories that had already been consumed, but when Elena entered with her magnificent three-layer German chocolate cake, the protests disappeared. Susan could see that Elena was pleased with the guests' response to her masterpiece.

The group remained seated around the table for another two hours of idle talk. Then everyone pitched in to help clean up. Afterwards the guests gave some indications that they were about to call it an evening and leave. Vera Banks was already searching for her coat when the doorbell rang unexpectedly. When Susan opened it, Owen Forsythe was standing there.

"Hi, I know you weren't expecting me, but I thought I would just drop in to wish you a happy Thanksgiving. I didn't get a chance to see you at the office this week and—Oh? Am I interrupting something?" Looking over her shoulder, he spotted the women. "I didn't realize you were having company. Maybe I better go and I'll call you later."

Just as he started to turn away, Susan grabbed him by the arm. "Don't. Please stay. We've got plenty of food and besides, it's awfully good to see you. Everybody's just getting ready to go and I'd appreciate your company."

"That's right," Vera Banks joined in as she put on her coat. "We were going to go this very minute, right girls?"

Vera's banter helped Owen to feel more at ease and also acted as a cue for everyone to make their exits quickly and unobtrusively. Minutes after Owen came in and sat down, the guests were gone and even Elena had been good enough to disappear into her room.

"Wow, I sure know how to keep a party going, don't I?" Owen quipped when they finally found themselves alone. "They cleared out of here so fast, I feel like a fugitive from a leper colony."

"That's exactly what I wanted them to do." Susan smiled. "And I'm really pleased that you came to see me. It's a great surprise."

"Good. I'm glad I came because I wanted to have a chance to talk to you alone."

"Oh? What did you have in mind—business or pleasure?"

"Pleasure, I hope." He took her hand and led her to the sofa. "I've missed you."

"That's nice to hear," Sue beamed with gratitude.

"Hmmm. I had hoped that you would return the compliment."

Sue thought his voice turned more serious. "Well, I've honestly missed you, too. I hope you're going to believe that, even though it required a prompt to get it out."

"I'm glad. Now it'll make it easier for me to say this." He turned to look at her squarely and she admired those fascinating gray eyes again, almost as if she were seeing them for the first time. "I've been thinking about us a lot more since the New York trip and wondering what to do about us."

"Do about us?" Sue felt her stomach lurch forward uncontrollably, afraid of what his statement implied.

"Yes. You see, I got the feeling that you were looking for some kind of commitment from me. . . ."

"No, I wasn't!" she interrupted. At least she didn't think she had been at the time.

"No? Well, maybe I got the wrong impression because I do recall a lot of talk centering around people being involved in relationships but not really caring in a deeper way about their partner?"

"Yes, I did say that and I still think that's a fair statement to make."

"Doesn't that mean you were looking for something more from me?"

That was a question that she knew would be coming, but somehow it unnerved her. "That's just it, Owen. I didn't know what I wanted from you or even what I wanted from myself at that time . . . and I guess I decided that you felt the same way. I also felt that we needed to come back to San Antonio, go about our business, and let some time pass so that we could clarify our feelings more accurately."

"All right, that's fair enough. I think I've been able to clarify my feelings about the two of us."

"You have?" Just where was it all leading to?

"I think I'm a pretty good judge of character," he went on, "and I hear you saying that you don't want to be tied down by marriage on the one hand, and you don't want a cool, distant relationship either. Am I right so far?"

"Well, yes, I guess so," Susan replied cautiously.

"I'm glad to hear you agree because that's pretty much the way I feel, too. I know you're aware of my views about marriage. After all, we both had a try at that and we know what that's all about. Instead, I got to thinking that maybe we could try living together for a while. That's what I see as the best alternative for the two of us. In a way it is a commitment, but without all of the legal strings attached. And if some time in the future we decide we want to make it permanent we always could do that, too. Sue, why don't we give it a try?"

Susan swallowed hard before reacting to his proposition. She wanted to be as diplomatic as she possibly could. "Owen," she began, "I'm really very flattered by all this, that you should want to share your life with me so intimately, but I don't think I'm ready for a move like that." Not wanting to hurt him, she tried to couch her refusal as softly as possible, but he had forced her hand and there was nowhere else to go. Her back was against the wall now. . . . His offer left her no choice but to look as deeply as she could into her true feelings for him, and at this moment they just weren't deep enough to permit her to accept what he was proposing.

"Why not?" Owen appeared stunned more than hurt by her rejection.

"I guess I like my independence too much and doing things my own way. I don't have to tell you about the need for making a lot of compromises whenever two people get together."

Owen sat there silently for a long time, so long that Susan could have easily panicked waiting for something to happen. He was hurt, that was certain, and Sue wished there could have been some other way. But there wasn't.

"Well, you sure had me fooled this time. And quite frankly, I don't enjoy being a fool. Do you know what I think about all of this? I think you don't know what you want. On the one hand, you talk a lot about commitment and on the other hand you talk about freedom and your independence. Just what the hell do you want?"

"Wait a minute, Owen," Susan said in defense of herself. "I didn't ask you to come here with this proposition. You wanted my honest feelings, didn't you? I don't like this idea; I'm sorry; but don't get angry just because I'm not head over heels about what you've suggested. Maybe that kind of arrangement is just a little too cozy for me. I don't know. Maybe it's too much like marriage without any of the benefits. Do you know what I'm trying to say?"

"No, I don't and I'm sorry I brought it up." Owen got up to leave. "I really thought we understood one another a lot better than we do. I guess it's obvious now that I was wrong. Dead wrong. Forget I ever asked. Okay?" With that, he picked up his coat and walked out the door.

Susan dashed out in the corridor after him. "Wait! Owen, please wait!" He stopped and looked back at her. "I'm sorry, Owen. I didn't mean to hurt you. Come on back —let's talk some more, please?"

Owen looked bewildered as Susan took him by the hand and led him back into the apartment. When they settled themselves back on the sofa once more, she leaned over and planted a light kiss on his cheek.

"Am I forgiven?"

"Sure. I guess I moved too quickly."

"Look, Owen, I must have more time to think about this a little more. It was just too sudden, that's all."

"I suppose I really shouldn't have expected you to make a decision like that on the spur of the moment. I've been going back and forth on this idea ever since returning from New York. Once I came to grips with this thing I wanted to settle it with you. I was disappointed for that reason and I'm sorry if I pressed you too far. I want to be reasonable."

"Sometimes you're too reasonable," Susan said aloud without thinking.

"Am I?" his eyebrows lifted questioningly. "I just find that it makes life easier for everyone concerned."

Later, after Owen finally did leave, Susan reviewed everything that had happened several times over in her thoughts, especially the matter of his being so reasonable. Sometimes that was what took away some of the excitement in their relationship. He hadn't given her an ultimatum, not even a deadline. In the end, however, she knew that she would have to make a decision. If she did decide to move in with Owen, that would put an immediate end to all other relationships in her life, including Carlos. It would finally put an end to her infatuation with him once and for all. But although she told herself that that was a big plus in favor of Owen's proposal, it was also the major deterrent. Even with all the controversy between herself and that handsome Spaniard in recent days, it hadn't prevented her from thinking about losing him forever if she went along with Owen's suggestion. What would Carlos say if he found that she had done it? Damn him! He wouldn't care at all, would he? Would he?

Chapter Fourteen

After the Thanksgiving holidays were over and classes resumed at the university, Susan developed a strategy whereby she might increase her chances of running into Brett Sinclair. If they were to meet ostensibly by accident, it was likely that he would be more willing to talk about Elena honestly and openly than if Susan tried to confront him directly about Elena. At one time, Brett must have felt something for the young woman, and it was important to find out if there was anything left in his heart for her. If not, it would be interesting to know at least what he believed his responsibilities were and what he intended to do about them.

It wasn't hard at all for Susan to get herself in a position to bump into Brett. A visit to the registrar's office provided her with his roster of classes. Then it was just a matter of being outside the building at approximately the same time he would probably be exiting. Susan thought it might take two or three days before it would work, but it didn't. As luck would have it, he spotted her first as he was crossing the campus. Susan was really surprised that he was eager to seek her out.

"Hey, remember me? Brett. Brett Sinclair?"

"Of course, Brett. You . . . were Elena's friend." That was all Susan had to say in order to bring a sheepish look to Brett's eyes.

"I'm really glad to see you. I wonder if you have a few minutes? Do you have some time to talk? It's about Elena."

"I'm early for an appointment I had here," Susan lied,

"so I think I can give you more than just a few minutes. Is there some place we can talk?"

Brett pointed in the direction of the Student Union building and as soon as they sat down in a leather booth over coffee, he launched into an elaborate self-defense before Susan had even asked a single question. Clearly, he was bothered a great deal by what had happened, and he needed to talk it over with someone.

"I swear to you, Ms. Blaine, I really love Elena and I don't intend to give her up."

"Well, now, that's very interesting, Brett. If that's true, then why did you walk out on her?"

"Two reasons, I guess." He scratched his head looking as though he was about to confess a minor crime. "First, to be honest, I was scared. It was all a mistake, something we hadn't planned or expected to happen, and all I could see was that it was the end of school and my career. The whole bottom seemed to drop out on me and I guess I just panicked." He looked carefully at Susan hoping she wouldn't berate him for having those feelings.

"And what was the other reason?" Susan took a sip of coffee.

"The other reason was that I got angry, angry over the fact that she took me completely by surprise. It was just totally unexpected." Brett brought two clenched fists together to reveal his frustration. "I got angry because she was always giving me that business about how important it was for her to be free and independent and a liberated woman. And then, wham! All of a sudden it was all marriage and a family and all that stuff. It just wasn't in the kind of plans we were making, can you understand that?"

"Yes, I can see why you might feel the way you did. That's all quite understandable. But what I'm having a harder time figuring out is why you deserted Elena when you just told me you love her?"

"Desert her?" Brett bristled at Susan's suggestion. "I haven't deserted her!"

"She thinks you have," Susan countered.

"I know, I know," he said with regret. "That was stupid of me. I thought it would force her to get rid of the baby."

Brett turned his face away from Susan's, unable to meet her eyes after what he had just admitted to her. "I was wrong," he said in a low voice. "I've already been willing to tell her that."

"You have? When?"

Brett swallowed hard before he continued. "Well, I really didn't get a chance to. I tried to talk to her every day this week since I got back, but she doesn't want to listen to me. It's that arrogant pride of hers. She's determined that she's going to see it through all by herself."

"Yes, I know what you're talking about," Susan nodded. "The Obregon pride is something very formidable to have to cope with. But, Brett, believe me, she still cares for you. I know she does."

Susan's reassuring words helped to bring some light into the young man's face.

"Then tell me how I can get her back," he asked. "How can I get her to at least listen to me?"

"That's not going to be easy. Yet, I know she wants to marry you, and her family does, too."

"Maybe I should see her family?"

"I wouldn't do that if I were you," Susan warned emphatically. "At least not until the two of you have settled your differences. Believe me, take my advice. Right now her brother is not in a very receptive frame of mind about anything you might have to tell him. Just the mention of your existence is enough to set him off in a rage. I'm afraid if the two of you ever do meet, he'll really go mad."

"Not a very friendly guy," Brett mocked.

"No, I'm really serious about that, Brett. I think Carlos is so upset about all this that he just might get violent if he were provoked even the slightest bit."

"He'd better not try," Brett said with false bravado. "I've got a black belt in karate and I wouldn't like to use my training against one of my future in-laws."

Susan chose not to respond to Brett's overconfidence. Instead, she suggested an idea that had just crossed her mind as he was speaking, a way in which a confrontation between the two men could be avoided. Aware that Carlos was trying to locate Brett, Susan developed a strategy out loud. "If Elena thought that Carlos were threatening you in some way, wouldn't she come to your aid, wouldn't that melt away some of her stubbornness?"

"Oh, I see what you're saying." Brett looked enthusiastic. "But how are we going to work that out?"

"I don't know yet. We've got to give this some careful thinking. I'm relying on you for some help with this." It took over an hour of brainstorming and step-by-step planning before the co-conspirators worked out all of the details to their satisfaction. In the end, Brett wasn't completely convinced it would work but was willing to give it a first-class try. Finally, they shook hands as if they had made a solemn pact and went their separate ways to prepare for the night's coming drama.

It was late afternoon when Elena and Susan were preparing supper. The phone rang and Susan answered it, muttered something excitedly into the receiver and hung up abruptly. As hoped, Elena's curiosity was aroused.

"Who was that?"

"Carlos." Susan put on the best look of consternation that she could.

"Why, what did he want?" Elena asked.

"Oh, God. I really think there's going to be trouble now."

"What are you saying? What's the matter?"

"Carlos says that he has discovered the name of the young man that must marry you. And as soon as he is off duty, he's going to see him."

"*¡Madre de Dios!*" Elena cried out, bringing an anguished hand to her forehead. "We can't let that happen. He'll go wild. I have to get to Brett."

"But how? Do you know where he is?" Susan asked with a incredulous voice.

"Y-yes." Looking sheepish at her admission, Elena revealed she had seen Brett on campus recently and that he'd informed her he had rerented their old rooms in the hopes that she would return.

"Well, then, there's no need to worry, Elena. Carlos will be on duty for at least another hour—"

"But what if something happens and he should leave

early?" Elena cried as she struggled to get her coat on quickly.

"Be careful, Elena, please." Susan felt strong pangs of guilt over the ruse she and Brett and invented, but it was the only solution they had come up with.

With Elena's car speeding down the street and out of sight, Susan went quickly to the phone and dialed the number she knew from memory.

"Randolph Air Force Base," an impersonal voice answered.

"Extension three-forty-two please," Susan asked hurriedly.

Six long rings made her stomach churn. Finally, someone answered.

"Major Obregon, please. It's very important."

Three minutes passed. Then four. Susan grew fearful that Elena's prediction might come true. If for some reason he had gotten off duty early and had already left the base, Carlos would never appear at Brett's apartment. And Elena would almost certainly become suspicious about the fake phone call from her brother.

"Hello?" It was Carlos, and Susan breathed easier. When she told him that she could help him locate Elena's boyfriend, Carlos promised to be there in less than an hour. *So far, so good,* Susan thought.

"So you've finally decided to tell me where he is." Carlos appeared supremely confident when he arrived. That annoyed Susan, but she was striving desperately to maintain an atmosphere of calm.

"Yes, but first I must have a promise from you that you are not going to do anything rash, that you're going to be reasonable when you see this young man."

"And if I don't?"

"Well, then we can forget the whole thing," Susan said flatly.

He studied her with a powerful gaze. "Very well. You have my word. Now who is he and where is he?"

Reminding him of his promise, Susan told him Brett's name and then launched into an explanation of the plan that she and Brett had engineered in order to bring the young couple back together again. When she was finished Carlos provided little in the way of a reaction and Susan was worried as they left for their fateful rendezvous.

Throughout the entire ride to Brett's apartment Carlos maintained a stony silence, answering Susan's questions with the briefest of monosyllables. By the time they pulled into the parking lot, his face bore that forbidding look she knew so well and she clutched as his arm nervously, not really knowing what he might do. She wanted to remind him of the promise he had made earlier, but decided it would probably be of no avail anyway. Carlos rapped on the door that had the number fourteen painted on it, and when it swung open, Brett was standing there to greet them. He held out his hand in friendship.

"Hi, Ms. Blaine, Major—"

Before Brett could finish his greeting, Carlos's fist lashed out without warning and struck him in the face. The boy reeled backwards and slumped to the floor with blood streaming from his mouth. Both Elena and Susan let out cries of protest simultaneously as Carlos stood over his fallen victim. Elena threw caution to the winds and wedged herself between the two opponents, cradling Brett in her arms.

But Carlos wasn't content to let it stop there. Pointing an intimidating finger at Brett he railed out loud, "I ought to kill you for what you've done, you bastard, but I gave Ms. Blaine my word I wouldn't." Clenching and unclenching his fist, looking as though he could barely restrain himself from continuing the beating he'd begun, Carlos walked away from the two women who now encircled him. Susan followed him with her eyes but stood frozen in angry silence.

"Don't look at me that way!" he exploded. "I had to do it. If I didn't, I would never be able to forgive myself, or him for that matter. Do you understand what I'm saying, Susan?"

There was almost a pleading quality to the look in his eyes, and the depth of the conflict and inner turmoil he appeared to be suffering was somehow sensed by Susan. Like the last sparks of a colossal volcano, Carlos's temper was beginning to subside almost to a simmer. This moment of violence was making him see the futility of what he was trying to do, his inability to control his sister's life and the decisions she and she alone had to make. It was something he couldn't articulate clearly, something only his eyes seemed to be able to reveal to Susan.

All she could do was nod to let him know that she recognized what he was feeling.

Elena helped Brett struggle to his feet and he touched his swollen jaw as he faced his assailant once more. "If you'd ever been in love, Major, you'd know that there's only so much that can hold back a man and a woman from loving one another. I don't know what you're planning to do, but I'm not about to give your sister up now or ever. I love her and I need her, and if that doesn't suit you, then I'm ready to go to battle for her. You might have to carry me out of here on a stretcher if you plan to try and stop me."

Carlos saw the courage in Brett's eyes and then looked at his sister. "No, no more violence. There's no point to any more."

"I love him, Carlos," Elena cried out. "I do love him."

"And I love her," Brett reaffirmed. "I want very much to marry her, if she'll have me." Elena rushed into his arms and they embraced one another. Tears of joy came to Elena's eyes on hearing Brett's words.

"You see, Carlos? You see? There was no need for all of those threats, for that violence. We will be married after all. That should please *Mamacita* and you should be pleased, too."

"All right, all right." Carlos nodded his tentative approval. "But you should both think carefully about this wedding and how you are going to plan it."

"I have given it some thought already," Brett interjected. Then turning toward Elena, he said, "I think we could first be married in a civil ceremony and then have a church wedding later with all of the pomp and circumstance you want."

Carlos was skeptical. "Do you think a large wedding really is feasible?"

"Well, I have a large family back home in Massachusetts, Major, and my mother would be very anxious to have everyone included."

"On the way over here, Ms. Blaine told me that your father has threatened to disinherit you if you marry before graduation," Carlos said, changing the focus of their discussion. "What about that? How will a formal wedding fit in with that?"

"Nothing will come of it. I've already talked with my mother about it and she promises to handle my Dad. If there's one thing my mother can do, it's wheedle almost anything out of my Dad that she wants. I'm sure it'll all turn out okay."

Torn between pride and anger, Carlos looked askance at the young couple. Angry enough to let her go, proud enough to hope that his sister would wed within the respected traditions of the Obregon name and that her ancestral home would be protected from insult. "I have a suggestion. I'll fly you both to Las Vegas where a civil ceremony can be performed with a minimum of waiting. When we return, Elena, you know Mother will arrange for a religious service at the family church with perhaps a small reception at the hacienda afterwards. If the family believes that you've been secretly married for some time and only found it necessary to tell them because of the child, well and good. Nothing more need be said to anyone."

Carlos's suggested plan surprised all of them into momentary silence. But Susan was the first to respond. "But Carlos, how is your mother going to react to all this? Is she going to agree to it?"

"If you think she won't, then you haven't read her very well, Susan. The Obregon name is at stake and she will do most anything to protect its honor. And the Obregon honor can best be protected by a secret ceremony in Vegas. Later a family wedding from the hacienda will help to satisfy our time-honored traditions." That aside, Carlos looked for more objections but saw only silent faces. "Well, how does all of that sound to you people? Does somebody have a better idea?"

Brett shrugged his shoulders and looked at Elena. "It's okay with me, I guess. What do you think, Elena?"

Elena was looking solemnly at her brother. "Carlos, that's kind of you to suggest it. Thank you. Thank you so much."

Carlos turned to Susan. "You're going to accompany us, too, aren't you? Elena will need you as a witness."

"Oh, yes," Elena agreed, smiling. "Please, Susan, you must."

"I thought you'd never ask," Susan said cheerfully. "And I think a little celebration is in order here. Brett, you're not going to disappoint us and try to make us believe that a member of Psi Omega doesn't have a bottle of something to drink around here? I think all of us could use a little drink."

"Comin' right up," Brett said, taking the cue eagerly.

A few drinks helped everyone take the edge off their frazzled nerves. Later, when their little party broke up and Susan and Carlos were driving home alone, the conversation turned naturally to the happy outcome of the night's events.

"I'm really pleased with the way things turned out tonight," Susan began. "I think Brett will be good for your sister."

"Perhaps," was Carlos's unenthusiastic response.

"He's really a nice guy." Susan tested the waters a little more as Carlos shifted gears. "Don't you think so?"

"How can you ask me that?" he growled.

"Oh, come off it, Carlos," Susan said, dripping with sarcasm. "You know, I wasn't going to say this, but on second thought I think I will! If it hadn't been *your* sister, Carlos, you probably would have found nothing wrong with Brett's macho behavior. Isn't that right?"

Carlos was silent for a long time. "Maybe you're right," he finally said. "Maybe it does depend on the girl."

Susan was surprised at his willingness to discuss it so rationally. "Yes, any girl but your sister. Did you ever stop to think how unfair that has been to Elena? I hate to say this, but you are a perfect example of 'don't do as I do but do as I say.' "

"All right. All right! So I was rough on her. But you've got to remember my upbringing. I know what you're thinking—that I believe in a double standard."

"Well?"

"It's true. I have believed in a double standard until now."

Susan's head spun around to face him. "Until now?"

"Don't think I have totally abandoned all my beliefs and traditions, though. I am willing, however, to concede that they may need some re-examination . . . some modification, if you will."

"Why, Carlos, I never thought I would live to hear you say that." Susan was genuinely stunned.

"Neither did I, but I have been giving it a lot of thought since this whole mess with Elena broke loose. . . . Between you and my sister, two women who mean the world to me, damn it, what choice do I have?" A smile came to his lips, a smile tinged with irony as he stopped his car in front of the apartment complex and came around to help her out. But when he opened the door, she didn't move. She just sat there staring straight ahead.

"What's the matter?" he asked.

"I think I'm utterly speechless." Susan was still trying to decipher all that his statements just implied.

"Well, I think that's enough talking for one night, anyway," Carlos said, gently taking her arm. "Maybe I've said too much already. I hope I don't wake up tomorrow morning ready to retract everything I said tonight."

"Oh, I can't let that happen. This is a subject for future discussion."

"After Brett and Elena are married, we'll have plenty of time." Susan wondered if he intended to keep that thin promise.

Three days later, the two couples climbed into a Piper Navajo and took off for Las Vegas with Carlos at the controls. It was a smooth flight in a clear, bright sky high above the occasional puffy white clouds that drifted underneath. When they landed, a rented car was waiting for them, and the foursome drove directly to the home of a justice of the peace who performed the short ceremony. There was an awkward moment of silence when it was over, but Susan helped to break it with enthusiastic congratulations and kisses for the young bride and groom. Carlos followed suit with a brief handshake for Brett and a warm hug and kiss for his sister.

Afterwards, Carlos drove them to the M.G.M. Grand Hotel where he had reserved the bridal suite for the newlyweds. First, however, a celebration dinner with champagne was served in a luxurious dining room. Following this, Carlos and Susan accompanied the new husband and wife as far as the elevator to bid them farewell. With tears in her eyes, Elena rushed into her brother's arms to thank him for everything he had done. To Susan's surprise, Carlos's eyes were misted, too, as he held his sister tightly against his chest whispering reassurances in Spanish to her until she regained her calm.

Susan heard him say, "You're on your own now, *muchacha.* I'm glad you've found a husband who loves you and will take good care of you." He held her away from himself, took out a handkerchief, and wiped away her tears. "Just tears of happiness, that's all. There. Now on your way, *querida.* And you, Mr. Sinclair," he said with a warning smile as he turned to Brett, "look after her well or you'll have me to reckon with."

"Aye, aye, sir," Brett gave back a mock salute and then rubbed his bruised chin. "I doubt I'll ever forget. Come on, Elena," he said giving her hand a tug, "let's go before he tries to induct me into the military on my wedding night."

Just as the elevator doors closed, Susan heard them call out in unison, "Thanks, Susan." She felt her eyes grow moist and when she glanced at Carlos, he was dabbing his eyes with his handkerchief, too. Susan slipped her arm inside his, realizing his embarrassment.

"Sorry," he apologized as he quickly put his handkerchief away.

"You don't have to be sorry because of a very human emotion. Oh, I know, I know," she said trying to make light of it. "You're going to tell me that it's all right for a woman to be emotional, but it's not for a man."

"Well, I'm not going to tell you anything of the kind, Ms. Blaine. And I'll bet that's going to surprise you, isn't it?"

"As a matter of fact, it does."

"Good," he said, pleased with himself. "Look, I've had about all of the heavy stuff I can take for one night. What do you say we go into the casino and relax a little bit before we think about flying back to San Antonio?"

"Why, sure. That sounds like fun to me, but to tell you the truth, I don't know much about gambling. I've never done any. It certainly looks exciting." Susan's eyes scanned the massive hall full of blackjack tables, roulette wheels, and crap tables crowded with noisy customers eagerly putting down their bets.

"Come on, let's see if we have any luck," he said, enticing her. "Tell you what, why don't you watch me play for a few minutes and learn how the game is played. Then if you feel confident enough, you can try it on your own. Blackjack's not hard to learn."

Carlos was a careful player, watching the house at several tables before finally selecting one for play, and he was good at calculating his chances of beating the dealer once he began. Several times in a row, he came up with a twenty-one, the winning hand against the dealer, and Susan squeezed his arm with delight, urging him on.

"Just a small win," he whispered back to her. "The house usually wins it all back by the time the evening is over. But you know something? I'm glad you're here. I think you're bringing me good luck." He kissed the tip of her nose lightly and turned back to concentrate on the game.

After watching Carlos for some time, Susan grew restless, wanting to try her own luck at blackjack. Promising to return shortly, she wandered off in search of a table.

When a space did open up at one, Susan cautiously ventured up to it. Then, getting cold feet, she turned away, but the dealer had spotted her and beckoned her to sit down.

"Don't be afraid, little lady." He winked encouragingly as he shuffled the cards in the shoe. That was about all the inducement she needed to take a position at the table. Feeling a little self-conscious, she fumbled in her purse, pulled out four tens and laid them down. With startling quickness, the friendly dealer snapped up the forty dollars and laid eight five-dollar chips in front of her. Just as swiftly the cards were placed in front of her, barely giving her time to think about the decisions that had to be made instantaneously. Luckily, she won her first three hands and she stacked the chips in front of her, her confidence rising. Then just as suddenly, her luck changed and she lost the next seven hands in a row. Before long, she was down to one last chip. That, too, was finally drawn up by the smiling dealer who was urging her to stay on and try again. Susan was no longer up to his challenge. Hastily sliding off the stool, she backed away. In less than twenty minutes, her forty dollars was gone, making her wonder what would have happened if she had continued to play.

"How'd you do on your own?" She hadn't seen Carlos approaching.

"Not too great!" she was forced to admit and told him what had happened. When he roared with laughter at her story, she asked him defensively, "Well, how did you do after I left?"

"Oh, I won a few dollars," he lied.

"How much is a few dollars?" she wanted to know.

"About a hundred and twenty."

"Oh," Sue said, deflated. "Well, I guess somebody has to win."

Carlos chuckled lightly, careful not to hurt Susan's feelings any further, and led the way into the casino bar where he ordered a martini for her and a scotch and soda for himself. They had barely taken one sip of their drinks when a shapely blonde sidled up next to Carlos. She was wearing a tight sequined outfit that identified her as one of the members of the chorus line, and Carlos was rather diffident in making his introductions.

"Bunny Johnson, I want you to meet Susan Blaine."

"Gee, nice ta meetcha. You and Carlos fly in for the weekend?"

"Not exactly," Susan smiled with constraint.

"Well, as long as you're here, stick around and enjoy yourself. Carlos sure knows how to show a girl a good time."

"Really?" Sue gave Carlos a sidelong glance while he continued stirring his drink carelessly, not looking up at all.

"Tell you what, Bunny. How about if I buy you a nice drink so that you can keep quiet before you get me into trouble with my girl here?" Carlos squirmed a bit in his seat.

"Oh, gee, now don't take anything I say seriously, Suzie. Carlos never did, right, hon?" The showgirl laughed out loud and gave him a nudge in the shoulder. Susan found herself warming towards the wide-eyed, leggy dancer. "Listen, I'd like ta have a drink, but it's almost time to go on stage. What can ya do? Can't even find time for old friends. That's show biz, I guess. I gotta get goin'." Before she left, Bunny made them promise to visit her backstage if they had time. They gave assurances that they would try, while knowing secretly that they probably would not.

Carlos glanced at Susan out of the corner of his eye.

"Your Bunny's okay," Sue acknowledged, playfully hoping to embarrass him.

"Mine? I think you're jumping to conclusions. Just a friend, that's all."

"Uh-huh," Susan answered with amusement. He was actually flustered and she found herself enjoying it.

Carlos waved for the bartender's attention. "I think I better order another round of drinks before we start talking?"

"And just what are we going to discuss that's so important that you have to ply me with liquor first?"

"I'm about to launch into a serious discussion about you. And me. And the two of us."

"Indeed?" Susan arched a brow. "Sounds pretty important."

"Yes, I think it is. Let's begin with you first." His smile revealed his gleaming white teeth and she started to melt with anticipation. "You have to be the most maddening, infuriating woman I have ever known."

"I am?"

"Without a doubt." He held her chin between his index finger and thumb. "The more time I spend with you, the more you seem to enjoy challenging me."

"When is the good news coming in this discussion?"

"The good news is that you are also the sweetest, most generous, and most beautiful woman I've ever known."

"Mmm. I do sound complicated."

"That's exactly the word I would use."

"Let's see, I think I heard you say sweet, generous, beautiful, and complicated. Is that a good combination or a bad one?"

Instead of answering Carlos looked around the noisy barroom. "This isn't the place to answer that question." He stood up and started to leave. "Wait here, I'll be right back."

Moments later, he returned dangling a room key in front of her, and holding his hand out to her. Susan felt her heart pound and she hesitated for an instant. Her mind was swimming with reasons for not accepting his offer, yet none of them could control the desire that was beginning to swell within her. Grasping his outstretched hand, Susan accompanied him to a suite on the ninth floor where he tossed off his dark suit coat and loosened his tie while Susan kicked off her shoes and curled up on the sofa.

"Come here," he growled passionately as he slid next to her and swept her into his arms, kissing her hungrily with a long ardent kiss. But a knock at the door drew them apart.

"Oh, I forgot," he brought his hand to his forehead. "I ordered some drinks and a snack," he explained, giving her a light peck on the cheek before letting the bellhop in.

"Mmmm." Susan uncovered the silver tray to find an interesting assortment of hors d'oeuvres.

"How about some champagne?" Carlos asked, bringing the cooler towards the table.

"It'll do in a pinch," she teased while filling up their plates and Carlos poured the bubbly liquid in their long-stemmed glasses. "What are we celebrating?"

"Us," he claimed confidently raising his glass high in the air. "To our reunion."

"I'll definitely drink to that." Susan's glass tinkled against his and their eyes locked as they sipped. He moved closer to her and ran his warm hand along her back in a circling motion drawing her nearer to him. Susan nuzzled next to him and rested her cheek against his chest.

"There's something I've been wanting to say to you all day."

"Oh, must you?" A little twinge of fear moved around in her stomach. "You're not going to break this glowing mood coming over me, are you?"

He stared directly into her eyes. "I hope not. I . . . just wanted you to know that it's taken me a long time to realize what hell I have put you through. You've been very, very patient with me and have been willing to put up with a lot. You've had to overcome a lot of bad images that I guess I've been harboring about Anglo women. It was very difficult for me to avoid putting you in the same category instead of appreciating you for what you are as an individual. But you forced me to do that from the beginning because somehow you really never fit the mold. You're not some cool, calculating, grasping female, the kind I've come to expect. You were warm and loving right from the start and I failed to recognize it all along. Why, you showed my sister more compassion than her own family did. You helped arrange the reconciliation between Elena and Brett."

"Carlos, please—" Susan tried to interrupt.

"No, let me finish, *amada mía,* because I want your forgiveness for my foolish pigheadedness, for not admitting what I felt in my heart was true about you." He knelt down beside her on the sofa and slid his arms around her waist.

"Oh, Carlos, you're making me feel embarrassed. I haven't been all that wonderful either."

"Darling, don't—"

"Wait. Let me say something, too, about all of this. When I came out here to San Antonio, I had my own set of preconceived ideas about what a man and woman's relationship should be like. And I was determined that everything had to fit into my scheme of things and I was going to make all the rules. So I guess I've had some lessons to learn, too."

He looked deeply into her concerned eyes and gave her a smile of recognition and appreciation. "So we both seem to have learned something from all of this."

Smoothing back a lock of his blue-black hair, Susan drew his head toward hers and his grip tightened around her. Lips met in a burning kiss that kindled their passions, and Carlos lifted her into his powerful arms. Striding into the bedroom, he lowered her gently to the bed and released her beside him. Still kissing her, Carlos slowly undid the buttons of her pink blouse and removed it. His fingers found their way under the front hook of her cream-colored bra, and it opened revealing her tantalizing breasts. They locked in a deep embrace and his hands moved about her back, and then the tips of his burning fingers glided forward until they found a path toward her eager nipples. Slowly, gently, he stroked them until she arched her back to receive his rushing mouth in an ardent exploration. Her entire body was now trembling with expectation as his questing hands artfully removed her garments until all that she wore were her skimpy bikini panties. Then gradually, they slid away too, and he continued to kiss and touch and nuzzle at random each curve of her body until she was on fire. A sensuous smile crossed his lips as he stopped briefly to permit his eyes to travel over her lovely body, and in spite of herself, Susan blushed.

"My God, you are beautiful," he rasped, his hand trailing blistering heat over her flesh. "Never be embarrassed by my love for you."

Breathless with passion, they frantically divested him of his clothing. Then Susan lay back inviting him to come to her. Tantalized beyond endurance, his body now lowered against hers and they moved in delicious rhythm, first ever so slowly, then faster and faster. With explosive force he plundered and drew her up to meet him again and again in a searing union of love.

"I love you," they cried simultaneously as they climbed

to a final ascent before spiraling down and down until only an afterglow remained.

Their passions spent, they lay locked in each other's arms, Carlos's head resting against her warm breast. Finally, he rolled off her but encircled her waist as they lay side by side.

Murmuring "I love you" Susan punctuated each affirmation with a little kiss. Again and again she repeated her love ritual covering his chest, then his face with brief kisses until she heard him snickering with suppressed laughter.

"What are you laughing about?" she asked, raising her head to see what was the matter.

"Nothing, it's just that your hair was tickling my nose."

"Oh, I like that! I'm offering words of love and you concern yourself with a little tickling hair." Slapping his rump playfully, Susan rolled off the bed and began gathering her lingerie from the floor.

"Stop!" Carlos shouted with laughter, and she looked over her shoulder just in time to see him make a lunge for her. Squealing with delight, Susan made a run for the bathroom, but Carlos was there first barring her way.

"You ought to be ashamed of yourself," she said pointing at him, "running around like that."

"Look who's talking!" he said, moving closer to get an arm around her once more. "But I like you this way."

"Yes, but at least I'm attempting to maintain some modesty," she claimed, backing away and holding her lingerie at strategic locations.

He stalked her mischievously, like a tiger seeking its prey. Letting out a screech of excitement, Susan tried to dart away from his path, but he gave chase and cornered her next to the bed.

"And now, my beauty, you must pay the forfeit." He twirled an imaginary moustache, and she let out a giggle. With a catlike sweep of his hand, he clawed the lingerie from her hands, tossed it over his shoulder and toppled her onto the bed. But before he could pin her down, she was scrambling away.

"Oh, no you don't," he laughed, grasping her leg before

she was able to get free. She yelped as her captor yanked her towards him and finally pinned her wriggling body under his. "Mmmm, you smell good," he murmured into her ear and teased it with his tongue, sending a tingling sensation down the entire left side of her body.

"Carlos!" she sighed, wrapping herself around him, drawing his long lean form tightly against her so that her every curve and valley was a part of him. She had thought that their playfulness would lead to nothing further, but now she was shocked at how quickly that love-coil deep within wound itself tighter and tighter threatening to break through the floodgates of desire once more. Her hands wandered blindly through the field of thick hair on his chest, around his muscular back and upwards to his neck. Now both hands gripped firmly his lush hair and she felt his hot breath meander maddeningly over her. Gradually his lips traveled relentlessly towards hers muttering love words on his way until they joined again and Susan gave herself up to his desire.

"Mi vida," she heard him say as they lay quietly, molded as one, before the sensuous rhythm of love began and repeated itself and quickened into a crescendo of ecstasy.

When the magic of the moment finally subsided, he brushed back her hair and whispered, *"Mi alma,* marry me, marry me." His words clanged through her brain, and she found herself unable to answer. Carlos sat up to look at her curiously.

"What is it?" he asked seeing the reluctance in her midnight blue eyes. "I'm asking you to marry me. Aren't you going to give me a reply?"

Susan came to a sitting position beside him hugging the bedsheet around herself. "Carlos," she stammered, "I do love you . . . but there are many problems we have to overcome."

"None that we should not be able to solve," he argued.

"I'm not so sure about that. Some of them are not going to be easy."

"Such as?"

"Such as your mother's attitude for one."

"You won't be the first woman to have a difference with her mother-in-law," he said, trying to make light of her objection.

"Actually, I think it's more than that," Susan continued. "It's your way of life, your relatives, your friends—*raza*, if you will. I would be worried about how all that might affect you and me."

"Don't you think I've considered all that? I'm aware of those possible problems, but together we should be able to deal with them."

Susan wanted to believe him but wasn't convinced. "I'm divorced. I'm not Catholic. Is that something your family's willing to accept?"

Carlos grasped her firmly by the shoulders and shook her lightly. "Stop throwing nothing but obstacles in the way!" He glared at her, then was sorry for his reaction. "Susan, Susan." Carlos brushed his mouth against hers. "No more conflict, no more angry outbursts . . . not now, not tonight. Let's talk about it calmly."

"All right, Carlos, let's try. Let me start by explaining how I feel about things that are important to me—like my job, for instance. I really enjoy working and I don't want to have to give it up."

"Who said that you'd have to?" he asked.

Susan looked back at him in disbelief. "Am I hearing this? Is this *the* Carlos Obregon that I know talking now?"

He shook a finger to reprimand her. "Don't be snide and don't jump to conclusions, Susan. Naturally, I would expect our marriage and family to be uppermost in your mind. But that doesn't mean that you wouldn't be able to work."

"Maybe that's the rub for me, Carlos. I like my work so much that I don't know if I'm willing to make it secondary in my life behind a home and family."

"Are you telling me that you don't want a home and family ever?"

"No, I do . . . sometime."

"And when will that be?"

"I—I don't know. I'm just not sure."

"Looks like you're confused to me. You don't seem to

have a firm commitment to anything. You've got to make up your mind, Susan. Until you've decided what it is you do want, then talking about marriage is kind of pointless, I guess."

His use of the word *commitment* struck her as very ironic. Deeply distressed, Susan bowed her head. "I'm sorry, Carlos."

"So am I," he sighed in disappointment and made as if to leave the bed, but Susan grasped his hand.

"Carlos, can't we think about this a little longer? I need more time."

"Time? How much time? A month? A year?"

"Be reasonable!" she cried.

"How much longer do you want to have us play this game of emotional seesaw, up one minute and down the next?"

"Carlos, be patient with me. I do love you."

Again he breathed deeply out of frustration. "And I love you. *Niña mia,* I think you must decide and soon what it is most that you want from your life. There's no need for me to tell you that all of life is often a compromise. And it is learning to live with these compromises that makes a good life, one of give and take. Nothing comes easy in any man's or woman's life, but out of struggle comes love. That is what I truly believe. Would we have chosen to fall in love with one another if there were no conflict, if it were easy? I don't think so. If love is to mean anything, it probably has more to do with sacrifices and changes in two people's lives. If there is no sharing, there cannot be any love." He rested his hand on her shoulder, a benign smile on his lips. "We've wrenched and torn at the fabric of each other's souls, haven't we? But do you know something? I believe the two of us are better because of it. I know that I've learned a lot from you, a lot about my own shortcomings, about my narrow ideas of what a woman should be. I know now that a woman can't just be a sexual toy for a man or be a servant for him and his children without any regard for herself as a person. You've taught me a great deal, Susan, and I want you to know that I love you for it."

Tears stood on the edge of Susan's eyelids when he was

finished. "I think I've come away with something, too, Carlos. More than anything else, I realize now that there is great pain in loving someone with different beliefs and a different background than your own."

"Maybe," he pondered out loud, "a little bloodletting between a man and a woman is a good thing if it helps them come to a better understanding of one another. It might even make the bonds between them a lot stronger, enough for an entire lifetime." He paused, then bent over to kiss her forehead and then her trembling lips.

"Don't make me wait too long for my answer, *mi vida,*" he whispered. "I cannot."

Susan squeezed her eyes shut to hold back the tears, but she could not prevent them from seeping through.

"Muchacha, don't cry." He cradled her in his arms. "It will be all right. I know we will work it out."

His reassurances could not prevent her from sobbing against his shoulder until she was limp with fatigue. Finally, Susan fell into a deep sleep, completely exhausted. When she woke with a start some time later, Carlos was still there next to her with his arm locked around her. She looked at him quietly as he slept, so virile, so handsome, so utterly maddening throughout all of their tempestuous relationship. Something had held them together this far, something she could not clearly identify. And she was glad that it had. But now he had given her what amounted to an ultimatum and she needed an answer soon, an answer which might part them forever.

Chapter Fifteen

FOR THE NEXT few weeks Susan pursued an inward jour-
ney trying to sort out her life. While her daytime hours
were largely absorbed by the demands of her work, a certain portion of herself she kept reserved to herself. The approach of her twenty-ninth birthday heralded the close of
youth's folly, she decided. It was time to put aside childish
whims and to set her course solidly towards mature goals.

Often Susan had to fight herself from being stampeded
by Carlos's warning not to keep him waiting too long. His
theories about marriage and the relationship between a
man and woman had made a burning impression on her
mind and heart. She was drawn to Carlos like steel to a
magnet, and she responded almost mystically to his notion
that pain as well as joy were the cement that bind together
a man and woman for a lifetime. But there was something
almost threatening in his concept. She wasn't sure she
could handle that heavy approach to life.

Whenever she felt trapped by Carlos's demands, Owen
would surface in her thoughts as the safe alternative to the
drastic obligations Carlos imposed. And Owen was a very
special man. From the day she was first hired, he had always been in her camp. He had supported her both profes-
sionally and emotionally. As her boss, his counsel had
been readily available whenever she sought it and always
without strings. As her lover he had been tender and passionate without creating unreasonable demands. She felt
safe but free with him. She could walk through life with
dignified composure beside Owen—at least for the time
being. Yet Owen had disturbed her peace of mind, too. He

had been right when he told her she didn't know what she wanted.

Good Lord! There were times when Susan felt paralyzed and incapable of arriving at a decision. *What's the matter with me?* She felt tormented with doubts about her stability. *Am I becoming incapable of making a rational decision?*

Now stop it! She chided herself for a silly fool when she stood back from such melodramatic monologues. Still and all, Susan felt it necessary to arrive at a coherent life plan. What did she hope to be or have at age forty? If she didn't come up with a clear-cut goal, chances were she would arrive at middle-age still foundering in the waters of indecision.

She joined the Y and went to the gym three nights a week to work out and to swim. She was pleased to feel her body toning up and recovering the elasticity that she had enjoyed in her early twenties. And for her mind, she purchased a half dozen classics at the bookstore and delved into Jane Austen and George Eliot with relish. She really looked forward to quiet hours with books and records in her own apartment.

For entertainment she went on the town with Vera and a few women she had met at the Center and sampled San Antonio nightlife on weekends, but for the most part Susan preferred long intervals with no one but her own thoughts for company. She found living alone wasn't lonely or threatening. It was encouraging to discover that she was good alone. Maybe the single life was the path for her. And maybe it was merely a relief to be free of emotional turmoil for a change. Susan told herself to take all the time she needed to make up her mind. This was her *life* she was deciding.

Maria Vargas came to see Susan at Forsythe's one rainy afternoon in early January.

"Come in and take off that dripping coat." Susan led her client into her office and waited while Maria slipped off her coat and hung it up to dry. "Sit down, Maria, and tell me how things are going for you."

"Mrs. Blaine, they couldn't be better." Maria was full of smiles.

"Wonderful. Tell me everything. You sound happy."

"I'm going to get married!"

"Well, well, well. Who's the lucky guy?"

"Michael Sullivan." Maria nodded her head. "That's right. An Anglo and an angel."

"Good grief. I didn't think such a combination was possible."

They laughed companionably, while Maria told Susan about meeting Mike at Grayson's where she had been working as a secretary for the past two months and how the wonderful Mike treated her like a queen and how eager they both were to get married and start a family.

"Do you plan to have children right away?"

"You bet we do. We want at least six kids."

"What about your job?"

"I can't wait to quit. I'm not the career type, Mrs. Blaine. Maybe it's just my upbringing, but a home and family are what I've always wanted. Men can have the rat race. It's all theirs with my blessing."

"You certainly sound like you know what you want."

"I sure do."

"Well, I'm glad for you, Maria." Susan sat back and tapped her pencil thoughtfully on the desk. "What about the Harmon case? You know that the hearings were held on the amendment and it's been properly certified as part of the city code now."

"I know. That's why I'm here, Mrs. Blaine. I want to drop the case. It doesn't seem very important to me anymore."

"I see." Susan rocked in her chair and remained silent for a minute. "I suppose I could withdraw the exception if you're certain you don't want to go through with it. But the case is docketed to be heard again next month."

"I know, but"—Maria shrugged her shoulders—"who cares. That bum got what he deserved from all the bad publicity. I don't want to drag it out."

"I feel sure you could win and be awarded damages." Susan tried to remain objective.

"I suppose so. But Mike wouldn't like it. He'd rather let the whole thing fade into the past. And to be honest, so would I. It's funny, but now that I have a real man in my life, it just makes this other thing seem pretty stupid." She stopped suddenly, her face coloring red. "Oh, please, Mrs. Blaine. I don't mean you didn't do a good job or anything. I only . . ."

"It's okay, Maria. No offense taken. I understand. Your perspective has changed recently. Your priorities aren't the same, right?" Susan hoped she sounded cool and unemotional.

"Right!" Maria smiled happily. "Gee, you get the drift right away, don't you? I guess that's what makes you a good lawyer. You should keep at it," Maria suggested magnanimously. "You're the kind of woman who belongs in a man's world."

Susan wasn't sure that that was necessarily a compliment and decided to cut the interview short. A little more of Maria's backhanded praise might send her to the nearest bar seeking a stiff drink. She sat at her desk after ushering Maria Vargas to the door and swiveled her chair around to stare out of the window at the ominous gray sky. *Well now, Ms. Blaine, super woman lawyer of the year. What do you make of that?*

Susan was still wondering what she made of the Vargas episode that night while she curled up on the couch with *Middlemarch* and listened to the somber melodies of Beethoven on her stereo. Was she really the android Maria made her feel she was that afternoon? Was there some feminine quality lacking in her emotional apparatus that led her to this present condition—a woman alone at night and competing with men by day? Was she merely a mixed-up feminist who was trading the hearth and home for a sterile independence? Or, like Dorothea in her novel, a misguided fool concealing her need for fleshly love in high-minded pursuits?

She closed her book and went to bed but not to sleep. Maria Vargas seemed to have upset the tenor of her days. She dreamed of Carlos that night. Susan was driving her

Datsun with Carlos seated beside her. But he got out of the car and she couldn't find him. The landscape was strange and alien and the faster she drove the more frantic she became.

The next morning Susan rebuked herself for letting Maria Vargas throw a wrench into her serenity. Who was to say Susan couldn't have a career and a man too? Owen was perfectly willing and available to lend himself to the modern woman's design. She could have her cake and eat it too. If she wanted to.

But did she want to? She saw Owen frequently at work, but he didn't press his attentions on her. He sensed that she was taking time out to evaluate her life and reach a decision. He was decent enough not to take advantage of propinquity to plead his cause. Owen let her have her time-out without more pressure.

Susan would catch his meaningful gaze on her from time to time, but that was all. He had a code of honor that he never breached. The next move was up to her.

If Maria Vargas caused a ripple on the surface of Susan's sea of tranquility, Madeline Stanton caused a ground swell. She came to Susan, a fifty-three-year-old career woman, seeking to have a will drawn up to dispose of her considerable assets on her death.

"I have no family—no close family—to inherit. Only a few distant cousins back East."

"Do you have other beneficiaries to be remembered as well as your relatives?" Susan was taking notes on Madeline's replies to the standard queries in such matters, but a part of her mind was assessing the attractive woman seated across from her desk.

Madeline Stanton was well groomed and smartly attired in a dark wine suit with a Chanel jacket revealing a mauve silk print beneath. Her gold bracelets and earrings were undeniably genuine and her manicure was perfect.

Besides her private residence and several apartment buildings, there was a sizable stock portfolio, jewelry, and antiques totaling several million dollars. Madeline had made her fortune largely in real estate and was still an active businesswoman running her own brokerage firm with a staff of twenty employees.

Although Madeline presented a dignified exterior and manner, she seemed inclined to confide in Susan.

"I was an only child. My parents married late in life and they treated me as an adult from early childhood. To tell the truth, I don't think I was ever really young. My parents died within a year of each other when I was eighteen, and they left me a little money which I proceeded to invest in business, and I started making money right from the start."

"You were raised in the East, weren't you?" Susan questioned, finding herself drawn into her client's personal narrative and really wanting to learn about the events that had led Ms. Stanton to her present situation.

"I married when I was twenty-five, but it didn't last very long. I was too independent in an era when a good wife stayed home and raised babies. Frank wasn't a mean man, but he wanted the traditional home life. You know the scenario: He would make the money and I would spend it. But I was too absorbed in my own career—I had a talent for making money and I couldn't see any sense in dropping it. So I left him."

"That must have taken a lot of courage in those days."

"Not really. Not for me. I was too busy learning and growing to waste time wondering if it were right or wrong. There was so much to discover. I've traveled all over the world in the past twenty-eight years. I've met so many interesting people and I've seen so many beautiful places—the Greek isles, the Pyramids—I have friends in Paris and Rome as well as New York and San Antonio. My life is full and satisfying. I've had everything I wanted. What would it have been if I'd stayed with Frank?"

"What *would* it have been if you had?" Susan asked boldly.

"Very dull, my dear. Very apple-pie, down-home America. Frank still lives in Jamestown, with his wife, Irene. He owns a furniture factory; he's done quite well. Raised five sons. One's a doctor. Nice family."

"What about his wife. Irene?"

"Precisely. What about his wife? Irene is a plump, middle-aged *hausfrau* from all reports. Oh, very happy, I presume. But still a *hausfrau*. That was never for me. I have no regrets, Susan. Life at best is a compromise. I'm satisfied with the choices I've made. Not everyone can say that."

But Susan wasn't so sure about Madeline's conclusion. Travel, sights, people, and places were wonderful adjuncts to life, but were they the core? Weren't they too peripheral? Something was missing and to Susan it seemed suspiciously like love.

What about love? Love for a man. Love for children and a family. Love for a home and a place and people. Those seemed the core of life to Susan, the hub around which the rest should revolve.

Is that so? Susan asked herself. Since when did a home and family take center stage in her value system? What about her career?

It's funny how Maria and Madeline came along to draw such a picture in contrast for Susan. Actually neither woman's path seemed a valid option for Susan.

She wanted part of each life-style, she supposed. And that entailed quite a balancing act. Maybe it wasn't possible. But she had to try.

One thing she did know, she didn't want to be a Madeline Stanton when she reached the age of fifty. Susan was grateful for the object lesson presented by the meeting with Madeline. The more she weighed the impact of that encounter, the more she was left with an impression of emptiness and rootlessness. One should have a home, a place, loved ones.

Loved ones.

Someone to love. Someone to make that home with her. Someone to make a place where she belonged, a place for storing memories and sinking roots.

And who was that someone for Susan? Was it Carlos? It was his face she looked for constantly through the hours of the day, in the office, on the street, at her door. It was his voice that called to her heart and haunted her dreams. It was his touch that she yearned for with an intensity that grew daily once she admitted it to herself.

What did it matter that Carlos was the choice of difficulties, of trials and pain? With him she felt alive and in touch with her deepest needs as a woman.

With Owen life would be smooth and even, but lacking in an intensity sufficient to bind their lives together.

Susan stopped by Owen's office on a Friday afternoon and asked him if he would like to have dinner with her at her place that night. His eager acceptance left her feeling blue, but she had decided that she couldn't keep Owen dangling any longer. The wheels of resolve had finally turned in her mind and the first step was to make a clean break with Owen.

He arrived at her door bearing a bottle of champagne and Susan almost lost heart when she realized it was meant for a celebration. But she steeled herself against weakness and turned the conversation to themselves as they sat over coffee following their steaks and baked potatoes.

"That was a mighty fine dinner, little lady. Your culinary talents almost match your fine jurisprudence. You're a damned fine woman, Ms. Blaine."

"That's high praise coming from you, Mr. Forsythe." Susan felt momentarily at a loss. This was tougher than any courtroom confrontation. "Owen, I'm sure you know I didn't invite you over tonight just to display my domestic virtuosity. We both have been waiting for me to work things out in my mind"—she cleared her throat—"about us."

Owen picked up the direction of Susan's opening statement and smiled ruefully. "Don't look so miserable, my dear. I'm a grown man. Just lay it on me straight. I won't crumble."

Susan smiled and breathed easier. "You're such a brick, Owen. I must be crazy to let you slip out of my clutches."

"Is that it, my darling Sue? Am I slipping out of your clutches?"

Susan nodded her head yes and reached for Owen's hand. He studied her silently. Susan felt sure that he was contemplating a deeper plunge and offering marriage. But he didn't.

"I suppose that Carlos Obregon has a part to play in this little drama?"

"Yes, he does," Susan admitted with straightforward candor. She owed Owen honesty, above all else.

"I must admit I'm not too pleased to hear that, Susan." He searched her face for her feelings. "Even if I weren't in the running, I would have to say that I think the major is the wrong man for you."

"I know, Owen. And the hell of it is that you may be perfectly right."

"Then I won't elaborate. I think you know the objections before I raise them."

"Indeed I do." Susan smiled again to keep herself from crying. She really didn't want to send Owen away. And the thought of Carlos frightened her. Maybe she didn't have the courage to carry out her decision.

Susan said good night to Owen with tears in her eyes. And she wept into her pillow that night when she recalled their parting. *Well, Carlos Obregon*, she whispered, *I'm certainly learning the lessons of pain.*

On Saturday, Susan made a date to meet Carlos at the Capistrano Mission the following afternoon.

There was a touch of frost in the January air although a bright sun cast sharp shadows that etched the mission stones clearly against a sapphire blue sky. A slight breeze rippled the beech leaves over Carlos's dark head where he sat waiting for Susan to arrive.

She caught sight of him before he noticed her, and she stopped to study his poised figure outlined against the ancient landscape. He seemed remote and contemplative—an integral part of a timeless setting both gracious and cruel. Carlos belonged in this land of dramatic contrasts, of burning sunshine and thorny vegetation, of soft shadows and melancholy music. It was all very seductive and beautiful, but alien. It would take a large measure of courage and persistence to build a successful life with that tempestuous man waiting for her.

She was both eager and frightened, and she called his name.

"Carlos."

He looked up and she saw the pleasure in his eyes as he discovered her approaching. He rose to his feet but did not walk towards her. Instead he waited, seeming to drink in Susan's presence as she moved nearer to him.

They smiled at one another, then kissed ardently and drew back to study each other. They didn't say much, but strolled hand in hand beneath the stone cloisters, peering through grilled windows and arched doorways, letting the peace of centuries wrap them in its tranquility before speaking on the subject that had brought them together.

At last Susan spoke the opening words of negotiation between them. "Are we doing the right thing, Carlos?"

"We must be," Carlos answered simply.

"How can you be so sure?"

"Because there is nothing else to do," he replied, selecting his words with care. "We did not meet by accident, *querida*. We had no choice in the matter."

"Carlos, don't talk like that. It's that kind of idea that makes me want to pull back."

"Very well, my sweet. I won't say such things. I'll let you discover them for yourself." Silence fell between them.

"What will I discover?" Susan finally asked, in spite of herself.

"I thought you didn't want to hear." Carlos chuckled.

"I don't really. But I must. Do you understand?"

"More than you think, my darling. You don't have to be afraid to hear about our future together. We're going to have a glorious life . . . all the wonders of love to explore for a lifetime."

"You mean it, don't you, Carlos? You're not just mouthing pretty phrases?"

"Your doubts astonish me, Susan. I can't believe you don't feel the power of our love." He turned her to face himself, holding her shoulders and searching her face.

"Oh, Carlos, please don't be angry," she whispered. "I do feel our love . . . so much that I doubt my senses."

"Trust your heart, my darling." He kissed her tenderly.

"I will devote my life to your happiness, Susan. You'll never regret marrying me," he promised earnestly.

Susan's heart swelled with love at the fervor of his pledge. "Carlos, what would you have done if I had decided against us?"

"I would have come after you and kidnapped you."

"No, I mean it, seriously. What would you have done?"

"I would have continued to pursue you until you relented."

"I might not have," Susan replied.

"Yes, you would. You were mine since that night at the hacienda. We might not have realized it then with our minds, but in our hearts we knew."

"You place so much reliance on the heart."

"Of course I do. The heart doesn't lie. It is only our minds that confuse us. We never go astray when we follow our hearts."

"You almost convince me," Susan whispered fervently.

"Just give me time, and I will."

"Will a lifetime do?" Susan asked.

"Nothing less, my darling. Nothing less." Carlos pressed Susan to his beating heart.

AVON CONTEMPORARY ROMANCES

Avon's new series of contemporary romance novels each feature a heroine faced with difficult choices about her life when she finds the man who may not be quite perfect, but who is just right for her.

PAPER TIGER
Elizabeth Neff Walker
An attractive, intelligent newspaper columnist is forced to assess her career's importance when she is pursued by two men—her good-looking editor-in-chief and a strapping outdoorsman. 81620-2/$2.75

DANCING SEASON
Carla Neggers
An independent cafe owner must choose between a charming, world-famous ballet dancer and her older brother's attentive, easy-going best friend. 82602-X/$2.75

BEST LAID PLANS
Elaine Raco Chase
Pursued by a dynamic real estate tycoon, a beautiful, vivacious boutique owner must reassess the importance of career and take a closer look at an old friend—a handsome, charming lawyer. 82743-3/$2.75

AVON
CONTEMPORARY
ROMANCES

LOVE FOR THE TAKING
Beth Christopher

Beautiful Sondra Blake is at the peak of a successful flight career when two suitors—a dashing, freewheeling Beverly Hills lawyer and a down-to-earth antiques dealer—vie for her love. Torn by her conflicting emotions, Sondra struggles to choose the love that will embrace her heart but not imprison her spirit. 83311-5/$2.75

BALANCING ACT
Pamela Satran

Attractive assistant fashion stylist Kim Davies is on the verge of sacrificing her career for handsome lawyer Steven Carswell when she unexpectedly wins professional acclaim, and realizes that she wants both her career and a family. When a sensitive co-worker declares his romantic feelings for her, Kim wonders if either man can understand that her commitment to her career in no way lessens her commitment to love. 83659-9/$2.75

UNTIL LOVE IS ENOUGH
Laura Parker

Now single after six years of marriage, a beautiful 26-year-old woman returns to college in Dallas, Texas to complete her studies. When an attractive young professor encourages her to expand her goals and a dashing corporate executive woos her with his protective love, she is forced to re-evaluate her own desires for love and independence. 83865-6/$2.75

AVON Original Paperbacks

Available wherever paperbacks are sold or directly from the publisher. Include $1.00 per copy for postage and handling; allow 6-8 weeks for delivery. Avon Books, Dept BP, Box 767, Rte 2, Dresden, TN 38225.

Cont. Rom. 5-83

Dear Reader:

If you enjoyed this book, and would like information about future books by this author and other Avon authors, we would be delighted to put you on the mailing list for our ROMANCE NEWSLETTER.

Simply *print* your name and address and send to Avon Books, Room 419, 959 Eighth Ave., N.Y., N.Y. 10019.

We hope to bring you many hours of pleasurable reading!

Sara Reynolds, Editor
Romance Newsletter